PRAISE for…

Ava Comes Home
*She expertly manages a page-turning blend of down-home comedy
and heart-breaking romance.*—Cape Breton Post

Shoot Me
*… possesses an intelligence and emotional depth that reverberates
long after you've stopped laughing.*—Halifax Chronicle Herald

Relative Happiness
*Her graceful prose…and her ability to turn a familiar story into
something with such raw dramatic power, are skills that many veteran novelists
have yet to develop.*—Halifax Chronicle Herald

Vagrant Press is an imprint of
Nimbus Publishing Limited
PO Box 9166
Halifax, NS   B3K 5M8
(902) 455-4286
nimbus.ca

Printed and bound in Canada

Cover design: Heather Bryan
Author photo: Morrison Powell

This novel is a work of fiction. Names, characters, places, and incidents are either the product of the author's imagination or are used fictitiously. Any resemblance to actual persons, living or dead, events or locales is entirely coincidental.

Library and Archives Canada Cataloguing in Publication

Crewe, Lesley, 1955-
Hit and Mrs. / Lesley Crewe.
ISBN 978-1-55109-725-1

I. Title.   PS8605.R48H57 2009   C813'.6   C2009-902860-3

 Canada Canada Council | Le Conseil des Arts
for the Arts | du Canada

NOVA SCOTIA
Tourism, Culture and Heritage

We acknowledge the financial support of the Government of Canada through the Book Publishing Industry Development Program (BPIDP) and the Canada Council, and of the Province of Nova Scotia through the Department of Tourism, Culture and Heritage for our publishing activities.

This book was printed on ANCIENT FOREST
Ancient-Forest Friendly paper   FRIENDLY™

LESLEY CREWE

Hit & Mrs.

To Anne

Have fun!

Lesley Crewe

Vagrant PRESS

For Linda.
"You're the best…"

CHAPTER ONE

The girls grew up together during the sixties in Notre Dame de Grâce, on the outskirts of downtown Montreal. Each of them kept a picture that was taken in the summer of 1965. They were ten years old and looked as if they hadn't seen a comb in weeks, with missing teeth, knobby knees, and skinny arms protruding from ugly striped t-shirts and dirty high-waisted jeans.

Their friendship had been sealed forever six months earlier, on February 14, 1965, in Mrs. Glencross's fifth grade class. They were the only four girls who didn't get a valentine. The pretty girls called them the Losers. The Losers called the pretty girls every foul name they could think of, but not so horrible that they incurred the wrath of God or The Blessed Virgin.

Linda was the only one who didn't get teased about her name. Bette was Better, Better the Bedwetter. Gemma was Aunt Jemima, since the pretty girls were horrible spellers, and Augusta was Augusta Wind. Linda tried to call herself Lin the Pin so she would fit in, but it didn't last long because it wasn't very good.

To grow up in NDG was to be immersed in a veritable melting pot of ethnic cultures. Linda and Augusta went to Sunday school and Girl Guides together at Wesley United Church. Gemma's Italian relatives grew vegetables on every square inch of the tiny lawns in front of their duplexes and had a jungle of tomato plants in their backyards. The Jewish families, Bette's included, had little shops up and down the business district, while the French, Poles, Greeks, and Irish were scattered around like tossed birdseed.

Their customs may have been different, but their families were all in the same boat. None of them had much money, so the kids made their own fun. The streets and alleys were their playgrounds. They biked, played dodgeball and Red Rover, skipped rope, and jumped hopscotch on the sidewalks out front.

All the kids on their street spoke a smattering of everything, but when two of them got in a fight they were instantly reminded of whom they belonged to. It was as if war had been declared between their countries of origin. Threats were made, beatings promised, and nationalistic loyalties defended to the death, or at least until the next day.

Once the supper dishes were put away their parents and grandparents sat on balconies and front porches calling over to one other. Their mothers gossiped in groups at the end of the gate while their fathers smoked and told dirty jokes or talked about hockey and their adored Montreal Canadiens.

Finally twilight would fall and streetlights would come on. That was the signal for the Losers, grimy with dirt, spit, and old gum, to come in for their baths; then homework and if they were lucky a half-hour of television, *I Love Lucy* or *Bewitched*. They were usually asleep before their heads hit the pillows.

❀

Forty years later, the Losers were now the Book Bags. They held their regular monthly book club meeting on the second Tuesday of every month, but emergency meetings were called when necessary.

It was on the first Monday of the month when Linda Keaton's husband phoned her. "This is my new address if Wes wants to get in touch with me."

The pencil in Linda's hand snapped in two. Why wasn't it her husband's neck? "You think our son wants to get in touch with you? You're screwing someone his age. He thinks you're pathetic."

"Just tell him, please."

"Tell him yourself, you bastard. That's if you can spare five minutes out of that slut's bed."

"Get help, Linda." Stuart Keaton, MD, hung up.

Linda looked at the phone. "Don't worry, you horny creep. I'll get help. I'm phoning a hit man."

She called her friend Bette.

"Bette?" She burst into tears. "Emergency meeting tonight, okay?" She hung up because she couldn't talk anymore.

❋

Bette Weinberg put down the phone. Thanks to the heat from the bakery ovens, her face was as red as her hair. Well, not quite. There was enough grey in her hair to make it a shade duller. All she could think of was that miserable skunk Linda was married to. But before she called the others, she had to serve the customer who waited impatiently in front of her. She stood on tiptoe to see over the glass counter.

"Mrs. Pink, we're out of marble rye. I told you that twenty minutes ago."

"You call yourself a bakery?"

"You call yourself a customer? *Oy vey.*"

Mrs. Pink grinned as she looked to the heavens. "Sheesh, I come back tomorrow."

Bette grinned too. "Yeah, you come back tomorrow. I'll give you a marble rye so big it'll kill your husband."

Mrs. Pink leaned against the door to open it. "Don't make promises you can't keep, Bette." The bell tinkled its goodbye. Bette grabbed her cell and punched in the numbers.

"Gemma, we're having an emergency meeting tonight at Linda's. The pig must have called her. She's in a state."

Gemma Rossi stirred a pot of tomato sauce as she cradled the phone against her neck. Her oldest kids hollered at each other in the background.

"*Basta,*" Gemma yelled over her shoulder. Quiet reigned just as her husband walked in the kitchen.

"Why are you yakking on the phone? Where's dinner?"

"Look, I can't talk now, Bette. Pick me up at seven." She hung up and pointed at the nearest female child. "Get your father a plate."

"Why me?"

"Why not you?" Gemma rushed from the kitchen and shut herself in her room. She picked up the phone.

"Augusta? There's an emergency meeting tonight. Linda's in a bad way."

Silence.

"Augusta, put down that stupid paint brush and answer me."

"Sorry, I have to…"

"…paint the Sistine Chapel. I know. Do it tomorrow."

"I'll try and get away. I have to check and see what the girls are doing."

"You're the mama. You tell them you're going and if they don't like it they can throw themselves off the roof."

"You're a broken record."

"We'll pick you up around seven-thirty."

❧

Bette grabbed her car keys off the hall table. It was a dark walnut monstrosity, as was all the furniture in the apartment above her father's bakery shop. It stood against hideous wallpaper that had once been very nice but had yellowed from years of tobacco smoke.

One by one her five brothers had married and left the family prison with nary a backward glance. Bette, being a female and an old maid to boot, was automatically elected warden. Her job was to run the family business and remain on bedpan duty until their parents croaked.

She couldn't remember being asked if she wanted the job.

Her mother rolled behind her in her wheelchair. "Where are you going at this time of night?"

Bette turned and looked at her watch. "Ma, it's ten to seven."

"It's April. It gets dark in a hurry. You shouldn't drive after dark. What if your father has a heart attack while you're out in your precious car?"

A voice yelled from the living room over the blare of the television news. "Why am I the *schlemiel* who gets the heart attack? Do me a favor, Ida. You have the heart attack."

Mother and daughter ignored him.

"Look, Ma, Linda's having problems. I said I'd go see her."

Bette's elderly wrinkled mother, jet-black hair notwithstanding, made a face and dismissed Bette with a wave of her hand. "Problems. That woman's got no problems. She lives in her fancy house, in her fancy neighborhood, married to her fancy doctor husband. What problems does she have?" Her mother pointed a finger at her. "Don't forget, she grew up in this neighborhood too. She ain't so fancy schmancy under her expensive suits. Her shit stinks too."

"Oy Ma, you've got a mouth like a stevedore."

"She got a body like one too," yelled her father. He broke into laughter at his own joke, before he coughed up a lung.

Her mother rolled herself backwards and parked in the living room doorway. "At least my big mouth works, Izzy, unlike that tiny thing you got between your legs."

Bette turned on her heel. "I'm outta here." She slammed the door, stormed down the stairs, and hopped into her very clean, black 1994 Chev Impala. She bought it as a gift for herself ten years before, to celebrate her fortieth birthday. Well, not so much to celebrate, but to keep from jumping off the Mercier Bridge.

She was careful to back gingerly out of the narrow stretch of pavement that served as a driveway. It was really the lane between two rundown buildings: Weinberg's Bakery on the left, Weinberg's Laundromat on the right. Bette's life was caught in the middle.

It took five minutes for her to hop over to Draper Avenue and collect Gemma. Gemma lived in the downstairs flat of her duplex. Her husband, Angelo, a devoted son, installed his sainted mother upstairs. Bette and Gemma had a favorite pastime called "A hundred new and improved ways to kill an elderly relative and make it look like an accident."

Gemma was waiting by her front door when Bette pulled up. She reminded Bette of a round tomato, firm and soft all at the same time. Bette once told her if she gained any more weight she was in danger of looking like the original Mrs. Rossi. Gemma went on a diet for a month after that. It was just the motivation she needed. But it wouldn't matter how much Gemma weighed. Her olive skin, big brown eyes, and dark shiny hair always deserved a second look.

Her two youngest were with her. She kissed them goodbye and then cuffed the backs of their heads when they clung to her coat. They moped back indoors.

Gemma hurried down the steps, yanked the door open, and did what she always did—slammed the car door shut with a resounding thunk.

"Must you do that?"

"Sorry. I forget this car is alive and has feelings." Gemma grabbed her seatbelt as Bette looked in the rearview mirror and then over her shoulder. She pulled out and her marvellous car purred down the street.

Gemma gave a great sigh and sank into the velvet upholstery. "Thank you, God, for getting me out of the house."

"Tell me about it. Not that I want Linda to suffer."

"I wonder what the schmuck did now?"

"He's still breathing."

The two old friends laughed as they drove to Westmount to collect Augusta. Westmount was the crème-de-la-crème neighbourhood in Montreal. The mansions built on the mountain were nothing short of spectacular, with iron gates and huge trees that hid the thick stone facades just enough to buffer the families who lived in them from the great unwashed in the streets.

But Augusta's address was deceptive. She was perilously close to the edge, in more ways than one. She didn't live with the rich; she taught their privately schooled children how to paint.

She and her husband, Tom, had a very nice brick house on a street with other very nice brick houses. Their flower beds and bushes were straight from the garden centre that sprung out of the pavement at their grocery store parking lot every spring, all middle-class hopes and dreams. A solid, forever kind of place.

Until Tom died of a heart attack on his front yard at the age of forty-seven while mowing his weed-free bluegrass lawn.

❀

Bette found a parking spot relatively close to Augusta's house. Unlike Gemma, Augusta wasn't waiting by her front door.

"I'll go," Gemma said. "She's probably forgotten, knowing her."

"Or those brats are making her life miserable," Bette yelled after her friend.

Gemma marched up the walk and grabbed the wrought-iron railing to help her up the front steps. She thought how attractive Augusta's front door was, with its lovely seasonal greenery arranged in a huge wreath. The soft light that shone from above made it look like a work of art. Gemma wished she could create something like that, but knew it was a lost cause. It would be torn from the door in a matter of minutes, with the hubbub of five children and their many friends galloping in and out all day.

Or her mother-in-law would set fire to it.

She rang the doorbell and walked in. "Only me." Gemma looked at the mess on the floor in the front porch. There were thirty shoes at least, not one of them with a mate. She rolled her eyes and ventured into the kitchen. "Gussie, let's get a move on."

Augusta looked up from the table. Her lovely face looked tired and that glorious mop of butterscotch hair was in its usual mess, held up with whatever comb she picked out of the wicker basket by the phone. Gemma still found it hard to look into Augusta's big green eyes. The sadness and aching loneliness were still evident, even three years after the day she cradled Tom's head in her lap for the very last time.

"Sorry, Gemma. I have to figure out how to get the girls to swim class."

Augusta's teenage daughters sat at the table with their arms folded. They threw resentful glances in Gemma's direction.

"If you let me get my driver's licence, Mother, we wouldn't have this problem. Everyone I know is driving," Augusta's eldest cried.

Gemma heard Bette blow the horn. "We'll drop them off on the way."

"But how will they get back? The mom who usually does it is in Florida this week."

Gemma wanted to shake her. "Gee, then I guess they'll have to miss it."

The girls whined immediately. Gemma walked over to her friend, hauled her out of the chair, grabbed her coat, and escorted her like a prisoner to the front door.

"We'll be at Linda's," Gemma told the girls. "You know the number. Your mama will be home around eleven. Have those dishes done by the time she gets back. And clean the cat's litter box. I can smell it from here."

She shut the door in their astonished, sulky faces.

Gemma didn't let go until she pushed Augusta into the car. They were finally on their way.

❀

They sat in their usual positions around Linda's gorgeously decorated family room, with its perfect blend of casual, modern, and vintage furniture. Glorious colours in the carpet, sofa pillows, and drapes were purposely made to look as if Linda was so secure in her own style that she could afford to be a little daring. Trouble was, it cost a lot of money to get it that way. But she never bragged about it. She was Lin the Pin, not Lin the Pin Cushion.

They each held a large glass of wine. Bette only ever had the one when she drove. Gemma and Augusta usually downed four or five glasses between them. It was obvious from Linda's state when she opened the door that she'd had a whole bottle to herself before they got there.

Her usual chic blonde bob was dishevelled and the skin on her face was blotchy. She hadn't even bothered to repair the damage, which meant Linda was in a bad way. She never went anywhere without a perfectly made-up face. When she got up and started to pace, her wine sloshed on the fabulous Indian carpet beneath her feet.

"Look at me. I'm fifty next month. Fifty. And here I am in my big house in the West Island surrounded by what? My husband and my son? Take a look around. They're missing in action."

She paused to take another huge gulp of wine. "Where are they, you ask? Hubby is now living on Lakeshore Boulevard in a condo with a nurse bimbo named Ryan. That's right. *Ryan.* She was the freshest of the new crop that just graduated. She's so young, she's got a guy's name. She belongs to that new generation of females who have stupid boy names like Mackenzie and Dylan and Taylor. No doubt she spells it with an *i*. Rian. With her perky tits and cement ass."

She drained her Chardonnay. "And where's my darling Wes? He's so angry and mortified he doesn't even like to come home. So where does that leave me? Alone."

Linda finally sat down like a rag doll and let her wine glass fall to the floor. "Wes blames me, you know. He thinks it's my fault his father ran off with a girl young enough to be his sister."

Augusta leaned over and put an arm around Linda's shoulder. "No, he doesn't, sweetheart. He's angry right now and it's easier for him to be angry with you. Believe me, I can tell. I've had a lot of practice."

Linda gave Augusta a grateful glance.

Bette spoke up. "This is ridiculous. I say we go over to that condo and face the little bitch. We can pick her up and throw her out the window into Lake Saint-Louis. And while we're at it, we can scoot back to my place and do the same thing to Izzy and Ida."

"And ruin their perfect marriage?" Linda said.

Gemma twirled her glass around. "We'll do Mama Rossi after that. Trouble is, I'd be next, since my husband loves me so much. Apparently, no one on the planet has a great marriage anymore."

"I had one," Augusta said.

Gemma gave her a sad smile. "Yes, you did."

Bette leaned over to grab a handful of cashews from a crystal dish on the ottoman in front of her. "What's Angelo done now, Gem?"

Gemma poured herself another glass of wine. "He hasn't done anything, that's the problem. I ask him to fix a leaky sink and he does, at his mama's. He finally tells me that we're going out to dinner, so I get all dressed up. Guess where we go on my big night out?"

Her friends shrugged.

"We go out the door, turn left, ring the doorbell, and get buzzed upstairs to Mama's. He's angry that I'm upset and his mother tells him I'm a *desgratiata*."

"Translation, please?"

"A big bitch."

Bette shook her head. "I had it backwards. We'll do Mama Rossi first and then the Ryan slut. Thank God I never married. What a nightmare."

"It's not always like that," Augusta reassured her. "Sometimes it's wonderful."

Linda touched the wedding band around her finger. "That's why I don't believe there's a God. Why did Tom die? What did he ever do but love you madly?"

"I don't want to talk about it."

Linda took her wedding band and threw it across the room and out the door. They heard it clink on the ceramic kitchen floor. She wiped her hands together as if she were dusting them off. "There. Good riddance to bad rubbish."

"I say we do something for ourselves," Bette said. "Let's forget miserable parents and in-laws and ungrateful kids and two-timing husbands. When's the last time we did anything for us? Other than fire the latest Oprah Book Club Selection out the window."

"You're right," Gemma nodded. "We're almost fifty. Life is passing us by."

Linda leapt up off her overstuffed couch. "We're all fifty this year. That's worth celebrating. Sort of. We should take a trip together."

"Where?" Augusta asked.

"Where have you always wanted to go?"

"New York."

Now Bette hopped out of her seat. "New York for a long weekend. We could go to Broadway."

"I've always wanted to see a show on Broadway," Gemma said. "I'd love to see *Mamma Mia*, wouldn't you?"

Augusta joined into the spirit of things. "I want to see the MoMA and the Metropolitan Museum of Art. What could be better?"

"Macy's and Bloomingdale's," Linda answered. "Not to mention Saks Fifth Avenue."

Bette hopped up and down. "Let's do it. What are we waiting for?"

The four friends reached out for each other and did a little dance around the ottoman. Linda's cat ran under the couch.

"Wait," Gemma said.

They stopped dancing.

"I can't go. I hate to fly."

"You've never flown," Bette said.

"Exactly. Because I hate to fly."

Augusta's face fell. "And what about the girls?"

Gemma turned to her. "What about the girls? Your mother will be around. She can stay with them for a few days."

"I'm not sure. She's sort of frightened of them."

They let themselves go and looked at each other, their excitement draining away.

"I can't go," Bette said. "I can't afford it."

"Neither can I," Gemma admitted. "My secret cache in the fridge only has two hundred dollars in it."

"Your secret cache is in the fridge?" Linda asked.

"It's in a yogurt container, and since they all hate yogurt they never open it." Gemma was quiet for a moment. "But I'll try and get the money somehow if you promise me you'll go, Augusta. You and Linda need this. The girls can live without you for seventy-two hours."

"But you don't like to fly."

"Don't worry," Bette said. "We can dope Gemma up the wazoo. I have a cocktail of tranquillizers at my disposal; necessary ammunition for living with my folks. "

The friends eyed each other hopefully again. Finally Augusta said, "There's still the money issue, though. Even if Bette and Gemma could raise the money for airfare and their share of a hotel room, that would still leave them with nothing left to go anywhere. We don't want to wander aimlessly around New York City with no money. And anyway, the tickets for *Mamma Mia* alone would cost a fortune."

Four glum faces returned.

"Well, it was nice while it lasted," Bette sighed.

Linda snapped her fingers. "I've got it. Just a sec, I'll be right back." She tore out of the room. The other three held hands in a mini vigil of hope. Linda roared back into the room with her hand behind her back, then whipped it out in front of her and held up a Platinum Visa Card.

"Dr. Viagra forgot to take this with him."

Nobody moved.

Linda kissed the card. "Let's call this a Fuck-You-Charlie, Going-Away Present. What do you say?"

"New York City, here we come!"

The Book Bags did a conga line all around Linda's very expensive house.

CHAPTER TWO

Gemma's bomb exploded at the supper table. Might as well freak everyone out at the same time.

She let them get well into their meal. A family with full stomachs was easier to deal with, so she waited for the chance to slip her news into normal conversation. But that moment never arrived. Everyone's tongue flapped a mile a minute and no one listened to a thing anyone else said. Finally she couldn't stand it.

"I'm going to New York."

Her husband, mother-in-law, and five kids dropped their utensils on their plates and then sat in stunned silence for a good ten seconds. You'd think she told them the Pope was at the door.

"What?" Angelo croaked.

"I'm going to New York, whether you guys like it or not."

Angelo's mother bit her knuckle, then spat, *"Putana."*

Gemma glared at her. "I'm a slut? Is that what you said? I don't have to take..."

Angelo interrupted her. "What's in New York? Another man?"

Gemma got up from the table. "As a matter of fact, there is. I met Donald Trump at the grocery store a couple of days ago. He wants me to run away with him. Didn't I tell you?"

Angelo's mother proceeded to wring her hands and howl.

"Don't go, Mama," said her youngest. "I'll miss you."

Gemma reached over and cupped her daughter Anna's heart-shaped face in her hand. "I'm not going forever, only a couple of days. Mama will come back and bring you a present."

Anna looked relieved. "Really?"

Gemma nodded.

"You can't go," her husband said.

"I can't? Watch me."

She turned away and went to the sink. Angelo got up and followed her. "How you get the money? I'm not giving you money. You want to take food from the mouths of your children?"

Gemma spun around and faced him. "Is this the eighteenth century? I need your permission to go somewhere for a weekend?"

"You do if you take the money from this family. I work too hard for my paycheque to go and give you a good time in New York."

The old woman screeched from the table. *"Porca putana!"*

"Do you hear the way your mother talks to me? Do I deserve this kind of treatment?"

Angelo turned to his mother and pleaded. "Mama…"

His mother continued to give Gemma the evil eye, but at least she closed her mouth.

Gemma proceeded to wash the dishes in the sink, to give her hands something to do. She wasn't nearly as confident as she looked. "Well, you'll have no worries on that score. It's Linda's treat. I don't have to pay for a thing."

That took the wind out of his sails, but not for long.

"You still can't go."

"Angelo, I'm going. The kids will be fine and your wonderful mama can cook for you while I'm away. You won't change my mind." She looked back at her mother-in-law. "You'll have your baby boy all to yourself for four days. That should make you happy."

The old crone in black muttered under her breath. Gemma had no doubt it was a curse.

❁

Seinfeld was over. Izzy turned off the television. Ida released her parking brake and started to roll away to bed.

"I'm going to New York." It was Bette's lucky day. Both her parents looked like they were going to have a heart attack. "You can't stop me. I'm going and that's that."

Ida looked at Izzy. "She's lost her mind. Call a doctor. Call Herschel Levy's son…"

"He's a proctologist."

"And she's a pain in the ass. What do you mean, you're going to New York? What's in New York?"

Bette stood up. "You two aren't, for one thing."

Ida grabbed her chest. "Do you hear the way she talks to her mother? That I should live so long to hear a grown daughter treat her mother like dirt." She appealed to the ceiling with her upturned hands. "What did I ever do to deserve such disrespect? Where are my sons? Where are they?" She beat at her breast like an overexcited chimp.

"That's a good question, Ma. Where are they? When was the last time any of them came over to visit?"

"They're busy. They look after their families, just as you should look after us. What do you think they'll say when they find out you've abandoned us?"

Bette walked over to the doorway. "Knowing them, probably 'Oh shit, who's gonna take care of them now?'"

The astonishment on her parents' faces gave Bette a stab of satisfaction—but a small one, because she knew she had to come back, and the disappointment of that reality was bitter.

Her father took a coughing fit. Her mother tore at her dress. "Do you see this heart?"

Bette sighed.

"It's broken," Ida sobbed. "Do you hear me? It's broken."

Her father pointed at her mother. "You broke your mother's heart. What kind of daughter breaks her mother's heart?"

"Cut the crap. I'm only going for four days."

Her parents looked at each other.

"Did she say four days?" Izzy said. "I think she said four days."

"You wanna give your mother a stroke? Why didn't you say four days? Why you need to go for four days, anyhow? Who can do anything in New York in four days? Where you get the money to go for..."

Bette had had enough. "What I do in New York is my business. How long I go is my business. How I can afford it, is my business. I'm fifty, Ma. Not fifteen."

Her father, who was so skinny his shirt collar was three sizes too big for him, fumbled for his cigarettes. "Who's gonna feed us?"

Bette folded her arms across her chest. "You haven't eaten since 1982. Four more days won't matter."

Ida grabbed her stomach. "I starve to death in four days."

Izzy answered before Bette had a chance to open her mouth. "We could live off your fat for years."

"Why, you…" Ida rushed towards Izzy, but Bette quickly grabbed the wheelchair's handles from behind and held on tight. "Let me at him."

Bette wished she could do that, but this nightly ritual needed to be played out. It was their only source of entertainment.

"Come to bed, Ma."

Ida reached for Izzy and he ducked out of the way. "You're slowin' down, old woman."

"I give you slow." She kicked him.

Izzy hopped around. "She *kicked* me."

"I thought you were lame, Ma."

"Every so often, God give me strength."

Bette closed her eyes. "Amen to that."

Augusta made homemade pizza and bought the ingredients to make ice cream sundaes for dessert. She planned what she would say when the girls came home from school. She would be firm.

Once they'd smacked the last of the chocolate syrup from their lips, Augusta spoke. "I thought I might go on a trip to New York."

"Wow," Summer said. "That will be fun. When do we go?"

"We'll miss school," Raine grinned. "Cool."

"I won't go to any museums," Summer added. "I know you, Mom. You'll make us prance around and look at stupid art. I need to go shopping."

Augusta cleared her throat. "I'm going. You're not."

She tried not to panic at the sight of their stricken faces. The two of them looked so much like Tom, with their strawberry-blonde hair and smattering of freckles. She'd never left them alone before. Not since their father died.

"It's only for a long weekend. I'm going with Linda, Bette, and Gemma. A sort of slumber party for our fiftieth birthdays."

Summer frowned and twirled a dessert spoon in her hand. "You're a little too old for slumber parties, aren't you?"

"I don't think it's very nice that you won't take us," Raine said. "When do we ever get to do anything wicked?"

"You do lots of nice things," her mother answered.

"Right," Raine said, "Did we go to Disney World like the rest of the planet? No. You won't take us. Daddy wanted us to go. Don't you remember?"

Augusta blinked. "I don't want to fight about this. It's a few days away with my girlfriends. It's not a big deal."

Summer crossed her arms. "You don't love us; otherwise you'd take us too. It's not fair."

"Don't be silly." Augusta knew what would happen next and tried to stay strong.

Raine looked up with tears in her eyes. "I don't want you to go, Mom. What if something happens? We'd be orphans."

Augusta's stomach did its customary flip. "Nothing will happen, girls. New York isn't far away."

"Daddy died on the front lawn. That's not far away either," Summer said. "You can't guarantee nothing will happen."

"Yeah, Daddy wouldn't want you to leave us alone. He never left us alone."

Augusta's head throbbed and the muscles in the back of her neck seized. It wasn't worth it. Nothing ever was. She brushed her bangs out of her face and reached over to pick up a plate and take it to the sink.

"Fine. I won't go if that's the way you feel."

"Go if you want to. Don't let us stop you." Summer got up and left the kitchen.

"Yeah, don't let us stop you." Raine followed her sister out of the room.

It passed through Augusta's mind that she was left with the supper dishes again. She should tell them to come downstairs and help, but right now they were the last people she wanted to see.

No. Not true. Now that she wasn't going, that honour would go to Gemma.

❋

Linda picked up the phone and dialled. She let it ring six times. She was about to hang up when an out-of-breath voice said, "Yeah?"

"Hi darling, it's Mom." She heard heavy breathing. "Hey Mom, what's up?"

Linda sat on the breakfast stool by the island in her kitchen. "Nothing really, did I catch you at a bad time?"

There was a pause. "No…no…I just got in the door, that's all."

"Oh. Well, I've called to tell you I'm going to New York for a few days with the girls."

"Hey, that's great. Have a good time."

Linda got the distinct impression Wes wanted to rush her off the phone and it ticked her off. She wasn't the sort of mother who bugged him every day of the week.

"Thank you, I will. Don't you want to know when I'm leaving?"

Another pause and then Linda was sure she heard whispering. "Hello. Wes? Are you there?"

"Yeah, Mom, I heard you. You're going to New York. I'm glad. You deserve it. Have a great time and call when you get back."

She heard a female voice giggle and coo. Wes made shushing noises. Fabulous.

"I'll leave my travel information on the fridge door, just in case you…"

"Great. Great. Bye, Mom."

She heard another groan and then the fumbling of a phone being hung up.

She clicked the phone off and sat with her thoughts in her silent kitchen. Her eyes wandered to the pictures she'd framed of Wes's drawings when he was in elementary school. He begged her to take them down, but she refused.

When had he become a man? She couldn't have been paying attention, or she'd have seen it. To think back was a blur. She hadn't noticed the years of her life falling away like leaves in an autumn gale.

The cat jumped up on her lap and nuzzled against the underside of her chin, his motor on full throttle.

"You won't leave me, will you, Buster?"

Buster did his best to assure her he wouldn't.

She sat for a long time; she had nothing to do. Then she heard the dogs bark next door. That reminded her she hadn't asked her neighbour, Mr. Harris, if he'd look after Buster while she was away. No time like the present. She peeked out her window and there he was, carrying a bag of lime to the small greenhouse near the back of his property. He had a glorious garden. He was a crazy Englishman who wore the most outlandish outfits. Who else would wear a bowtie to trim the hedge?

The neighbours felt sorry for him. His wife had died two years before, and since they had no children, he cut a lonely figure. The women on the street often found themselves at his door with a casserole dish in hand. He'd offer his thanks with such enthusiasm that they'd rush back to their kitchens to replenish his larder with similar treats.

He never went anywhere without his two fat Shar Pei dogs, Winston and Churchill. She watched him bend down to give the wrinkled creatures an affectionate rub.

She put Buster on the floor and went out on the deck.

"Clive."

He turned around and gave her a big grin and a wave. She hurried over and went through the gate to his yard.

"Good morning, Linda. How are you on this fine spring day?"

"Great. Hi Winnie, hi Churchill."

"Be polite, boys. Say hello to Linda."

The boys wiggled their bodies.

"Clive, I hate to bother you, but would you mind looking in on Buster while I'm in New York for a few days? I don't leave for a couple of weeks yet, but I wanted to give you plenty of notice."

Clive tipped his cap. "It would be my pleasure."

"Thank you." She smiled at him and noticed for the first time what lovely blue eyes he had.

"Are you and Dr. Keaton going on holiday?"

Linda hadn't told anyone about Stuart, other than Wes and the girls. She struggled for a moment, because her tongue was suddenly too big for her mouth. "Actually, Stuart and I are no longer together. He moved out three weeks ago."

She watched Clive's face register shock and it relieved some of the tight pressure in her throat.

"Oh dear, I'm sorry to hear that, Linda. You must be very upset."

To her absolute horror, she started to cry.

Clive and his dogs looked around frantically as if to escape, and she thought she would die of embarrassment, but soon realized he was only searching for a handkerchief, which he passed to her as soon as he took it out of his pocket and shook it.

"It's clean. Well, as clean as I can make things. I put it in the wash with a pair of black pants and it's never been the same."

Linda didn't know what he was babbling about. She felt like an idiot. She took the handkerchief and then grabbed him, leaning against his slight chest and bright blue bowtie.

"I don't know what to do. I'm so lonely. How do I do this? I don't want to be alone. I've never been alone and now I have no one. Even my son is away, having sex at this very moment and not even thinking about me."

Clive patted her shoulder awkwardly. "There, there. I'm sure that's a good thing. One wouldn't want to be thinking of one's mother while having sex."

Linda looked up into his perfectly serious face and started to laugh. Thankfully, he joined her. When she couldn't laugh or cry anymore, she blew her nose and felt much better.

"My humble apologies, I don't usually wail at the drop of a hat."

Clive put his hands in his pockets. "You're never prepared when someone is lost to you."

She sniffed and fiddled with the handkerchief. "I feel terrible, bleating on like this. You know first-hand how awful it is to be alone."

He nodded and then smiled. "But I have the boys."

The boys wiggled at his feet.

"And we'll make sure Buster is well provided for until you come home. I hope you have a good time. Sometimes a change of scene is just what you need. Don't worry; we'll be here when you get back."

She thanked him again. He went his way and she went hers.

He said he'd be there when she got back. At least someone would notice if she never returned.

❋

Gemma sat at her kitchen table with Anna, reading aloud one word at a time. Anna spelled it back to her. She had a test in the morning.

The phone rang. One of the kids answered it upstairs and yelled, "MAMA."

Gemma picked it up. "Hello?"

"Houston, we have a problem."

"Bette? What problem?"

"Augusta isn't coming with us."

Gemma slapped her own forehead. "*Santa Maria*, I knew this would happen. We have to go talk to her."

"I'll pick you up. I need to get out of here anyway."

"Why?"

"Ida's on the warpath. She found a *Playboy* magazine under Izzy's mattress."

"Why do you insist on calling your parents by their first names?"

"So I can pretend they're not my parents. See you in five."

Gemma hung up the phone. "I have to go out, Anna. Get your sister to ask you the last six words. You know them all so far. Good for you."

Anna beamed. "Are you going to Augusta's?"

Gemma nodded and got up to leave.

"Why are her kids so mean to her? I'd never be mean to you."

"Life is complicated, Anna. Sometimes people lose their way. When that happens, you have to rely on your friends."

"And you're Augusta's friend."

Gemma smiled and kissed her. "Bed by nine."

It took them twenty minutes to get to Augusta's door. This time, Bette came in with her. Augusta didn't look surprised to see them, just worn out. The three friends sat in the kitchen. The girls were upstairs with music blaring.

"Tell me it's not true," Gemma said.

"Look, I'm sorry, there's no point. I wouldn't have a good time anyway. They're right. What if something did happen? In today's world, you never know. Then who would look after them? I'm not like you, Gemma. I don't have a husband and relatives all over the place. There's Mom and that's it. I have to be careful."

Bette and Gemma looked at each other. It was Bette who spoke first.

"You could fall down the basement steps with a load of laundry, too. It amounts to the same thing."

Augusta hid her face with her hands. Bette jumped out of her chair and put her arm around her friend. "I'm sorry, I shouldn't have said that."

Augusta took her hands away. "No, you're right. That's the problem. I'm always afraid something's going to happen, to me or to them. I'm walking on eggshells all the time. It's hard."

Gemma straightened her back. "Life is hard. Everyone has something they're terrified of, but you keep walking anyway."

"I'm tired of walking."

"Then you should've laid down beside Tom and died too."

Augusta gasped.

"Gemma, don't," Bette said.

"No. I'm sick of this, Augusta. For three years I've watched you get smaller and smaller. Do you think Tom would've wanted you to be so afraid of your own shadow that you stopped living?"

Augusta gave her a dirty look, but it didn't matter. Gemma couldn't stop now. "And I know something else. Tom was a great papa and I think he'd be horrified if he knew how these girls blackmail you. You have got to stop apologizing for the fact that you lived and he didn't. Of course they're angry about it. But it wasn't your fault, so they have no right taking it out on you."

Augusta's shoulders slumped. "I know. I just don't know how to fight it."

"One day at a time," Bette said. "That's how I get through life. Otherwise I would've blown my brains out years ago."

The three friends smiled at each other.

"You're coming with us," Gemma said, "because if you don't go, we don't go. It's as simple as that. And you know how much Linda needs this right now."

"All right, but how do I tell the girls?"

"Do you mind if you leave that up to me?"

"I'm such a coward."

Gemma rose from the table. "Make some tea. I'll be down in a minute."

She left the kitchen, walked up the stairs, and poked her nose into Summer's bedroom. Summer jumped, as if she'd had a fright. "Why are you here?"

"Get your sister, please. Then come back in here. I want to talk to you."

"Why…"

"Just do it."

Summer stomped past her and did as she was asked. A minute later, two girls with mutinous faces sat on Summer's bed.

Gemma took a deep breath. "Do you girls love your mother?"

"What kind of silly question is that?" Summer asked.

"It's a simple one. Do you or don't you?"

"Of course we do."

Raine nodded in agreement.

"Well, from where I'm standing, it sure doesn't seem like it."

"Look, this is none of your business. You have no right to come in here and tell us what to do."

Gemma took a step closer and pointed her finger at Summer. "I have every right. I've been your mother's friend for forty years. I love her and I care what happens to her. She used to be a happy person. She laughed all the time, full of joy and wonderment. She loved to paint and create things. I've always wanted to be like her."

They were silent.

"But not now. Now she's a scared little woman who worries all the time. And you've made her that way."

"That's ridiculous."

"Is it? Were you happy for her when you heard she had the chance to go to New York with her best friends? Did you make her feel good about it?"

Summer's face grew dark. Raine's eyes filled with tears.

"For three years, she's stayed by your side. She wanted to have four days to herself. Four. How long will you keep her a prisoner here? How long are you going to make her pay for your father's death? You two weren't the only ones who lost someone that horrible day. She lost her lover and her best friend. They were so in love they couldn't see straight. All of us wanted what she had with your father. Believe it or not, as much as you miss him, she misses him a thousand times more."

Augusta's daughters burst into tears. It was awkward. Gemma passed them a box of Kleenex. "Now go downstairs and tell your mama to have a wonderful time in New York."

For once, they didn't argue with her.

CHAPTER THREE

Bette gave up. It seemed her parents were determined to extract their pound of flesh before she left for New York. So be it.

"You need to go to Epstein's Pharmacy and renew all these prescriptions." Her mother wheeled toward Bette with a lapful of pill bottles.

"Are you kidding? There have to be forty containers here. How old are these?"

Ida shrugged. "You want I should keel over on the floor when you're gone? You'd deny a dying woman her pills?" She clapped her hands together in prayer and shook them. "Oy, the pain, the shame of it. A daughter who pushes her mother down the stairs the first chance she gets."

"First I deny you pills and then I push you down the stairs. You should be on Broadway, Ma. Why don't you come with me and audition for Neil Simon?"

Ida stopped with the hands and her eyes widened. "I can come with you?"

Bette opened the fridge door to take out the cream cheese for her morning bagel.

"You know when you can come to New York with me? When pigs fly."

Izzy walked in the kitchen. "You hear that, Ida? You better grow some feathers."

"This from a man who can't close his own fly or his big yap."

Bette slammed the fridge door. "Will you two knock it off? Why can't you be happy for me? Is that too much to ask? I'm having a little holiday. When was the last time that happened?"

"Holiday," her father said. "In my day, no one had a holiday. We worked, seven days a week, eighteen hours a day. You sit on your bum downstairs and hand people bread. For this, you should have a vacation?"

Bette pointed her finger at them. "I don't need a vacation from work. I need a vacation from you two."

Ida pursed her lips. "Fine. Go. When you come back to find our carcasses on the floor, you'll be sorry."

Her father lit a cigarette and took a big drag. "When you pick us up off the floor, remember, I want Howard Lipshitz's Funeral Home to handle the arrangements."

Ida spun around. "Lipshitz? That idiot?"

"What's wrong with him?"

"His name says it all, you can't trust a word he says."

"Ma, you'll be dead. It doesn't matter what he says."

"Oh, you'd like that, wouldn't you? You'd like me to be dead and have a big fat liar drag me away like an old mattress."

Bette stabbed the cream cheese with her knife and spread it over the bagel. She sat down at the table and looked at her mother. Her mother looked back.

"I can't win, can I?"

Her mother entwined her fingers and twirled her thumbs.

"I didn't think so."

Bette called Linda the first chance she got. "Is there any way we can extend our trip?"

"For how long?"

"Three years."

"What did they do now?"

"Does it matter?"

"I feel for you, kid. I really do."

"Listen to me. All I do is whine and there you are with your own problems."

"At least my problem lives five miles away."

"Are you sure about this, Linda? Are you really going to charge everything to his credit card? He'll find out, you know."

"Stuart hasn't come up for air in a month and a half. The only thing he's thinking about at the moment is his dick. No, you don't have to worry on that score. I've always handled the finances. He wouldn't know a bill statement if he fell over it. And besides, he's got about ten credit cards. By the time he realizes anything's up, we've come and gone."

Bette felt better. "Oh, I can't wait. So it's definite, then? We leave next Monday?" She heard Linda rattle papers over the phone.

"I've got everything booked right here. When we arrive at La Guardia, we'll take a taxi to the Waldorf Astoria and whisk ourselves up to our fabulous room and voila. New York City on a platter."

"The Waldorf Astoria. I can't believe it."

"We're going first class all the way, baby. I want to see it all and do it all."

"Can we really do everything in four days?"

"Why not? Who's going to stop us?"

They laughed until they were giddy.

Gemma packed and repacked her suitcase. She didn't have a thing to wear; nothing but flowered tents. She grew more despondent by the day.

"What about this, Anna?" She held up a square cloth with a little opening in the top and a huge opening at the bottom.

"I like it."

"You like everything. What do you think, Sophia?"

Sophia cracked her gum. "It looks like a flour bag."

Gemma dropped her dress on the floor. "I knew it. What am I going to do? Linda says we're staying at the Waldorf Astoria. That sounds fancy. I'm not going to fit in."

"Then stop shopping where Nonna shops," Sophia said. "That's why you look sixty."

Gemma's mouth dropped open. "You think I look sixty?"

"Well, fifty-five, then."

Gemma fell back on the sofa. "*Mamma mia*. Get me the phone, Anna."

Anna hopped up and ran out of the room, returning lickety-split on her spindly legs. Gemma punched in Augusta's phone number.

"Hello?"

"Emergency meeting tonight. You and me at the mall."

Four hours later, Gemma was stuck inside a pricey outfit with her hands over her head. Augusta laughed so hard she couldn't breathe.

"Will you stop that and help me outta this thing?"

Augusta stayed seated. "I can't get up. If I do, I'll pee my pants."

A muffled cry of frustration came from underneath the black jersey knit covering Gemma's face. "If Bette were here, she'd help me."

"Good idea, I have to call her. This is priceless."

"Augusta…"

Augusta finally struggled to her feet. "All right, all right, bend down a little and I'll grab the top."

Gemma's hands flapped helplessly while Augusta grabbed the material and gave a big yank. The rip was heard throughout the back of the store. The two of them held their hands over their mouths so they wouldn't have hysterics, but it was a lost cause. They both snorted when a prissy voice called out from the other side of the door.

"Are you ladies having any trouble?"

Gemma looked in the mirror at her sticking up hair and sweaty red face. "No. No trouble. Thanks."

"This is a store of repute. We won't have it sullied with unsavoury behaviour."

Gemma blinked at Augusta. "What did she say?"

"Don't, Gem…"

Gemma threw the door open and stood there in her bra and panty girdle, her round rolls bulging out of both. She confronted the stick figure in a suit. "What did you say?

"Ah…I…"

Gemma planted her hands on her hips. "That my friend and I have *sullied* your establishment?"

"I heard a rip."

Gemma reached over and grabbed the dress from Augusta's hand. "If your clothes were bigger than a size two, maybe that wouldn't happen."

The snob put her nose in the air. "We don't carry gigantic sizes."

Gemma turned and looked at Augusta. Augusta turned and looked at the snob. "I think you'd better run."

Two days before they left, the Book Bags gathered for their regularly scheduled meeting, once again held at Linda's since her house was empty. They didn't discuss the book on their May roster, Joanna Trollope's latest novel. They sat around the kitchen table instead with their maps, brochures, travel guides, pamphlets, and subway routes.

By some unspoken agreement, Linda was the leader. Probably because she was booking as many things as she could over the Internet, before their journey even began. It gave her something to do. A woman can only scrub so many floors in the run of a day. And she was paying for everything, after all. She'd paid dearly.

"Right," she said. "Here's the agenda."

"We have an agenda?" Bette said. "That sounds official. I thought this was supposed to be fun."

"It will be fun." Linda fanned out all her paper. "But New York is a big city. You have to know where you're going, or at least have a vague idea of where everything is. Otherwise, we'll go around in circles, and we don't have that kind of time."

"You walk five miles a day," Gemma said. "I can't keep up that pace, and I certainly don't want to see your swinging ass a mile ahead of me the whole time."

Augusta poured club soda into everyone's glasses. "Look, we all know what'll happen. Bette and Linda will spin like tops around the whole city and you and I, Gemma, will mosey along. We don't have to do the same thing. We'll see *Mamma Mia* together and eat our meals together, but other than that, let's go where we want. My ideal time is to browse in a museum. I really don't care if I go to Bloomingdale's."

"Well, I'll come with you, then," Gemma huffed. "I'm never shopping again."

Augusta passed the glasses to her friends' outstretched hands. "Which is just as well since you're banned for life from Chez Simone's."

"She's banned for life?" Bette asked. "What happened?"

"You don't want to know."

"Can we get back to this, please?" Linda said. "Now, we leave on Monday evening. Since we don't get in until after 7:30, by the time we get a taxi and drive to the Waldorf, it'll be too late to do anything but settle in for the night. Just as well, since we want to get cracking early the next morning."

Bette rubbed her hands together. "I can't wait. Four nights without the snoring dynamic duo."

"Tuesday and Wednesday will be our free days. We'll see all the sights, like the Empire State Building, Radio City Music Hall, the Statue of Liberty, Times Square, that sort of thing. Thursday night we have our tickets for *Mamma Mia*. I booked third-row centre seats. We'll have a late meal afterward and then head back to the hotel. We leave Friday morning. How does that sound?"

"It actually sounds like a long time, now that you say it," Augusta said. "I thought it was four days, travel included?"

"It's four nights. Monday, Tuesday, Wednesday, Thursday. You'll be back home in time to take the girls to the movies on Friday night. An extra day doesn't make that much of a difference, surely?"

"I guess not. I'll buy them something for every night I'm gone."

"That will be hard to do if you don't want to go shopping," Bette pointed out.

"I'm sure they have gift shops in museums."

"I can see their faces now," Gemma said. "'Thanks for the Monet fridge magnet, Mom.'"

They laughed together and raised their glasses. "Look out, New York. Here we come."

❈

They agreed to meet at the ticket counter at the airport. Linda and Augusta were taking taxis over, but Gemma told Bette that Angelo would drive the two of them there. Might as well save a few bucks.

It took Bette ages to pack; her mother kept getting in the way. She had to go around the wheelchair every time she wanted to put something from her closet into the open suitcase on the bed. She finally gave up and tackled the items in her bureau instead.

"What's that? Is that a black bra?"

"So what if it is?"

"Since when do you need a black bra?"

"What business is it of yours?" Bette hid the bra further down in the suitcase.

"What do you get up to in that fancy car of yours? Are you a hussy?"

Bette sat on the end of the bed. "Repeat that one more time. I don't believe what I just heard."

"A hussy. One of those women who wiggle around men."

"You are clinically insane."

"What? I can't ask my daughter a simple question?"

Bette jumped up and went around the wheelchair to go and look in the mirror. She pointed at herself. "Mom, look at me. I'm short, I'm pudgy, I've got curly red hair, I live with my parents, I work in a bakery, and I stutter in front of men. Do you honestly think I'm a catch? Do you honestly think that every time I drive away I'm meeting men so I can wiggle around them?"

"Stranger things have happened," her mother shrugged.

"Not that strange." Bette looked around. "You're making me lose my concentration. Where was I?"

"You were stuffing a black bra in your suitcase. What's wrong with the ones your cousin Bernice gives you?"

"Bernice is a stick. She wears a 32A. Besides, I think it's disgusting that she gives me her castoffs."

"Bernice has no social life either. It's not like her bra is being fondled by strange men. They're practically new."

Bette grabbed her own boobs. "I wear a 38DD. How am I supposed to breathe if I wear hers?"

"You younger generation are way too picky. I suppose you've got black panties in there as well?"

"Can you get her outta here?" Bette yelled to her father in the living room.

"I've been trying to get her out of here for fifty-nine years. It hasn't worked yet."

Bette pointed at the bedroom door. "I want you to leave my room this minute. I have to get ready."

"Fine." Ida reversed back into the hallway. "Treat me like dirt."

Bette shut the door in her face.

The doorbell rang and Ida drove down the hall and through the kitchen. She stopped at the top of the steep narrow stairs that led to their apartment. "Come in."

Gemma opened the door and looked up. "Hi, Mrs. Weinberg. Is Bette ready to go?"

"Not yet, she's too busy packing her hoochie-mama underwear."

Gemma struggled to keep a straight face as she climbed the stairs. When she got to the top, Ida stared at her accusingly.

"You don't need to worry about Bette, Mrs. Weinberg. We'll take good care of her."

"I'm so relieved the Three Stooges are accompanying my daughter to Sin City."

Gemma plastered on a smile. Ida didn't stop staring at her. Finally, Gemma looked at her watch. "Perhaps you could tell Bette I'm here."

Ida put her chair in reverse and continued to stare at Gemma as she rolled back down the hall. She stopped in front of Bette's door.

"Gemma's here. Hurry up or you'll miss your stupid plane."

Bette opened the door. "I'm coming, I'm coming."

Ida wheeled toward Gemma again as Bette trailed behind with her suitcase. She and Gemma made excited faces at each other.

"So," Ida said to Gemma. "What happens if you get lost?"

"What makes you think we'll get lost?"

"You two couldn't find your way out of a paper bag."

"Mrs. Weinberg, please don't worry. We'll make sure Bette gets home safely."

Ida gave her famous shrug. "What, me worry? I never worry."

They continued to look at each other.

"What if you get mugged?"

"Why would we get mugged?"

"You two got mugged on Royal Avenue, didn't you?"

"Ma, stop. That was in sixth grade and it involved a Popsicle and a package of spearmint gum." She stopped in the doorway to the living room. "See ya, Pop."

Pop coughed and waved. Bette continued up the hall.

Izzy finally got his breath. "Wait." He came out of the living room with his cigarette between his lips and fumbled around in his pocket.

He took out an old wallet that was clipped to his belt by a chain. "Here. Take a few dollars. In case you get raped." He passed her the folded up money with his nicotine-stained fingers.

"For pity's sake, I'll be sure to have a good time being raped, mugged, and lost in New York."

"Listen to your father."

"Okay. Thank you, Pop." She took the money and gave him a quick kiss. He blew smoke in her face.

Gemma reached for Bette's suitcase. "Let me get that. I'll take it downstairs. Goodbye, Mr. and Mrs. Weinberg. We'll call you tonight and let you know the room number where we're staying."

"Staying, schmaying. Don't bother. I'll be dead."

Gemma lugged the suitcase downstairs. Bette looked at her mother.

"You won't be dead. I'll bring you back a present."

"Present, schmesent. Don't bother. I'll be dead."

Bette rolled her eyes and sighed. "Goodbye, Ma." She turned to go.

"What? You give your father a kiss and I get the brush off?"

"Pop gave me money. You said you'd be dead. There's a big difference. Look, I gotta go." She leaned down and kissed the top of her mother's head.

Her mother grabbed her around the neck for a moment, so hard Bette nearly toppled over, and then she pushed her away. "Go."

Bette rushed down the stairs and hurried into the back of Angelo's car. Gemma turned around in the front seat. "How on earth do you survive?"

Bette let out a long, relieved sigh. "Valium."

"May I ask how your mother gets down those stairs in a wheelchair?"

"She hasn't been outside since 1990."

"How much did your father give you?"

Bette opened her fist, counted the bills and then looked at Gemma in amazement. "There's six hundred dollars here."

"Don't think *you're* getting six hundred bucks," Angelo told his wife as he manoeuvred through traffic. "I don't even have sixty bucks."

Gemma tweaked his cheek. "Poor Angelo. Too bad you don't eat yogurt."

Angelo gave her a look. "Huh?"

Before they knew it, they pulled up to the terminal at Montréal–Trudeau Airport. People everywhere piled out of cars, hauled luggage, and hugged their loved ones. Car horns honked as people jostled into and out of the few parking spaces by doors. A parking attendant yelled or whistled his disapproval and made grand hand gestures at people who didn't pay any attention.

Bette and Gemma jumped out of the car and traffic backed up behind them. Angelo helped them with the bags, but the attendant shouted at him to get moving.

"*Vaffanculo,*" Angelo shouted back.

"Angelo!"

"What? The guy's a *bastardo.*" He closed the trunk and stood awkwardly by Gemma. Bette gave them some privacy.

He looked lost. "So, have a good time."

Gemma grabbed his upper arms and shook him. "Hey, you'll be fine. Your mama will see to that. Take care of the kids. Make sure Sophia brings that new boy right to the door before they go to the movies. Put the fear of God in him. And tell Anna to remember to feed the fish and get Mario…"

He grabbed her and hugged her tight. "Come back."

Gemma was shocked. She pulled away and put her hands on his cheeks. "What do you mean? Of course I'll come back. I'll tell Donald Trump to get another woman. This one's taken."

He nodded and wiped his nose with the back of his sleeve. "Get outta here."

She laughed and grabbed her luggage. He got in the car, gave the parking attendant the finger, and took off.

Bette joined her. "He loves you, you fortunate girl."

"Nah, he just likes to have his back rubbed before he goes to sleep."

They hurried through the entrance. People came at them from every direction, most intent on getting somewhere as fast as possible. There was already a lineup to check in. They strained to see

Augusta and Linda, but they weren't there. That's when Gemma realized their first mistake.

"Linda's got all our tickets. We can't get in line yet."

"That's right. How stupid are we? They should be here by now."

At that moment, Linda was stuck in traffic about a mile away. She was late leaving because she couldn't find the spare house key to give to Clive. Why hadn't she taken care of that days ago? She rooted in all the junk drawers, on top of the fridge, and in every basket she could find. Her taxi honked the horn outside. Buster accompanied her as she raced around the house.

"Buster, what am I going to do?"

Buster meowed. He wasn't sure.

"Oh, forget it." She picked up her pussycat. "Be good. Mommy will be home on Friday. Don't scratch the new settee." She kissed him, put him down, and raced to the front door to set the alarm. She closed the door, gestured to the taxi driver that she'd be one second, and rushed across the lawn to Clive's. Thank God he worked from home. She rang his doorbell and heard Winnie and Churchill warn their dad he had company.

Clive came to the door. At 7:30 in the morning, he had on a bowtie. Maybe he slept in one.

"Ah, the happy traveller is off."

Linda shoved her keys in his hand. "I'm not so happy. I couldn't find the spare keys. You'll have to take mine. You know the code to get in. I've left enough food for Buster to keep him going for a year. Just make sure he has fresh water every day. The scoop for the kitty litter is by the box."

"Go. We'll be fine."

"Thank you so much. You're a doll." She turned and ran down a couple of steps before she stopped and looked back. "Oh, my schedule is on the fridge door and my son's phone number is there too, just in case. He might drop by or he might not, I have no idea what's he's doing."

"Probably having sex."

Linda laughed over her shoulder. "Isn't he lucky? I wish it were me. Bye."

"I wish it was you…er…me too."

She gave him an astonished look. "Clive, behave yourself. Not in front of the boys." She tore down the walk, jumped in the taxi, and waved goodbye.

Meanwhile, on the other side of the city, while Augusta waited for her taxi to come, she quizzed her mother on everything that could possibly go wrong. The girls stood nearby, as if to stay by their mother for as long as possible.

"All the emergency numbers are by the phone. 911 obviously, poison control, the weather report, the doctor…"

"The weather report? Why do I need that?" her mother asked.

Augusta was distracted. She should have called for a taxi earlier. She stood by her front window and willed the taxi to show up. "Sorry, what?"

"The weather report?"

"In case of freezing rain, snow, whatever."

"In May?"

Augusta ignored her. "I have the number of the hotel on the fridge. The airline schedule is there too. I'll call when we get there."

"It's okay, dear. Calm down. We'll be fine. Won't we, girls?"

The girls didn't look like they'd be fine.

Finally a taxi came up the street. "Oh, it's here." Augusta hugged and kissed her girls at the same time. She kissed her mom last. "You'll look after them, won't you? They'll be all right?"

Her poor mother gave her a sad smile. "If you're going to do this, Augusta, please go and have fun. The girls will be fine. I'll be fine. I promise I'll watch them like a hawk."

Augusta felt her eyes well up with tears. She had to leave fast. Everyone stood by the door as she got in the taxi. She waved at them through the side window and then out the back window as the taxi drove off. The girls ran out on the lawn and waved back. They got smaller and smaller. When she couldn't see them any more, she let out a sob.

"You okay, lady?"

She searched through her purse for a Kleenex. "Yes, I'm fine." She saw the driver glance at her in the rearview mirror. "Really, I cry all the time."

He didn't look reassured.

As fate would have it, Linda and Augusta arrived within ten seconds of each other. They paid their taxi fares and smiled when they saw each other.

"We're here. We're really going." Linda pulled her suitcase behind her. "The other two must be inside. Let's get this show on the road."

Augusta felt much better seeing Linda's happy face. Everything would be fine. She had nothing to worry about.

CHAPTER FOUR

Gemma was flying.

And by the time they got in the air, she was as crazy as a moose.

"Just what the heck did you give her?" Linda worried. She and Bette watched from their seats across the aisle as Augusta attempted to wrestle a glass of wine from Gemma's lips. She only ended up spilling it on both of them.

Bette bit her bottom lip. "Nothing too horrible, the usual stuff."

"Well, the usual stuff must be a horse tranquillizer. How many did you give her?"

"Two."

Linda gave her a look. "Are you nuts? Gemma doesn't take aspirin for a headache. You've probably given her an overdose."

"Oh God, do you think so?"

They glanced back at their friend. Gemma giggled as she leaned her seat backwards as far as it would go. The businessman using his laptop behind her wasn't amused. He tapped her on the shoulder.

"Would you mind? I can't work if your chair is back this far."

Gemma swivelled in her seat. "So stop working."

"Just put it up a little," Augusta said under her breath. "It's only polite."

"You know what your problem is, Gussie? You're way too polite. You're so polite people walk all over you." Gemma stuck her nose back between the seats and addressed the businessman again. "This isn't your office. It's a plane, so get over yourself."

Augusta slapped her arm. "Turn around and shut up, Gemma. You're going to get us kicked off this plane."

"Can they do that? I thought you weren't allowed to open a door in mid-flight."

"Oh hell, I can't wait to get to New York."

Gemma took off her seatbelt and stood up. "I have to pee."

Augusta leaned toward Linda and Bette across the aisle. "Will you guys please help me?"

Bette got up. "I'll go with her. I feel responsible."

Bette manoeuvred past Linda and helped Gemma crawl over Augusta and the young student sitting in the aisle seat. He looked as though he wanted the floor to open up and swallow him whole. The plane gave a small lurch and Gemma ended up in his lap.

"Oh dear, are you all right?"

"Fine."

"You shouldn't be travelling alone. Where's your mother?" She patted his head.

Bette grabbed her elbow. "For the love of God, get off of him and come with me."

Gemma stuck her tongue out at her. One of the flight attendants got in on the act. She hurried over and asked if she could be of assistance. Between the two of them, they hurried Gemma down the aisle and into the bathroom. Bette waited outside the door.

"Sorry about this. My friend is afraid to fly and I gave her a tranquilizer. I think it was too much for her."

"That's okay. I've seen worse." The attendant rushed away and Bette stood guard; first on one foot, and then the other. She peeked back down the aisle and saw Linda and Augusta craning their necks at her. Linda pointed to her watch. Bette shrugged. That's when the turbulence started.

Bette grabbed the door handle. "Hurry up, Gemma."

There was no response.

Bette knocked on the door. "Gemma."

Nothing.

Bette knocked louder. "Gemma, are you all right?" She rattled the handle. "Hey, are you okay? Gemma!"

There was a muffled thud. Bette panicked. "She's unconscious." She pushed at the door and nothing happened. She peeked out into the cabin and signalled for the flight attendant. Linda and Augusta thought she was waving at them. They bolted out of their seats. Now there were four people in front of the bathroom door.

"You must go back to your seats, ladies," the flight attendant said.

"The seatbelt sign is on."

"But I heard a thud and she's not answering the door," Bette said. "Oh my God, what if she's dead?"

Augusta covered her mouth with her hand.

"Don't be ridiculous," Linda said. "She's fallen asleep."

"Excuse me, everyone." The flight attendant pushed past the three friends and opened the door in a jiffy. They found Gemma slumped over, sitting on the john with her panties down around her knees.

"Is she breathing?" Augusta asked.

As if to answer the question, Gemma gave a great snore.

They sighed together in relief. Between them, they got Gemma looking a little more dignified—which wasn't easy in a space the size of a pantry. Bette and Linda held Gemma up by her arms while Augusta quickly pulled Gemma's underwear back up where it belonged.

Linda stared at Gemma. "Am I seeing things? Was that a thong?"

Augusta nodded. "Sophia told her she looked sixty so Gemma bought a few as an experiment."

"Well, the experiment has gone awry."

The attendant suggested they put her in one of the empty first-class seats, so as not to hump her down the aisle and over the mortified student again. They led their sleepy friend over to a comfy seat and tucked her up in a blanket. The attendant told Augusta she could sit in the seat beside her. The student looked mightily relieved when Linda and Bette returned to their seats without their friends.

Just their luck, the plane circled over New York for a good hour— but since it was dark, there was no view to pass the time. Not even the famous lights of the city were visible. The captain came on to tell them it was overcast and unseasonably cold in the Big Apple. He didn't have to tell them it was windy. The plane bucked as it made its descent. A roller coaster would be hard pressed to come up with a better ride. Linda and Bette held hands through the descent, but Augusta was forced to bite her nails alone. Gemma snored on.

They finally landed, and as the other passengers filed out of the plane, Augusta shook Gemma awake. Gemma gave a great yawn and smacked her lips a couple of times.

"Aren't we in the air yet?"

"We're in New York, you ninny."

Gemma shook her head. "We are? Where have I been?"

"Out cold." Augusta stood and waited for Bette and Linda to join them. Gemma also stood but quickly sat down. "My head is throbbing."

The businessman with the laptop went by and gave them a dirty look.

Linda and Bette hurried up the aisle. "Are you okay, Gem?"

"Not really."

Bette grabbed her hand. "Are you woozy? Sick to your stomach?"

Gemma adjusted her skirt and squirmed in her seat. "No, but I'll tell you this: These thongs are well named. I feel like I've got a rubber sandal up my butt."

Augusta grabbed her bag and coat from Linda. "Can we please get out of here? I need a drink."

They rushed out of the plane and into the La Guardia airport terminal, and hurried over to the luggage carousel. Augusta's suitcase came down with a broken wheel and the handle nearly ripped off, but she was lucky since Linda's didn't come down at all.

Linda stamped her foot. "I don't believe this. Now I have to report my bag missing. What a waste of time."

"Get them to deliver it to the hotel," Augusta said.

Gemma burped. "Remember that Visa card? Go get a whole new wardrobe. And while you're at it, buy me some antacids."

At that moment a young mother, struggling to carry a crying baby and two over-the-shoulder bags, bumped into the back of Linda's heel with a stroller.

"Ow!"

"Oh, sorry," the mother said.

Linda winced. "That's okay. Do you need us to hold anything for you? You look like you need help."

"No thanks." The mother walked away.

"This Miss Independent thing has gone too far," Gemma said. "Young women these days won't accept a stick to pull them out of quicksand."

Linda looked around. "Okay. I have to find the Air Canada counter.

Bette, I made arrangements with a car service to take us to the hotel. They're called 'black cars' or something like that. They're parked at the front of the terminal. Why don't you go and tell them to wait?"

"I don't think we should be separated," Augusta said. "Why don't we all go to the counter? The last thing I need is to lose one of you."

Linda rolled her eyes. "Fine. You're such a worry wart."

They wandered about, looking for signs to point them in the right direction. When they finally found the right place there was a line of people in front of every agent, so they had no choice but to wait. Finally, in desperation, Linda insisted Bette and Augusta go out to nab their car before someone else grabbed it. She shoved a piece of paper at them with the name of the car service on it. Gemma stayed behind. She sat and swayed on her luggage, nodding off every few minutes.

Bette and Augusta hurried through the airport once more. They followed the signs and eventually arrived at what looked like the main entrance. They went through the doors and saw cars and taxis and minivans, with people hopping in and out, and traffic being directed by parking attendants. But the wind very nearly knocked them off their feet and the rain didn't help matters.

"I'm not sure which one is our car service," Bette yelled into Augusta's ear.

"What does Linda's note say?" Augusta no sooner had words out of her mouth than the paper flew out of Bette's hand.

"Oh no." Bette started to run after it, but Augusta put out her hand to stop her.

"Never mind, Bette. It doesn't matter."

Bette brushed her hair out of her face. "Are you nuts? Linda will have a fit. She's already stressed about her luggage."

"She'll be along in a second. If we don't get the one she booked, we still have lots of cabs to choose from."

"I guess you're right. Let's wait inside."

So they trooped back indoors.

"While we're waiting, we might as well go to the restroom," Bette said.

"What if the girls come and can't find us? I think I'll stay right here."

"Good idea. You always were a camel."

"Listen, Weinberg, it's not my fault you don't do your Kegel exercises."

Bette grinned at her and walked to the nearest ladies' room, which was full of women and their luggage and coats. When she was done, she had to wait to wash her hands. A few beauty queens were doing their makeup in the mirrors, along with three elderly ladies who seemed to have all kinds of time. That's when she noticed the young mother, changing her baby's diaper on the pull-down changing table.

"He's lovely," Bette said.

"Thanks."

"How old is he?"

"Three months."

"What's his name?"

"Keaton."

"Are you serious?"

The mother looked up and Bette said, "Oh, it's a lovely name. It's my best friend's last name. Isn't that funny? She's the one you hit with the stroller."

The girl nodded.

Bette filled in the silence. "It's our first time in New York. We can't wait. We're staying at the Waldorf, if you can believe it. Linda arranged it. The one you hit with the…"

Bette trailed off because it was obvious the mother wasn't listening to her. She looked distracted, or even ill. Bette washed her hands and got ready to go, when the young mother turned to her. "Could you watch the baby? I think I'm going to throw up."

"Sure, of course. It was probably the plane ride. It was pretty bumpy."

The young woman lurched into a stall, and from the sounds of it she was quite sick. Those in the bathroom looked at each other sympathetically. The baby started to cry, so Bette put her carry-all down next to the mother's bags and picked up the little fellow.

"Shh, don't cry. Mommy will be right back."

Little Keaton wasn't reassured. He was furious. He looked at Bette, screwed up his face, and let out a piercing scream. Bette jostled him up and down in her arms and made funny faces to try and get him to stop. It made things worse. She looked at herself in the mirror. "My record holds. I'm rejected by every male I meet."

The mother finally limped out of the stall. "Sorry, I'll be right there."

"That's okay," Bette shouted over the baby's cries. He had turned beet red by this point, and Bette was a little frantic, as if she were to blame for this kid's hysterical reaction. The mother threw cold water on her face. Bette wished she'd do that to the baby.

"I'm sorry, but I really have to go, or I'll miss my ride."

The mother wiped her face with a paper towel and reached over to claim her enraged child. He let her know what he thought of the whole situation. He barfed all over her.

"Oh God."

"Oh dear." Bette passed her some more paper towels. "He's not very happy, is he?"

"He can join the club."

A few other women got into the act, so Bette picked up her bag. "Good luck, dear."

"Yeah, thanks."

Bette went out the door with the wrong bag.

Two things happened then. Bette walked over to Augusta and told her about the uproar in the bathroom as Linda and Gemma showed up. And the young mother tidied herself as best she could and put her still-screaming baby in his stroller. She reached into the carry-all for Keaton's soother and just about fainted when she realized the bag wasn't hers. It was filled with someone else's stuff. It had to be the red-haired lady's.

She began to shiver almost uncontrollably, unsure whether to run after the woman or call her contact outside. In the end, she reached for her phone, because she couldn't run through the airport with a stroller without having people notice her. She took the stroller and the bags into an alcove. Her fingers were suddenly too big for the cellphone. She fumbled with the number a couple of times. "Work, goddamn you." She tried again. It rang once.

"Yeah?"

"I've lost the bag."

"*WHAT?*"

She started to cry. "It happened so fast. A woman grabbed it. It looked like mine, so she must have mixed them up."

"What woman?"

"I'm not sure."

"*What woman?*"

"She's short and has red hair. She's travelling with another woman named Keaton, who's tall and blonde, very pretty. I think there were four of them. She said they were going to the…where was it?…The Waldorf, I think. She just left. You can still catch her."

"You better hope I do." The phone went dead.

The young woman's teeth began to chatter. "What have I done?"

❁

Once the four friends reunited, the rush was on to find the car company that was supposedly waiting for them. They went out the door and looked around. Just then a black car sped up to them. The driver jumped out.

"Keaton?"

Linda gave a huge sigh of relief. "Oh, thank goodness. We have reservations."

"Yes. For the Waldorf?"

"That's right. Thank you."

"Yous guys are getting soaked. Why don't you get in?" He popped the trunk and reached for their bags. He stowed them away. "I can put your carry-on bag in here too." He reached for Bette's first.

"That's okay. I'll hold onto it." The others felt the same, so he slammed the trunk and Linda got in the front seat with him while the others crowded together in the back.

The driver took off with unseemly haste. As they peeled out, Linda said, "Whoa. After that flight, I have no intention of being killed on my way to the hotel."

"You're in New York, lady. This is the way we drive. If you don't like it, walk."

Bette clapped her hands. "Oh yes, we really are in New York. You sound like a real cabby."

The driver glanced at Linda. "Your friend's a genius."

For some reason, the four friends found this hilarious. The realization that they were actually on their way to Manhattan hit them at the same time. They chattered away like magpies.

The drive into the city was a Formula One race. It was thrilling and scary all at the same time. The rain-spattered windows made it hard for them to see clearly, and they fogged up the glass in their attempts to see if they recognized anything, but it was mostly just traffic and whizzing along the highway in the dark. They could have been in any big city. Linda consulted her Lonely Planet New York City guidebook. She tried to get her bearings; it seemed as if the drive was taking an awfully long time.

She wasn't the only one who had that thought. Augusta leaned over across Gemma and poked Bette. "I thought it was only a half-hour drive to get to the hotel?"

Gemma patted her arm. "You worry too much."

Linda addressed the driver. "Excuse me, are you sure this is the way to the Waldorf? If I'm correct, we seem to be heading in a northerly direction."

"Maybe you ain't correct, lady."

"There's no need to be rude."

"Let's get there, already," Bette said.

Augusta fiddled with her purse strap. "Lin, why don't you call the hotel and tell them we're running a little late? I know they guaranteed the room, but just in case."

"That's a good idea."

She was about to reach in her purse to grab her phone when the driver stepped on the gas and zoomed around a corner. They careened to the right.

"Slow down," they shouted at him.

He completely ignored them, as if they weren't there—and that was the scariest thing of all.

"What on earth are you doing?" Gemma said. "Are you crazy?"

He stepped on the gas even harder.

They couldn't believe what was happening. They held onto the door handles, and Gemma grabbed her friends on either side. They drove though a maze of streets, streets that were clearly nowhere near Park Avenue. And then, just as quickly as it started, it was over. They found themselves screeching to a halt under a dark overpass. The driver threw the car into park, reached into his pocket, and pulled out a gun.

"Gimme your bags. Now."

The poor guy never knew what hit him.

Augusta and Bette's screams alone would have alerted the authorities back in Canada. The other two did something more useful. Linda hit the gun out of his hand with her guidebook, and Gemma reached in her overnight bag, grabbed a can of pepper spray, and blasted the guy right in the face.

A cloud of noxious fumes filled the car. Then the battle was on to open the car doors, but in their rush to escape they kept re-locking them every time someone touched the control button. The windows opened and closed as if by magic.

"Leave it alone!" Linda said. "Let me do it."

Of course no one listened to her.

It was the driver who finally freed them in his panic to escape. Coughing hard, he pressed the right button at the right time and the five of them tumbled out the doors and into the night. He rolled around on the ground wheezing and gasping for air.

"Girls," Linda shouted. "Over here, over here."

The other three stumbled out of the darkness. Coughing, they ran toward Linda like chicks to a mother hen. Gemma ran around and blasted short bursts with her pepper spray. "Where is he? Let me at him." She rubbed at her eyes.

Augusta rooted through her purse for her cellphone. "Ohmigod, ohmigod, call 911. Call 911.

"I'll sit on him," Gemma said. "Lin, you tie his hands."

"With what?"

"Dental floss. I read that somewhere."

Their prey lay on the ground, struggling to breathe as he clutched at his throat.

Augusta tried to grab Gemma's arm. "Let's get out of here."

"Wait," Linda said. "I think he's in trouble."

"Who gives a shit? Let's kill him, the miserable bastard," Bette said.

Gemma advanced on him with her can. "You creep, you scared us half to death."

"Gemma, stop for a second," Linda said.

She stopped. And by then so had the guy on the ground. He just lay there. The women looked at him, and then at each other.

"I think he's fainted."

"I think he's faking."

"I think he's dead."

Augusta hopped up and down. "Call 911. Call 911."

"Is that all you can say?" Bette said. "Shut up with the 911 crap."

Augusta shivered violently, her hair plastered to her face thanks to the driving rain. "*You* shut up! Isn't that what we're supposed to do? We've been mugged. I thought the next logical step would be to call for help."

"Did we get in the wrong car?" Linda asked. "I don't understand it. He knew who we were and where we were going, so it must have been the right company."

"Well, I'm calling his supervisor when we get to the hotel," Bette said. "That's ridiculous, robbing people. They're in the taxi business. How can you make money like that? Their reputation would…"

Gemma threw her hands in the air. "Forget about taxis! We're getting soaked standing here. We'll die of pneumonia if we're not careful."

Augusta's teeth were rattling. "That guy hasn't moved. Someone has to do something. Lin?"

Linda took a few steps forward. "Why is it always me who has to do everything?"

"You married a doctor. You must have learned a few things over the years."

"I know how to throw a dinner party, not resuscitate a guy in cardiac arrest."

Gemma pointed at the guy. "Hurry up. If he wasn't dead before, he will be now."

Linda advanced on the prone figure, little by little, as if he might suddenly grab her ankle. She gave him a nudge with her toe, but he stayed still. She bent down and pushed his shoulder to turn him over, causing his arms to flop beside him. She reached out and put her fingers on his neck.

"He's toast."

"I killed him?" Gemma said.

"Apparently."

Augusta wrung her hands. "Oh my God, what are we going to do? My poor kids. I'm going to jail."

"Everyone stop talking for a minute and let me think," Linda said.

They were quiet for five seconds before Gemma asked, "How can a guy die from pepper spray?"

"You're a good shot," Bette said.

"We breathed some of it too," Augusta said. "We didn't die, but we may go blind." She blinked rapidly as if to make her point and her lip started to quiver. "You watch. We'll get the gas chamber. Whose stupid idea was this?"

"What idea?" Gemma asked.

"To come to New York and kill someone."

"I didn't do it on purpose, you know," Gemma said. "Did you want him to kill you? We're the victims here, not him."

"She's right," Bette nodded. "We can't help it if the guy was allergic to mace. Or maybe he had a heart attack. He's pretty beefy. We should thank Gemma for having the good sense to carry everything under the sun in that overnight bag of hers."

"Angelo gave it to me in case I met Donald Trump."

"Enough already." Augusta hopped up and down. "What are we going to do?"

"Call the police," Linda said.

"Can you believe this?" Gemma threw her hands in the air. "They'll want a statement and we'll have to go to the police station. There goes our first night in New York."

"I don't want to be here when the police come. Maybe they'll think we killed him," Bette said.

"We did kill him," Augusta said. "Oh God, can't we call the police and leave?"

Linda planted her hands on her hips. "Are you serious? We can't dump a body and take off. You didn't even want me to use Stuart's credit card to pay for this trip. Now you want to be involved in a hit and run?"

"Well, he started it."

Linda pointed at the body. "We'll have to move him, or he's road-kill."

"I can't touch him. I can't," Augusta said.

"Grab his shoe, then."

"But are we supposed to move a body?" Bette asked. "Won't the police want to draw a chalk line around him? You see that in movies all the time."

"Never mind, Bette," Augusta said. "I'm freezing. Let's just do it."

The friends gathered around the body. They each took an append-age and attempted to lift him off the road. They dropped him as a group.

"He's a dead weight," Bette said.

"Brilliant observation," Gemma replied, "but he's not going to weigh any less in the next two minutes."

"Let's drag him," Linda said. So they reached down and two wom-en took each arm and pulled with all their might. He moved another couple of inches.

"This is insane," Augusta cried. "We'll be here all night."

"We can't leave him now. Pull," grunted Linda.

They pulled, and he slid a few more feet towards the ditch.

"This guy needs to go on a diet." Gemma wiped the rain out of her eyes.

"Stop talking and pull."

They finally developed a rhythm and were a little more coordinated as they reached the edge of the road.

"Uh-oh." Linda stumbled backwards. "Damn."

"What's wrong?"

"My heel broke." She reached down and picked up her broken shoe, all the while hanging onto Gemma for balance. "Do you know how expensive these were? They're Jimmy Choos. Oooh, I wish this guy was alive, so I could kill him all over again."

The others let the man's arms drop in the dirt, so they could examine the damage.

"They're ruined." Linda leaned over the man. "Do you have any idea what you've done?" She put her newly flat shoe on and stuck the heel in her pocket. Just then, lights from an approaching vehicle came towards them.

"There's a car," Augusta said. "Flag it down."

"STOP! STOP!" They ran towards the car and waved their hands about.

The car slowed, but once the headlights hit the four banshees, the petrified woman behind the wheel put her foot on the gas and shot past them going eighty miles an hour, showering them with muddy water in her wake.

They stood like scarecrows for a few moments before beating the mud off their clothes with their hands.

"This goes from bad to worse," Linda said. "Now my Dior suit is ruined."

"Why didn't she stop?" Augusta cried.

"Would you? Look at us."

"Gemma's right. No one's going to stop." Linda headed for the car.

"Where are you going?" Gemma asked.

"To get my cell." Linda grabbed the phone out of her purse and hurried back to her friends. "I've never called 911 before...hello? Yes, I'd like to report a dead man. Sorry? No, we killed him, but it was an accident. He was trying to rob us. What? I have no idea where we are. We're under an overpass and..."

"Oh my God, look."

Augusta pointed down the darkened street. Coming at a fast clip was a gang of youths, headed straight for them.

"Oh, Jesus, Mary, and Joseph," Gemma yelled. "Hoodlums. Run!"

Linda ran back towards the car, limping on her uneven shoes. The other three took off in different directions. "Girls, get in the car! Get in the car!"

Linda hopped behind the wheel and turned the key. She forgot the engine was still running. A blast of metallic screeching put her in a panic and she shut the motor off.

The other three ran towards her. She turned the key once more. The engine sputtered. She tried again. No luck. Heart pumping out of her chest, Linda looked in the rearview mirror and saw the gang catching up to them. They were close enough for her to see their weapons.

"Get in the goddamn car now," she bawled out her open window as the engine roared to life. Bette dove into the front seat. Gemma was a little too slow for Augusta's liking; as Gemma tried to climb in the back, Augusta placed her foot on Gemma's ample backside, shoved her in, and then jumped on top of her.

Linda took off with the back door still swinging open, tires squealing. Two pairs of legs hung out over the side.

"Hurry, Linda," Bette shouted.

The car wove from side to side as it zoomed down the street and into the night.

The stickball players couldn't believe their eyes. Four crazy ladies jumped in a car and took off before they had a chance to help change their flat tire.

The catcher spied the body first. "Holy shit. There's a dead guy over here."

"Are you sure he's dead?"

The catcher felt for a pulse and nodded.

The second baseman pulled out his cellphone to call the police.

The pitcher stopped him. "Wait. What if the police think we did it?"

"But—"

"Do you want to take that chance? The guy's dead. There's nothing we can do for him now."

"Yeah, but…"

"We're black and the victim's white. Need I say more?"

They took off like scalded cats.

CHAPTER FIVE

"Can you see them anymore?" Linda kept her eyes glued to the unfamiliar road.

Gemma glanced out the back window. "No. They're gone. We're okay."

"We're not okay," Augusta said. "I'm sitting on a gun. What do I do?"

"Don't touch it," they yelled at her.

"But it might go off. Can't I throw it out the window?"

"No," Gemma said. "Your fingerprints will be on it. And what if a kid picked it up?"

"You're right." Augusta scooted over and practically sat in Gemma's lap to get away from it, as if it were a huge black bug.

"I have to stop for a minute." Linda pulled over and dropped her forehead onto her knuckles as her hands gripped the steering wheel. "I think I'm going to be sick."

Bette reached over and massaged her neck. "You're all right, Lin. Good job back there. I'd still be running if it wasn't for you."

"Where are we?" Augusta asked.

Linda raised her head. "I have no idea." She looked around. "There's a sign, but I can't read it."

"Just a sec," Bette said. "Pass me my purse, Gem. I need my glasses."

Gemma reached down and passed it over. Bette zipped it open, fumbled around inside, and took out a teddy bear.

"What the..."

Linda frowned. "What's that?"

"OMIGOD."

"What?"

"It's the wrong bag. It's the mother's bag. She has my bag. I had six hundred dollars in that bag. What should I do?"

"Stop saying *bag*," Linda said. "Calm down. Let's think."

Bette shook the bear. "What a goddamn night this has turned out to be. I can never go home now. Ida will run me over when she finds out about the money..."

Augusta interrupted her. "Look inside and see if her name is in there somewhere. I'm sure she'll get in touch with you. What mother wouldn't be frantic at the thought of her child's missing toy?"

"A young girl who looks like she could use six hundred bucks," Bette said. "Oh God, my glasses, my driver's license, my health card, and my money are all gone. Not to mention my airline ticket and passport."

No one said anything. It was too much.

Bette remembered something and patted down her coat. "I have my cellphone, at least."

Augusta squinted at the sign. "The only name I recognize is Harlem. Isn't this a bad neighbourhood?"

"According to the Lonely Planet, it's as safe as any part of New York," Linda said.

"Well, that's cold comfort," Gemma said. "We were accosted by a criminal ten seconds after we stepped outside the airport."

Linda finally shut off the engine. "We need to call the police. I'm tired of dealing with this alone." She reached once more for her cell.

"Wait," Gemma said. "You can't call. They'll want to know where we are and we don't have a clue. How will they get to us?"

Linda hesitated. "You're right." She looked around and pointed down the street. "That looks like a corner store at the end of the block. We'll ask what the address is and use their phone."

"Wait," Gemma said.

"Now what?"

"We can't leave the gun here. What if someone takes it? It's evidence."

"Well, we can't take it. What do we know about guns?" Augusta said. "We'll shoot ourselves in the foot or worse."

"If we're calling the police we should leave it here. We'll lock the car doors," said Bette.

"What if someone breaks into the car?" Gemma asked.

"What if, what if," Linda said. "We can't worry about every blessed thing."

"You can't leave a gun lying around," Gemma insisted. "It's not safe."

Linda turned around to face the back seat. "Fine. Take the gun and put it in your purse."

"But what about the fingerprints?"

"The police always pick it up with a pencil or a pen so the finger-prints don't smudge," Bette said.

"Okay." Gemma rooted through her purse and found a pen. "Crouch down, girls, just in case."

They hunkered down. Gemma gingerly lifted the gun and slowly placed it in her purse. By the time she closed it, she was in a lather of sweat. "Okay. It's done."

They sat up.

"Good job, Gemma." Augusta patted her friend on the back.

"Let's go," Linda said.

They got out of the car, took their suitcases from the trunk, and hob-bled down the sidewalk, all of them staying close to each other as if that would make them safe. They breathed a collective sigh of relief when they were inside the store. It was small, crowded, and dingy. The man behind the counter didn't look particularly friendly. Linda approached him first.

"Excuse me. May we use your phone?"

"No."

"No?"

"You heard me. There's a perfectly good payphone in the back. Use that."

"Fine. What's your address?"

Before he could answer, two men in hoodies came through the front door and approached the counter. The owner got up off his stool. "I got customers, lady."

Linda scowled and marched back to her friends, who stood around the coolers at the back of the store deciding what they wanted to drink.

"Do you want something?" Bette said. "We're dying of thirst."

"I'll have some water."

"So what's the address?" Augusta asked her.

"He wouldn't tell me."

"What do you mean?"

"He's busy. I'm going to have to go outside and look for a street sign. And he wants us to use that payphone." She pointed at the disgustingly dirty phone.

Bette passed Linda a bottle. "Do you want me to come with you?"

"Yeah, okay." Linda opened the bottle and took a quick swig before passing the bottle to Gemma. "Get the police on the phone. We'll be right back."

Linda and Bette started up the aisle, but they heard raised voices and a long string of cursing. Bette pulled Linda aside.

"Do you hear that?"

Linda nodded. They listened to the increasingly loud argument with growing alarm. They looked over and saw the other two beckon them to return, so they tiptoed back.

"Oh my God, do you hear them?" Augusta whispered.

Bette wrung her hands. "Is there a back way out of here?"

"Just be quiet," Linda said. "If we start running around, we'll call attention to ourselves. Crouch down and keep your mouths shut."

So the four of them sat on their haunches and looked like they were having a campfire at the back of the store. Augusta grabbed Gemma's hand. She was close to tears.

"If anything happens to me, Gem, please take care of my girls."

"It's okay, Gussie, I won't let anything happen to you."

"Put that knife away, you little punk, and get outta my store before I kill you."

"Open the motherfuckin' till or you're dead."

"NO. *You're* dead, you piece of shit."

"NO. *You're* dead, old man."

"Okay, that's it. I've had it." Gemma stood up. The others tried to get her to sit down, but she pushed them away. She reached into her purse and took out the gun. She pointed it at the ceiling and fired off a shot.

The ceiling tiles fell down around their ears in a cloud of white dust, which made them scream. Gemma dropped the gun, grabbed her suitcase and Augusta's hand, and rushed to the front of the store. "Get out of my way, you little bastards."

She was a raging bull, a raging bull with white powdery hair.

"Gemma, wait up." Linda and Bette grabbed their things and Augusta's suitcase and charged behind Gemma as she tore up the aisle with Augusta in tow. The two kids wearing hoodies took off out the door.

"What the hell are you doing to my store, you crazy bitch? I'm calling the cops. Look at my ceiling." The store owner jumped across the counter after them as they ran out the door. Their luggage bounced off the pavement behind them and made a terrible racket. The owner chased them with a cellphone in one hand and a baseball bat in the other.

"I'm never leaving the house again," Augusta cried.

After half a block, Linda looked over her shoulder and noticed the owner running back towards his store. He probably thought better of leaving his property unattended.

"Girls, he's gone."

Out of breath, they slowed to a fast walk.

"He's calling the police," Augusta said. "We should keep going."

"But I thought we wanted the police," Bette said.

Linda bounced beside her on her uneven shoes. "We do. But we don't want them arresting us for property damage. We'll call them about the other disaster when we get out of this disaster."

Gemma developed an interesting gait as she raced up the sidewalk. "On top of everything else, I'm getting a blister, and it's not on my foot."

Just then a police siren went off down the street.

"Hurry up, this way." Linda led them towards a dark alley on the right. "Let's hide in here." They gathered together with their bags, and as the siren got louder they pressed against a brick wall next to a stinking dumpster and rotting bags of garbage.

Bette jumped. "I think a rat ran over my foot."

They leapt about in a frenzied dance, but stopped when the two police cars whizzed by. That's when the drunk spoke up.

"Got a light?"

They screamed as one, and scared the poor bugger out of his wits. He threw his cigarette at them. "Take it." He lurched down the alley and away from them as fast as possible.

"Okay, I'm going to have hysterics in a minute if I don't get the hell out of here *now*," Augusta said.

Gemma pointed. "There's a bus and there's a bus stop. Who cares where it goes. Let's get on it."

No one answered her. They were too busy running for the bus.

It almost left without them, and if it hadn't been for an exceptional burst of speed from Augusta, it would have. She waded through puddles and managed to claw her fingers between the doors' rubber edging. "*Stop.*"

The bus stopped and the doors sprang open. Augusta leaned against the door, panting. "Hurry up, girls."

The others pushed their way into the bus with the suitcases.

"Spending the night?" the driver joked.

"We want to get to the Waldorf Astoria Hotel," Bette shouted as if he were deaf. "Do you know where that is?"

"Sure, lady, but it ain't anywhere near here."

It took forever to get there. They didn't even have the strength to talk. They looked out the window on occasion, but nothing held their attention except the couple making out in the back of the bus. That was on the first bus. When they transferred onto the next two, they were treated to the spectacle of a drug deal gone bad and a leering pervert. But it didn't matter. They were dry, off their feet, and headed in the right direction.

It was nearly midnight when they walked through the doors of the Waldorf Astoria. The doorman's eyes widened at the sight of them, with their white, wet, dishevelled hair and mud-splattered clothes. Linda's limp didn't help, and neither did Gemma's squirmy gait.

They walked up to the front desk. A perky girl plastered a smile on her face.

"Good evening, ladies. How may I help you?"

"We have a reservation under the name of Keaton," Linda answered in a monotone.

"Certainly. I'll check. One moment." She clicked a few keys and stared at the monitor.

"Mrs. Stuart Keaton?"

Linda went pale and the others froze.

"W-what did you say?"

The girl looked a little dismayed, as if she'd done something wrong but didn't know what. She glanced at her screen again. "I have a Doctor and Mrs. Stuart Keaton. Oh wait. I have Linda Keaton. Perhaps that's it?"

"Yes, that's it."

The clerk smiled. "Sorry. We have a lot of doctors here at the moment, what with the plastic surgery convention."

Linda looked at the others. She gestured for them to step away from the desk. They huddled together.

"Is this bloody nightmare ever going to end? How is it possible that Stuart is here with Ryan? I mean, what are the chances?"

"You know what, Lin?" Bette said. "Who gives a shit? I don't care if he's here. I need a room. I want a toilet and a sandwich. Is that too much to ask?"

Augusta bit her lip. "But if Linda doesn't want to be here, I don't think we should object. She is paying for it, after all."

No one said anything. They realized Augusta was right, but from the pathetic looks they gave her, Linda knew she had only one choice.

"All right, we'll forget the little prick, but do me a favour and eat every goddamn cashew you can find." She walked over to the clerk. "May I have the room key, please?"

The girl passed it over. "You're in room 715."

They trooped over to the elevator and didn't say a word. The door opened and they crowded inside. Linda hit the button and the elevator rose.

"I can't wait to get to our room and take off this bloody thong," Gemma said.

The minute she said it, the elevator stopped. They waited for the doors to open up, but they didn't. Linda pushed the button again. Nothing happened.

"What's wrong?" Bette asked.

"I don't know. It's not working."

They waited some more, but the elevator stayed still.

"I can't believe this," Linda said. "We're cursed."

"Open that emergency phone and tell them to get us out of here," Augusta said. "I need to pee in the worst way."

"You should've gone at the airport," Bette said.

Augusta gave her a look. "I'm glad I didn't. At least I still have my bag."

"God, don't remind me."

Linda picked up the phone and waited for someone to come on. "Yes? Hello? We're stuck in the elevator. Please hurry." She nodded a few times and put the phone down. "It'll be a minute. They said not to panic."

"Panic?" Bette said. "This is the best part of the trip. We're in a room at the Waldorf. Mind you, I thought it would be a bit bigger."

Augusta crossed her legs. "Don't make me laugh."

Gemma wiggled. "My ass is on fire."

Linda turned to face her. "You've been saying that for three hours. Take the damn thing off."

"I can't."

"Why not?"

"I'm a good Catholic girl. My mother would kill me if she knew I was in New York with no panties on."

"Your mother is safely tucked away in a cemetery in Quebec. She doesn't know."

"Oh yes, she does. She has eyes in the back of her head."

"She's *dead*."

"Makes no difference."

The elevator gave a jolt that almost knocked them off balance, but it thankfully continued to rise before stopping at the seventh floor. The doors opened and they filed out, all of them weary to the bone. They got their bearings and followed the signs to their room. Linda inserted the card and they shouted hurray when the door opened.

It shut behind them.

❄

Augusta's mother, Dorothy, drank her sixth cup of tea. The girls were on their fourth hot chocolate. They were up much later than they should have been, but Dorothy wasn't stupid. The novelty of going to bed at an ungodly hour would make the evening go smoother.

They were supposedly playing Monopoly, but their hearts weren't in it. Raine didn't even blink when she landed on Summer's hotel on Park Place.

The phone rang.

Raine knocked over her hot chocolate in her race to be the first one to the phone. "Hello? Mom?"

Her face fell. She held the phone out and pointed it at Summer. "It's for you."

Dorothy looked at her watch. "Who's calling you at this hour?"

Summer grabbed the phone. "Hello?" Her face lit up and she turned her back on her sister and grandmother. "Oh, hi Paul." She walked out the kitchen door and as far away as the cord would allow.

"Get off the phone. It's only a stupid boy."

Dorothy wiped up the chocolate mess. Raine helped her.

"Why hasn't Mom called? It's really late."

Dorothy flicked her cloth. "Oh gosh, a hundred things could have delayed them. The plane was probably late, or the traffic heavier than they thought. I know she's fine. She'll call us as soon as she can."

"Can't we call her?"

Dorothy sat down and brushed her hair away from her face. "Oh, I suppose we could, but I want your mother to go away without worrying about us. If we call in a panic, that will only upset her, don't you think?"

"I guess."

They heard Summer say, "I've got to go. See you tomorrow." She hurried into the kitchen and clicked the phone. "Hello, Mom?"

Raine jumped off her chair and stood by her sister.

"Yes. Hi. What? Oh, we're fine. We miss you."

Raine yelled at the receiver, "I miss you."

Summer nodded. "Mom says she misses you too. Sorry, what? Oh, nothing. We're playing Monopoly, but guess what? Paul just called me, can you believe it? What? God, mother, he didn't call too late. He's seventeen. Well, he failed a year, but he's really cute."

Raine hopped up and down. "Tell her I made 98 on my history test."

"Raine, settle down. You'll have your turn," her grandmother laughed.

They talked to their mother for a good five minutes before Dorothy was finally given a chance. She told the girls to get ready for bed before she took the phone. "So, dear, are you having a wonderful time? Well, that's great. You sound tired. Remember not to overdo it. You know how easily you get run down. Pardon? Of course, dear, I swear the girls are fine and you don't have to worry about anything. I'm here. Get a good night's sleep, honey, and we'll see you when you get back. Love you. Bye."

Dorothy hung up and smiled. Her daughter needed this trip badly. Dorothy was happy for her. They were going to have a wonderful time.

She started to clear away the Monopoly board.

❀

Angelo sat in front of the television, but he wasn't watching it. He did that so people would leave him alone. He heard the kids making a mess in the kitchen, but he didn't care. His mother would clean it up. She never let him lift a finger. The kids were supposed to be in bed, but he'd promised them they could speak to their mother.

He fiddled with his wedding ring. Every time the phone rang, his ears perked up, but it was never Gemma. What on earth was taking so long? Didn't she know he'd be here, worried? Visions of Gemma dancing in a nightclub filled his thoughts. She was always a good dancer. His hands gripped the arms of his chair.

There was a thump, thump, thump on the ceiling. His mother used her cane to let him know she wanted him. She complained she could never get through on the phone, since it was always busy. He couldn't disagree about that.

He rose wearily from his chair and walked out in the hall. "Anna."

Anna appeared in the kitchen doorway wearing her pyjamas. "I'm going upstairs to see what Nonna wants. Let me know if Mama calls."

"She'll call, Papa. She promised to buy me a present. Maybe she's still at the store."

He smiled at her. "That's probably it."

Angelo went out the door, turned left, rang the doorbell, and was buzzed upstairs. He trudged up the steps towards his mother at the top of the landing. She was wearing her long black dress. It's all she ever wore. She told him when he got married that she'd be in mourning for the rest of her life, and she meant it.

The only brave thing he'd ever done was to marry Gemma. Of course, they'd had to get married because Mario was on the way. But still.

Yes, Gemma was quite something when she danced. It made him ache just to think of it.

"So she call?"

"No."

"What I tell you. She's a *desgratiata*..."

"Mama, stop."

"No, I no stop. Why she run away and leave you with so many children? You have to work all day. You should be up all night waiting for her to phone?"

"I'm sure she got delayed. That happens on planes."

His mother turned away from him and walked into her kitchen. "It no happen when you no get on a plane."

Angelo followed her and sat at the kitchen table. He wasn't there two seconds before she put a plate in front of him. "Eat."

He pushed it away. "No thanks, I'm not hungry."

His mother looked shocked. "What? You no eat? Oh, this terrible woman, she make you sick..."

"Mama," Angelo said. "You've got to stop saying things like that. I'm tired of it. Gemma is a wonderful wife and mother, and she deserves a few days away with her friends. She works hard. She has five kids. You only had one. Think about it."

His mother looked shocked. Good. Maybe that would shut her up.

Just then a pounding came from the floor. Angelo jumped up and ran down the hall. "That's her. I told the kids to let me know when she called."

His mother ran after him with the plate of food. "Wait, you have to eat. You no get sick."

He ran down the stairs and out the door.

❊

The phone rang. Clive woke out of a sound sleep. The boys snuffled as he leaned over them to turn on the lamp and pick up the phone on the bedside table.

"Hello? Yes? Linda? Good Lord, is anything the matter? What time is it?" He squinted at his alarm clock and then sat up in bed. The boys were decidedly miffed at the interruption of their nightly routine.

"No, of course not, I don't mind at all. That's completely understandable. I'm sure Wes is fine. His cellphone is probably off. You know youngsters, never a thought for those sorts of things. Pardon me? No. I haven't seen his car in the driveway, but let me check again."

Clive put the phone down and pulled back the covers. The boys raised their sleepy heads amid the blankets. He crossed the room and looked out the window. Everything was as it should have been. The outside light was on, as he'd left it the last time he went in to check on Buster.

Buster hadn't been in a very good mood when Clive arrived earlier. He'd hissed and growled from the top of the fridge. Clive assumed it was the smell of the dogs on his clothes that put him off.

He shuffled back to the phone. "No, his car isn't there. But have you tried calling the house? Surely he would answer the phone if he was in."

Clive sat on the bed. "No, I don't think you're being silly. It's in a mother's nature to worry about their offspring. Why, the last time Winnie was a bit peckish I whisked him off to the vet only to be told it was gas. Of course, Linda. If I see the car in the morning, I'll run over and ask him to call you. I can even leave a note on the counter, asking him to do so. Will that be all right? Good. Are you having a nice time? That's lovely. Yes, I'll do that. No, it's no problem at all. Feel free to call me whenever you like. No, I mean it. Anytime. Goodnight, Linda."

He hung up the phone and looked at the picture of his wife that he kept by the bedside. Clive often talked to her. It made him feel better when he did.

"That was Linda. She couldn't get in touch with Wes. You always liked her, didn't you? So do I. I can't believe Stuart left her. He must be mad." Clive picked up the picture and kissed it. "Goodnight, petal."

He got under the covers, turned out the light, and snuggled in with his boys.

❀

"They should have called by now," Ida said to Izzy.

"Don't be such an old woman."

They sat on opposite sides of the television set. Izzy smoked. Ida popped candies in her mouth and crunched them noisily.

"I *am* an old woman. You want I should turn into one of your Playboy bunnies?"

"Please."

The phone rang.

Izzy bolted from his chair, and got to it first. "Hello?"

Ida pulled up beside him and wrestled it out of his hand. "Give me that."

Izzy grabbed it again. "Why should you get it all the time?"

Ida grabbed it back. "Because I endured thirty-six hours of labour, that's why."

"Thirty-six hours? Don't make me laugh. You dropped her like a hot biscuit."

They heard a screech on the other end of the phone. Ida put the receiver up to her ear. "Hello? Hello? Is that you, Bette?" She nodded. "It's her."

"Of course, it's her. Who else calls us in the middle of the night?"

"Who calls us, period? Hello, yes, I'm here. Where on earth have you been?" Ida nodded.

Izzy lit a smoke. "What's she saying?"

"The plane was delayed, so they had a late dinner, but they're in their room now."

Izzy grabbed the phone. "Did you get raped?"

Ida rolled over Izzy's foot and caught the phone as he dropped it. "What kind of a sick question is that? You and your dirty mind."

Izzy hopped around as he held the toes of his left foot. "You're a menace, you old bat."

The screech came once more. Ida put the phone back up to her ear. "Did you say something?"

"What's she saying?"

Ida put her hand over the receiver. "If you'd shut up for five seconds, maybe I could hear her." She uncovered the phone. "What? I can't hear you with your father yammering on every time I open my mouth."

"You never shut your mouth." He leaned towards the phone. "Isn't that right, Bette? She never shuts up."

There was a loud click on the other end of the phone. Ida and Izzy looked at each other.

"She hung up on me. What kind of daughter hangs up on her mother?"

"I'd hang up on you too, if you were my mother."

Ida put down the phone. "If I was your mother, I'd hang myself."

❁

"Why do I call my parents? Can someone tell me?" Bette asked no one in particular. The four of them sat on two queen-sized beds with their luggage all around them. None of them felt they could unpack until they'd talked to their loved ones and called the police.

Linda picked up the hotel phone. "Okay, we tell them it was an accident. We were clearly provoked. We don't normally run around killing people."

"What if they ask why we left the crime scene?" Bette said. "That's what might get us in trouble."

"Tell them a gang of thugs were running after us. What else were we supposed to do?" Augusta said.

"Do you think they'll believe us?"

"They should," Gemma said. "We're law-abiding citizens…"

"…who just killed someone," Linda said. "They don't know us from Adam. How would they know we're normal?"

"Because killers don't usually call 911 and confess," Bette said.

They agreed that was true. Linda dialled 911.

"Yes, I'd like to report a murder…"

Gemma hit Linda in the arm. "We didn't *murder* him, we killed him."

"Sorry, I'd like to report a killing."

Augusta shook her hands at Linda. "No, that sounds like murder."

"Sorry, I'd like to report an accidental death."

The other three nodded.

"I'm calling from the Waldorf Astoria...no, it didn't happen here... we were in a car...NO...it didn't happen at the hotel...it's not happening now. It happened before." Linda put her hand over the phone. "She thinks it happened here." She got back on the phone. "I'm sorry, I think you're confused...no, it's not an emergency...well, it was, but we tried to call before and we had to stop because bad guys were chasing us." Linda listened. "No, madam, this isn't a prank...a man is dead and he's on a highway somewhere in this city...I don't know where. I just flew in a few hours ago. On a plane...Look, we're at the end of our rope here. We haven't eaten, we haven't slept, we were mugged and chased by bad guys, we spent two hours on buses carrying a lot of luggage and we're fried. This is supposed to be a holiday and so far...what? Are you sure? But the guy is still out there...Okay, okay. What's the number?" Linda snapped her fingers. Gemma reached over and grabbed a pad and pencil by the phone and handed them to Linda. She started to scribble. "So we can call this number tonight? But...okay, fine. We'll call in the morning. So you're sure about this? Okay, thanks."

Linda put down the phone. "She says we can report it to the police in the morning, because it wasn't an emergency."

"Wasn't an emergency?" Gemma said. "What does she know, sitting on her ass in some cubicle? It was an emergency when that guy pointed a gun at us."

"I'm still trembling." Augusta held out her hands to show the others.

"I don't feel right sitting here in a fancy hotel when there's a man lying dead by the side of the road," Bette said.

"He was a bad man," Gemma said. "He could have killed us and eight children would've been orphans."

Linda sighed. "Bette, we're not going to feel right, period, after what we've been through. It scared the life out of us. We've done our best to report this to someone and the authorities told us we can call in the morning. I think we should order some food, unpack, and get into our pyjamas. It'll make us feel better. We can call or even go visit a police station tomorrow. What do you think?"

The other three nodded in agreement.

Linda stood up. "Since you three cowards didn't want to call, I'm first in the shower."

❀

Stuart lay on the king-sized bed and watched Ryan cavort around the room in her skimpy undies and small spaghetti-strap top. He was exhausted. How was it possible she was still raring to go?

She jumped on the bed and straddled him. "Don't be such an old bear, Stuart. Come on, we're in New York for God's sake. Let's go clubbing."

"I took you to dinner. We've shagged for two hours. What more do you want?"

"I want to go clubbing."

"I have an all-day conference tomorrow, in case you've forgotten. I told you that before we left home, so don't get all pouty on me."

Ryan flicked her streaked hair across his face, and then lowered her head and gently rubbed her lips across his. "Please. Pretty please. I'll give you what you want."

God, he hated when she did that. He'd have a heart attack at this rate. He put his hands on her shoulders. "No, Ryan. Now stop, I've had enough. It's been a long day and I have to get some sleep."

She huffed off the bed and stomped over to the chair by the window. "So I'm supposed to sit here and watch you snore and tomorrow I get to file my nails until you waltz in the door, is that it?"

Stuart got up on his elbows. "For Christ's sake, I told you before we left you didn't have to come. I'm not on holiday. I'm working, believe it or not."

She gathered her knees up under her chin. "Well, this sucks."

He didn't bother to answer her, opting instead to get off the bed and shuffle into the bathroom. Leaning over the sink, he looked at himself in the mirror. There were bags under his eyes, a symptom of all these late nights with Ryan. She was up for it twenty-four hours a day. He was up twice, maybe three times if he pushed it. How long would it take before he dropped dead?

He turned on the hot water and cupped his hands under the tap, splashing his face a few times before reaching for a towel. There wasn't one. They were all on the floor. How was it possible for one slip of a girl to need every towel in the bathroom? He muttered as he reached for the facecloth still folded in a triangle. Once his face was dry, he searched for his shaving kit so he could brush his teeth, but it was nowhere to be seen. The entire surface of the counter was covered with makeup, perfume, and huge black instruments of torture—a hair dryer, curling iron, and something that looked like a fat pair of tongs. He picked it up and wondered what it was for.

"Ah, screw it." He opened the bathroom door, shut off the light, and was about to fall back into bed when Ryan said, "I need ice. I'm drinking every bottle in this mini-bar, since you won't take me out. I deserve at least that."

"Fine." Stuart turned around and grabbed the ice bucket off the table, then opened the hotel room door and rounded the corner. He stopped dead in his tracks. Room service was pushing a cart into a doorway two doors down. He quickly retreated and shook his head. He could have sworn he'd seen Bette. He looked again, but she was gone. Maybe he was going nuts? Guilt was doing a number on his head. He went back to his room and shut the door.

"Hey! Where's my ice?"

"I don't want to go out in my bathrobe. The liquor's cold, any-way."

Ryan gave him a filthy look. "I'll get it myself, shall I?" She jumped up and grabbed the ice bucket.

"You can't go out like that."

"Watch me." She opened the door and sashayed down the hall. "Maybe I'll meet a bell boy and we can do it in the broom closet. At least that's exciting."

"Ryan, get back here."

"Make me." She kept going.

CHAPTER SIX

The bad guys were in a dither. The smuggled diamonds hidden inside the teddy bear had been snatched out of their hands moments before they were meant to be delivered. Heads rolled on the decision to use the young mother with the baby.

Then came worse news.

"The driver. He's dead," confirmed the voice on the phone.

Candy hit his forehead with the palm of his hand. "I knew it. I knew it. This just goes from bad to worse." He slammed the phone down and glared with his piggy eyes at the young woman in the chair in front of him.

"It's a professional job."

"It couldn't be. She was a lady. Look in the bag. Everything's in there...her passport...even her wallet has two hundred bucks in it. Who'd be stupid enough to leave that behind?"

Candy reached into his pocket, unwrapped three Life Savers, and popped them in his mouth. "She walked off with five million in ice, Gracie. I'd say she was very, very clever."

Gracie looked at him, wide eyed. "I did what you wanted. I brought the stuff over. What's going to happen to me? "

"If it were up to me, I'd kill ya, but higher-ups want to keep you for a while. You're the only one who knows what this broad looks like. You may come in handy. For now. Let's just say you're expendable, and so's your kid."

Gracie looked as if she might faint.

"Go over it again. You're sure there's nothing you can tell me about this woman? Did she say where she was going? Anything that would help track her down?"

She didn't speak.

Candy yelled in her face. "What do I look like, a priest? I don't got all day."

"No. Nothing."

"She didn't say a word?"

"She said Keaton was lovely."

Candy hit the table with his fist. He yelled for his beefy hench-men, whom he'd nicknamed Dumb and Dumber after a botched job in the Bronx. Candy wasn't the sort who let someone forget their mistakes.

Dumb came through the door first. He was all muscle, with a blank stare that registered nothing, whereas Dumber possessed a permanent sneer. He carried the baby out in front of him as if he were radioactive. "Yeah, boss?"

Gracie jumped up and grabbed her baby. Keaton held on to her for dear life.

"Your brat stinks," Dumber said.

"So do you," Gracie yelled at him.

Dumber put up his hand to slap her. Gracie flinched but didn't back down.

"Cut the crap." Candy crunched on his Life Savers and then put the rest of the roll in his mouth. "Yous guys take this chick to the safe house. Then come back here. We got work to do. We have to find this Bette Weinberg, and if not her, then her relatives. She'll give us the goods when she knows we have her family."

When Dumb and Dumber left, Candy got on the phone. He called a few associates, and one of them gave him the information he needed. Freddy the Fish lived in the east end of Montreal. He got Fish on the phone and gave him Bette's address.

"Rough up anyone who answers the door. I wanna know where this bitch is and I don't got a lotta time."

"I want a cut."

"Yeah, yeah. We'll sort out the details later."

Fish hung up the phone.

❁

Dumb and Dumber blindfolded Gracie and bundled her, the baby, and her belongings into the back of a beat-up van and drove to a run-down apartment. They parked in the alley behind and took her up the back stairs. After unlocking the door, Dumber pushed her inside. Only then did he take the blindfold off.

Gracie squinted for a minute and looked around at the slovenly surroundings. "Love what you've done with the place."

Dumber shoved her along the hallway. "Shut up, you stupid bitch." He opened a bedroom door and threw the stroller and bags on the floor before he forced her inside. "And that brat of yours better keep his yap shut too." Dumber slammed the door behind Gracie and locked it.

"This is a fine mess, isn't it buddy?"

Keaton bobbed his head up and down.

Gracie sat on the old mattress and propped herself up against the wall so she could nurse Keaton. He'd take a little and then doze off, which was just as well; it kept him quiet. And she needed him quiet. She didn't want to call attention to him at all.

Her fingers lingered on his silken hair. "You can't cry, little guy. I know you take after your big-mouth daddy, but you gotta listen to me. It's for your own good."

Gracie looked around. The room was dark and it smelled musty. She had no idea where she was, but one thing was certain: She had to get out of there or they would kill her and her baby. They'd also kill the lady who helped her in the bathroom, this Bette, and the Keaton woman. Gracie had been desperate enough to smuggle diamonds over the border, but she hadn't signed up for murder. That's why she wouldn't open her mouth to Candy about Bette. She had to get to the Waldorf and warn them.

She put her two fingers softly down Keaton's back and slid four one hundred dollars bills out of his diaper. "Thanks for not pooping on it."

In the first panicked moments in the restroom, she'd taken all six hundred of it, but quickly changed her mind. Everyone travelled with some money. Her plan had been to walk out of the bathroom and buy a ticket to anywhere, but as soon as she did she ran smack dab into Dumb and Dumber. They'd been in another car; when they saw their pal squeal off with four women they realized something had gone wrong with the plan and rushed into the airport to find Gracie. They took her by her arms and walked her quickly to the exit, Keaton still crying in his stroller.

Gracie needed to act fast. The longer they kept her here, the more that could go wrong. She lay Keaton down, and as she did, he filled his diaper. "That was good timing."

He grinned in his sleep.

It gave her an idea. She took off the diaper and put it to one side. Then she cleaned up her baby. There were still a few outfits and diapers in the other bag she'd taken on the plane, so she took what she needed and dressed Keaton in a couple of layers before laying the four bills across his head. On went his hat, which she tied snugly under his chin.

Next she placed him in his stroller, while she took the sheets off the bed, folding one of them to wrap it around her middle. The other sheet she smeared with baby poop. Then she picked up Keaton and smeared some on his clothes. She folded the stroller and laid it on the floor where it could be seen and left her knapsack open on the bed.

"Okay, buddy. You've got to help me. Stay very quiet."

She walked over to the closed door and pounded on it. "Hey. Hey! I gotta clean up my kid."

"Shut up," came a voice from under the door.

"Great. You want shit everywhere stinkin' up the place, that's your business."

"Aw, crap. It does smell like crap."

Dumber unlocked the door. "Holy shit, what a stink. Take that brat and wash him off. Don't you got no sense?" He gestured to Dumb. "Look at this mess. It's everywhere."

Dumb looked in and wrinkled his nose. "Some people just ain't brought up right."

Gracie pushed past them. "I don't need a lecture. I need some water." She made sure she pointed Keaton's little backside in their direction.

"Get that brat away from me. He reeks," Dumber winced.

Dumb pointed a finger at her. "Don't try nothin'."

Gracie rolled her eyes. "Where the hell am I going? My stroller's in the other room. I don't have any supplies for the kid and I don't have any money. Like I'm going take my baby out in the middle of the night? Don't be stupid."

"Hey, don't call me stupid."

"Sorry. I'm going to give him a bath, is that all right?"

"Hurry up."

They went back to watching their porn video.

Gracie closed the bathroom door and thanked God there was a window. She quickly took the dirty clothes off Keaton, unzipped her hooded sweater, and unwrapped the sheet from around her waist before turning on the water in the tub full blast. Then she picked up her sleeping baby and held him against her chest, slipping the sheet around the back of her neck and crisscrossing it over his body as tightly as she dared. The two ends wrapped around her waist and she tied it in the front. On went her sweater, which she zipped up over Keaton.

All set. She splashed a little water around. "Who's a stinky boy? Yuck."

Dumber yelled, "Make sure he's clean, and then wash that shitty sheet."

"I will, don't worry."

She climbed up on the radiator and pushed the window open. It wouldn't budge.

"Damn." She jiggled it and looked for a lock. It was painted shut, so she had to risk making some noise. She shoved at the window. It gave a little.

"What was that?" Dumb said.

"The toilet seat."

She whacked it again and it opened. "If we're on the tenth floor, buddy, we're screwed. I ain't Spiderman."

Keaton gave a little grunt.

"Shhh, baby. Just a little longer."

The men were moving around. She had to go—it was now or never. It was a good thing she was small; it was difficult getting out the window. It turned out she was at the back of a rundown apartment, with wrought-iron stairs zigzagging to the ground. "Thank you, God."

Gracie ran down the stairs as fast as she could and had to hang off the emergency ladder and drop the last four feet to the pavement below. That's when Keaton protested. She kissed the top of his hat. "Thanks, little man. You did a good job."

She disappeared into the dark.

❈

The phone rang. And rang. And rang.

Finally, a hand reached from underneath the duvet and groped for the phone, picking up the receiver and pulling it back underneath the covers.

"Mmm?"

"This is your wake-up call."

"Mmm." The hand tried to replace the phone but didn't quite make it, so the receiver fell to the floor.

The four friends snored on.

Around eight, Gemma threw the covers off her head. "What the hell is that noise?"

The other three showed signs of life and started to move around.

Bette yawned. "What noise?"

"It sounds like a buzzer."

Linda solved the mystery. She reached over the side of the bed and picked up the phone. "Oops." She replaced it on its cradle. "That must have been the wake-up call."

Augusta sat up and stretched. "We left one for seven. What time is it?"

"It's nearly eight."

"So what's the plan?" Bette said.

"Instead of calling that number, I think we should go to a police station. At least we'd see a bit of the city, because you know darn well that if we call they may send someone up here and we'll never get out of this room. What do you think?"

"I think you're right. Let's get a move on," Gemma said.

They quickly took turns showering and made coffee in their room. They'd eaten so late the night before that no one wanted breakfast. Gemma stared out the hotel window. "It looks like a great day out there. If we were in a parallel universe where everything went right, I wonder what we'd be up to today?"

Augusta joined her. "Having a wonderful time seeing the sights. I've always wanted to go to a hot dog stand, for some reason."

"Of all the places you could go, you want a hot dog from a street vendor?"

"They always look so good on *Law and Order*." Linda called the airline to see if her luggage had arrived but was told that no, there was no sign of it. Frustrated, she banged the phone down. "My suitcase is still having a wonderful time in Spain or Greece or the North Pole for all I know."

Since Augusta was around the same size, she lent Linda some clothes. When Linda came out of the bathroom a few minutes later, she pulled at her crotch. "Damn, I wish I didn't have such a long torso. I feel like I'm being carved in two."

She ended up putting Kleenex in the bra, and then stuffed some in the shoes Gemma lent her so they'd stay on her feet. She stood in the middle of the room. "Okay, this will have to do. Now, it's off to the police station first and then to the Canadian consulate to report Bette's missing passport."

"We might have to leave you behind, Bette," Augusta said. "Just think, you'll never see Ida and Izzy again."

Bette made a face. "That's the only good news I've had in the last twenty-four hours."

"If you girls don't mind," Linda said, "I'd like to do a little shopping. I need something to wear that's a tad more comfortable. I promise I won't be long, Augusta. I know you want to go exploring."

"That's okay."

Linda grabbed her guidebook. "I looked it up. Saks Fifth Avenue is only a couple of blocks away. We can walk along 50th Street and see Saint Patrick's Cathedral. You'd like that, Gemma."

"I'm not sure I would. I don't think I believe in Saint Christopher anymore. So far he's done a lousy job of keeping us safe."

Linda picked up her purse. "Of course, it all depends on whether I can get out of here unnoticed. You watch, I'll run into Stuart as soon as I put my big toe out the door. I really don't want to see his lying, cheating face on today of all days."

"You need a disguise," Augusta said.

"Not just her," Bette pointed out. "He knows all of us."

They decided to wear scarves on their heads and put on their sunglasses. Fortunately Augusta had an extra pair to lend to Bette, though they didn't suit her. Still, beggars can't be choosers, so looking every bit like spies or Jackie O. wannabes, they made sure the coast was clear before venturing out of their room. They quickly closed the door behind them and ran down the hall to wait for the elevator.

When it arrived they got in and held their breath every time the elevator stopped on another floor to admit more people, in case Stuart materialized, but fortunately they reached the lobby without any sign of him. Linda let out a sigh of relief before she realized the man standing outside the elevator waiting to get on was a colleague of Stuart's. She grabbed Bette's arm and spun around to face the back wall.

"Don't get off."

Bette knew something was wrong, but she didn't have time to warn the other two. Gemma and Augusta breezed out the door as Bette and Linda stayed put. When Gemma discovered they weren't behind her, she looked back. Bette stood like a statue and Linda was hunched in a corner.

"Are you coming?" Gemma asked.

"No, I don't think so," Bette said. "You go ahead."

The doctor hesitated and looked at Bette. "Is this your floor? Do you want to get off?"

"No, no, we love to ride up and down."

The doctor gave her a strange look and got on. Gemma and Augusta stood with their mouths open as the doors closed in their faces. Bette smiled brightly every time the doctor glanced over at them. Linda continued to look at her feet in the corner.

"Lovely day," Bette said.

The doctor nodded. "Yes, indeed."

"Great weather."

"Great."

"Are you married?"

Linda poked her in the ribs with her elbow.

"Er...yes, I am."

"Pity."

The doctor reached out and stabbed his floor's button again, as if to hurry the elevator along. The door finally opened and he rushed out as fast as possible. Linda turned around and collapsed in the corner. "Are you crazy? 'Are you married?'"

Bette shrugged. "You made me nervous. I didn't know what to say. It was the first thing I thought of."

"Oh God, this isn't going to work. Stuart's cronies are crawling all over this joint."

"It's not possible for him to know every plastic surgeon in North America. We'll be careful. Remember, you deserve to be here."

"Right."

They rode the elevator back down and missed Gemma and Augusta, who were on the one next door riding back up. After two trips, Linda called Augusta on her cell.

"Where the hell are you?"

"Where the hell are you? And what the heck happened back there?"

"Never mind, meet us in the lobby."

"Fine."

"Fine."

Having finally caught up with each other, they scurried out the door of the hotel, took off their head scarves, and stuffed them in their pockets. Linda consulted her Lonely Planet guidebook, and like a Sherpa guide, led her friends into the heart of the city.

Stuart leaned on the reception desk while one of the employees looked up the number of a local florist shop. He felt badly about Ryan. She looked adorable when she slept. He had leaned over and kissed her cheek before he left for his seminar. She'd groaned, but didn't waken. He'd make it up to her tonight. In the meantime, a bouquet of flowers might put her in a good mood.

As he glanced around, he saw two women standing by the elevator having a frantic discussion. The only reason he noticed them is that they wore head scarves and sunglasses. He wondered if they were famous people trying to avoid being seen. If they were, it wasn't the way to go about it. They stuck out like sore thumbs. He glanced away and then looked again. There was something familiar about them, but he couldn't put his finger on it. Then his heart raced a little. If he didn't know better, he'd say they looked like Gemma and Augusta.

He was losing his mind.

The two women got on the elevator before he could take a really good look. *Snap out of it, Keaton. You're seeing things. Everyone and everything shouldn't remind you of Linda. It's creepy.*

The girl at the desk interrupted his thoughts. She gave him the number for the florist. He thanked her and hurried away.

❀

Gracie and Keaton spent the night at the Vanderbilt Y on 47th Street as the Waldorf was close by, between 49th and 50th streets. She'd spent the money because she and her son were exhausted and needed a bed behind a locked door. Fortunately, she'd picked up a bite to eat and some diapers at an all-night corner store.

The sheet came in handy, as she didn't have anything else to carry Keaton in and he got heavier by the minute. With her sweater zipped over him, he looked as if she had him secured in a Snugli. To carry him in her arms would raise suspicion.

But she slept longer than she meant to, so she hurriedly drank the leftover milk and juice she'd bought the night before and unwrapped her muffin. Keaton looked at her with his big brown eyes.

"I have to eat so you can eat, little guy."

He waved his hands around and grabbed his foot, which he proceeded to stuff in his mouth. "No, you can't have toes for breakfast. Give me a sec."

He looked so cute. Gracie choked on her muffin and tears filled her eyes. "What have I done to you? I put you in such danger. Everyone's right, I'm a screw-up."

Keaton blew her a raspberry.

After her breakfast, Keaton had his. She bathed him and had a quick shower herself, after which she felt better, stronger. Courage was what she needed. People's lives were at stake, and she was the reason.

Gracie left the Y and hurried up the street. In no time she was in front of the Waldorf Astoria. Imagine being able to stay in a place like that. This Bette and the Keaton woman must have money. She walked through the doors as if she had every right in the world to be there, marching up to the desk to ask if there was a Bette Weinberg or a Mrs. Keaton staying there.

The receptionist said, "I'm sorry. There's no Bette Weinberg, but there's a Mrs. Stuart Keaton and a..."

"That's it," Gracie said in a rush. "Can you tell me what room she's in?"

The girl glanced up. "I'm sorry, but I'm not allowed to give out that information. I can phone her and see if she's in. Whom shall I say is calling?"

Gracie thought for a moment. She'd stolen four hundred dollars from Bette Weinberg and used some of it. If she said the mother from the airport, she was afraid the friends might call the cops, since she never tried to call Bette to give her back her bag. She'd have to wait and hopefully catch them coming into the hotel.

"No, that's fine. Thanks anyway."

She turned and started to walk away when a man passed her holding a bouquet of flowers. He went up to the desk and spoke loud enough for her to hear. "Delivery for Dr. Stuart Keaton's room." He passed over the flowers. The receptionist signed for them and beckoned for one of the bellmen. She told him to take the bouquet up to Dr. Keaton's room. He nodded and left with the flowers.

Gracie followed him.

She waited around a corner while the bellman knocked on the door. No one answered so he knocked again. Finally the door opened and there was a bit of a squeal. A woman said thank you. The bellman waited politely for his tip, but the door shut in his face. He gave the door the finger, walked back up the hallway, and disappeared. Gracie made sure no one was around before she approached the door and knocked on it.

A girl, not much older than her, answered the door in her underwear. She still had the flowers in her hand. "Yes?"

"Is Mrs. Keaton here?"

"Mrs. Keaton? No."

"But…this is Dr. Stuart Keaton's room, isn't it?"

The girl got snotty. "Look, what is this? Who are you? And what's that?" She pointed at the bulge inside Gracie's sweater.

This chick was pissing Gracie off. "It's my kid, if you must know. All I want to know is, where's Mrs. Keaton?"

Suddenly the girl dropped the flowers. "Do you know Stuart?"

"No."

"Don't lie to me, you bitch. This is Stuart's kid, isn't it? And you're here to blackmail him, aren't you?"

Gracie put her hands over Keaton as if to protect him. He snored under her chin, oblivious to all the fuss. "You're nuts."

The girl took a step towards Gracie. "How long have you been sleeping with him? How dare you follow us all the way from Montreal!"

Gracie backed up and stabbed her finger in the air. "You are out of your mind. Don't you ever come near me or my kid again." She turned and fled down the hall.

"You came near me first, you skank," the girl screamed after her. "You better stay away from Stuart, do you hear me?"

Gracie heard a door behind her open and an elderly voice say, "The whole floor can hear you. Stop making a spectacle of yourself."

"This is none of your business."

"You insist on making it my business."

Gracie thought she heard the girl say "Get stuffed, you old witch," but she wasn't sure. She was too far away by then. Opening the door to the stairwell, she sat on the steps to calm herself down. What had happened, and who was that weird girl? Maybe it was Mrs. Keaton's daughter.

Gracie realized the only hope she had of finding Mrs. Keaton and Bette was to stay as long as she dared down in the lobby. She hoped it wouldn't take all day. She'd have to wander out on the street, too. People would think it was odd if she hung around near the front door, and Keaton wouldn't want to be strapped to her for too long. If he threw a fit, people would notice them—and that thought made her shudder.

❋

The friends had a nice time as they walked up the streets of New York. They gawked at the buildings and the people and the yellow cabs. They stopped in the middle of the sidewalk to point at things, which ticked the natives off, but there were lots of tourists pointing cameras at everything they saw.

They almost felt like tourists, but knew they had to hold off on that for a little while longer. At least until the police matter was resolved. But they did take a bit of a detour and wandered over to see Radio City Music Hall and Rockefeller Center, since they were close by. It was exhilarating to see landmarks that were so familiar even though they'd never laid eyes on them in person before. They commented on the noise, the constant blowing of car horns and sirens, and about how small and insignificant they felt looking up at buildings that soared into the sky.

And then they had some luck.

As they walked, they noticed a police car parked by the curb and two burly police officers coming out of Starbucks with gigantic cups of coffee.

"This might save us a trip," Gemma said. "We'll tell them about the dead guy."

Linda agreed. "Good idea."

They hurried over to the policemen. "Excuse me, can you help us?"

They stopped. One of them sipped his coffee while the other one stood with his thumb resting on his belt. "Sure, ladies. Need directions?"

They shook their heads. "It's something much more serious. We'd like to report a crime," Linda said.

One cop looked at the other. "Well, crime is our business, so shoot."

"Well, you see there was this man and he had a big black car and…"

The radio came on from inside the police car. One of them reached in through the open window and grabbed the walkie-talkie. More static, and a mechanical voice relayed some sort of urgent-sounding message.

The cops jumped into the car. "Sorry, ladies, we have a B and E in progress." They sped away.

Linda shrugged at the others. "Oh well, we tried. We'll stay with our original plan and go to the police station."

It was a blustery day, which made walking difficult.

"I wonder if we should take a cab," Bette said. "I mean, if it takes us forever to get there, isn't that wasting time?"

"I suppose you're right," Linda agreed, "but I thought you'd want to see a little of the city, just in case some other catastrophe happens."

Augusta grimaced. "I don't like the idea of getting a cab. Look what happened the last time we jumped in one."

"Don't worry, nothing else will happen. We have to think positively. Surround ourselves with good karma, as it were."

Gemma looked up the street. "I'll pretend I'm Carrie from *Sex and the City*." She took a step into the street and held up her hand. A cab stopped instantly. "Wow, it really works."

They scrambled in and told the driver where they wanted to go. He took off like a shot before they could get their seatbelts on, swerving in and out of traffic lanes like a demented video gamer. They couldn't believe it when he zoomed through a red light, only to stomp on the brake pedal at the last second to avoid a collision with a bus.

They all came close to having heart attacks, but it was Augusta who jumped out of the cab first and dashed to the sidewalk. The others followed her, leaving Linda to throw some money at the driver and tell him he was an idiot. Augusta stood with her hand on her brow as she paced up and down the street. "I'm sorry, but that was ridiculous."

Gemma put her arm around Augusta's shoulders. "That *was* ridiculous. Surely they don't all drive that way."

"Well, I'm not about to find out. I'm staying on *terra firma*. You guys can take a cab if you want to, but I'm not."

Linda looked at the guidebook. "It shouldn't take too much longer. We can walk the rest of the way."

Unfortunately, she underestimated how long it would take. Suffice to say, Linda had major blisters on her feet from Gemma's shoes by the time they arrived at the police station. They wearily proceeded up the steps, opened the heavy doors, and walked into a large and busy foyer with all sorts of people milling around.

"Who do we talk to?" Augusta wondered.

Gemma pointed dead ahead. "Probably that important-looking guy."

Linda took a deep breath. "Okay, repeat after me. It wasn't our fault. It wasn't our fault."

"It wasn't our fault," they chimed as they slowly walked up to the officer who stood behind the glass partition of a huge desk that seemed to be on a platform. He looked very busy and kind of scary.

Bette whispered in Linda's ear, "He looks mean."

"Shhh." Linda cleared her throat. "Excuse me, officer?"

The huge man held up his finger. He barked some orders at a clerk and then picked up the phone to bark some more orders at someone else. He finally put the phone down.

"What can I do for you, ladies?"

The four of them quaked, but because her friends were looking at her, it was Linda who spoke.

"We'd like to report a crime."

He shuffled paper and wrote something down before he glanced at them again. "What kind of crime?"

Linda looked at the others. "Well, it's rather complicated. It's a kidnapping, mugging, sudden-death, car-theft sort of thing…"

"…not to mention breaking the speed limit…"

"…and unintended property damage…"

"…and don't forget the gun. The death was unexpected too, but it was self-defense."

He looked at them for a long minute. "Is that right?"

The four of them nodded.

"Well, I'll have you ladies sit over there on the bench and I'll call up one of my detectives and he'll be down shortly to talk to you. How's that?"

"That would be fine," Linda said. They started to walk away, and then she turned back. "Umm, do you think it will be soon? Because we have to go to Saks."

The look he gave her shut her up. They scurried across the foyer to sit on the bench by the far wall.

"Now you've made him mad," Bette said.

Linda pursed her lips. "All right, I'm sorry."

Augusta said, "I hope he doesn't hold that against us."

"You should've kept your mouth shut," Gemma chimed in.

Linda gave them a filthy look. "I'm sorry, okay? These jeans are so far up my va-jay-jay, I've lost my ability to think!"

They tried not to laugh but couldn't help it, and the more they tried to be quiet, the louder they got. The huge police officer wasn't impressed. He looked over and pointed at them. They stayed quiet after that.

Eventually, a man descended the staircase and went over to the desk. The big scary guy beckoned to them, so they got up and hurried over. He introduced the man. "This is Detective Ames."

Detective Ames nodded. They nodded back.

"Detective Ames, apparently you have a kidnapping, mugging, sudden-death, car-theft, property-damage, gun 'thing.'" Did I forget anything, ladies?"

They shook their heads.

Detective Ames quickly covered up his look of incredulity. "Right. Then we best get a move on. Would you ladies come this way, please?"

They followed him upstairs and down several corridors to a room full of desks and big men sitting at them. It was crowded, noisy, and confusing. He indicated the two chairs in front of his desk and pulled over a third. Linda pulled a little at her slacks and said she'd stand

Detective Ames went around the corner of his desk and sat in his chair. He took a form out of a pile and reached for his pen. Linda spoke before he had a chance to ask them anything.

"I know this sounds ridiculous, but we've been trying to report this for the last twelve hours and haven't had any luck at all."

"And why's that?"

"Because every time we start to tell someone, something happens and we can't. Take just a minute ago. We stopped two officers outside a coffee shop, but they had to drive away because of a D and C."

"D and C?"

Linda looked around. "Was that it?"

"It wasn't a D and C," Gemma tsked. "It was an ABP."

Detective Ames frowned. "An all-points bulletin?"

"Oh, maybe not, then."

"How about a B and E?" the detective suggested.

"That's it," Linda said.

"A break and enter."

Linda nodded. "Yes. That's where they went."

The detective cleared his throat. "Before we begin, I need your full names, addresses, and phone numbers." He pointed at Bette. "We'll start with you."

Bette gave him the information. "That's long distance, of course."

Detective Ames mouth went crooked. "I'll remember that." He pointed to Linda. "And you?"

Linda opened her mouth just as a man rushed into the room. "We have a bomb threat! Everyone evacuate the building."

"A bomb?" Linda cried. The other three jumped out of their chairs.

"We're being punished by God." Gemma made the sign of the cross and held her hands in prayer. "Hail Mary, full of grace..."

There was an instant mass exodus of people, most of them shouting out directions. Detective Ames stood quickly. "It's all right, ladies. In an orderly fashion, follow me and we'll have you outside in no time."

They felt better because he was so calm, and they quickly followed him like little ducks out of the room and down the first few corridors. The trouble was, they lost him after that. Someone ran up to him and said something in his ear. He looked concerned.

"I have to leave you." He pointed down the hallway. "You see the way we came in? You go to the end and turn left, all right? Then down another hallway and the lobby's right there. Someone will assist you."

Before they could say anything, he ran back the way he came.

The four of them watched him go with a look of panic. Naturally, it was Linda who mobilized them in the end. "This way, girls."

They started to run down the corridor, and then the huge policeman at the front desk happened to come around the corner. He frowned at them. "No running." He quickly disappeared.

"Don't listen to him," Gemma said. "Let's get out of here."

They came to the end of the corridor and looked both ways.

"What did he say?" Linda asked. "Was it left or right?"

"It was left," Bette said.

"No, it was right," Gemma said.

"Are you sure?"

"Yes, I'm sure."

So they hurried along the right corridor and then down another one, but the lobby was no closer.

"We've gone the wrong way," Augusta said.

"Look, there's a door with an exit sign," Linda said. "Let's take that."

So they hurried out the door and went down concrete stairs. They burst out of the exit and walked into a cement courtyard. A courtyard hemmed in with a chain-link fence.

"What's this? It's a prison yard...how do we get out?" Gemma asked.

"Grab the door before it closes," Linda cried.

Bette lunged for the door, but she was too late. It slammed shut.

Augusta threw her hands in the air. "I don't believe it. We're going to die in New York City surrounded by two hundred policemen."

"Why did it say it was an exit when it obviously isn't?" Bette asked.

"Technically, it is an exit, it just doesn't go anywhere."

Bette threw off her coat. "Well, I'm climbing this goddamn fence. Someone give me a boost and I'll go over the top and tell someone we're here."

They rushed over to her. "Good idea," Linda said. "But since you're the shortest, it makes more sense for Augusta or me to try it."

"I'll be the one who boosts you up." Gemma bent over to give them access to her back.

Augusta looked at Linda. "I'll go. You've got my new jeans on and I don't want them ripped."

"What the hell difference does that make?" Gemma shouted. "Our clothes are about to be blown to kingdom come. Now someone get on."

Augusta put her foot on Gemma's back and grabbed the chain-link fence. She hopped up and put both her feet on Gemma's back. "Are you all right?"

"Yes," Gemma said. "I'll push you up."

Gemma started to straighten up and Augusta reached higher. She lifted her right leg and almost got her toe hooked on the top of the fence. She tried it again but didn't quite make it.

Bette clapped her hands. "You can do it, Gussie."

Augusta was making a third attempt when the exit door flew open and their large desk sergeant appeared. "There you are."

In her relief that rescue was at hand, Gemma rushed over to him, leaving Augusta stranded on the fence.

"Gemma, get back here."

Gemma ran back.

"Hold the door," he shouted at Gemma. She turned around and did as she was told. The big cop ran over to Augusta and pulled her down.

"Everyone out."

He took them down several corridors and led them to the lobby. He was about to say something to them, but he was called away, so, shouting "Thank you," they ran to the front doors and burst out onto the sidewalk. Once there, they ran until they couldn't run anymore. They finally sagged against a storefront and waited until they could catch their breath.

"Can you believe that?" Linda said. "Is it my imagination, or do you think someone doesn't want us to report this crime?"

The others agreed with her.

"How many times have we attempted to let someone know about our stupid dead guy?"

Gemma stamped her foot. "This is ridiculous. We're in flippin' New York City and so far we haven't done anything. We're going to spend the entire time rushing from one police station to the next and before you know it we'll have to go home."

"Well, what do you think we should do?" Augusta asked.

"Before we do anything else we have to get Linda some clothes." Gemma pointed at Linda's feet. "She's got Kleenex hanging out of her shoes, for God's sake. She looks like a bag lady."

They looked at Linda's shoes and agreed. It was time to go to Saks.

❀

Stuart walked back to the hotel with a few other delegates from the conference. They chose to go out for their mid-morning break instead of staying in the hotel. It felt good to get a breath of air. He wanted to run up to his suite and check in on Ryan. He'd give her his American Express card and tell her to go nuts. They had a free evening on the roster and he planned to take her out to dinner. She could buy herself an outfit.

His colleague pointed out something and even though Stuart wasn't listening, he turned his head anyway. That's when he thought he saw Linda walk by on the opposite side of the street. No. He was seeing things again. He did a double take. She had already disappeared.

Get a hold of yourself, Keaton. He started to sweat. Maybe he *was* having a mid-life crisis. He'd heard his receptionist say so to one of the nurses in the office. He remembered being angry, but she was good at her job so he let it go. Still, it was definitely a burr under his saddle.

Stuart couldn't wait to get rid of his fellow doctors. They parted company in the lobby, where Stuart dashed for the elevator and willed it to hurry up to his floor. He got off and rushed to his room. When he took out his card and opened the door a pillow hit him in the face.

"Don't you come near me, you bastard."

He was incredulous. "What's wrong? Didn't you like your flowers?"

"How long have you been sleeping with her?"

Stuart was seriously confused. He came into the room and Ryan jumped on the bed, as if to get away from him. "Sleeping with whom?"

Ryan pointed her finger at him, her face full of tears. "Don't you dare deny it, you creep. You have a baby and you didn't bother to tell me? I want your babies. No one else can have them."

"I don't want babies. I don't understand what you're talking about."

"You don't want babies? What are *you* talking about? You said you loved kids."

"Yeah, other people's."

Ryan picked up another pillow. "I hate you, you stupid man."

Stuart reached up and pulled her off the bed. She struggled with him before he finally got a hold of her shoulders and gave her a shake. "Now calm down and tell me what's going on."

"A girl came to the door and she said she wanted to speak to Mrs. Keaton."

Stuart made a face. "What?"

"And she had a baby with her. She insisted on talking to Mrs. Keaton. I know what she's doing. She wanted me to know. You hid this from me and now you're caught. I bet this is your wife's doing. I bet she put her up to it. She wants to ruin every bit of happiness we have. The evil cow!"

"Don't be ridiculous. You're all over the map. Linda doesn't even know I'm here. And how would anyone else find me, much less a girl with a baby?"

"How should I know? But it happened, and you've ruined my trip." She shook herself out of his grasp. "As a matter of fact, you've ruined my life."

In a flood of tears, Ryan ran into the bathroom and slammed the door shut. Stuart stood there and looked around the room.

What had just happened?

CHAPTER SEVEN

Izzy and Ida didn't sleep very well the night of Bette's phone call, although neither one wanted to admit it. It was a little spooky knowing a young person wasn't at their beck and call.

It was mid-morning when Izzy walked in the kitchen with his sleeveless undershirt and boxers on. His cigarette had a two-inch ash hanging off it.

Ida was parked in front of the fridge with the door open, a carton of eggs in her lap.

"How did you sleep?" she asked him.

"Like a log. You?"

"Like a log. Do you want some eggs?"

"When was the last time you saw me eat an egg?"

"So I should stop asking?"

He walked over to the coffee maker. "I'll have coffee." He poured a cup and put five spoonfuls of sugar in it. No cream.

Ida shook her head. "You look like a skeleton. Why don't you eat some food?"

"I am. Coffee."

"Coffee's not food."

"Coffee comes from a coffee bean. That's food."

"The only thing keeping you alive is the sugar."

Izzy flicked his ash on a saucer. "The only thing keeping me alive is watching you eat."

Ida spun her wheels around to face him. "What are you talking about, you fruit loop?"

"One day you're going to explode, and I want to be here when you do."

Ida picked up a bread knife and stabbed the air. "One day, old man, I swear…"

There was a loud crash as the kitchen door was kicked in. A gigantic man stood in the doorway. Izzy's cigarette dropped from his lips into his coffee cup. Ida's eggs and bread knife fell to the floor.

Izzy jumped up, grabbed the back of Ida's wheelchair, and pushed her, hell bent for leather, out of the kitchen and down the hallway. Ida's screams pierced the quiet morning air. The huge man ran after them, but Izzy was faster than he looked. His knobby knees pumped like pistons as he turned left into the living room and back out to the kitchen. Ida grabbed a broom. The huge man was almost on them. Izzy turned left again to circle around and back down the hallway. Ida swung the broom. She hit her mother's vase and brushed the picture of dogs playing poker off the wall.

"Come here, you little shit," the giant man shouted.

"Don't you dare call my husband a little shit." Ida threw the broom over Izzy's head and knocked the guy right between the eyes. Didn't hurt him, though. He brushed it off, reached out with his beefy hand, and grabbed Izzy by the back of his undershirt, nearly ripping it off his skinny body.

Izzy fought like a tiger, but he wasn't very successful.

"Stop moving, you bony asshole."

Izzy still flailed about. It took a sock to the jaw to keep him still. He was knocked out cold. The intruder picked him up, threw him in a chair, bound him with duct tape, and put a strip of it over his mouth, all the while fending off Ida's wild punches and jabs.

"Leave my husband alone, you monster!"

He almost yanked Ida out of her chair when he grabbed her hands and wrapped tape around her wrists.

"Rape! Rape!"

"Shut up, you old bag. Who'd want to rape you?" He gave her hair a tug. "Tell me where I can find Bette Weinberg."

"Never."

He back-handed her in the face.

"Tell me."

"Never."

He went over and put a knife to Izzy's throat. "Tell me or he's dead."

"She's at the Waldorf in New York. She never should have gone.

It's all that Linda Keaton's fault. Just because she lives in Pointe Claire and has a plastic surgeon for a husband, she thinks she's better than anyone else."

The man picked up the address book on the table by the phone and opened it. He flipped through a couple of pages and ripped one out before he walked into the kitchen and stood by the backstairs doorway. Taking out his cellphone, he turned his back on Ida and relayed the information to Candy.

"Bette Weinberg is staying at the Waldorf. Linda Keaton's address is 4560 Fraser Street in Pointe Claire. I'm calling a friend. He can be over there in a matter of minutes. Right." He hung up and dialled once more. "4560 Fraser Street, Pointe Claire. We're looking for anything suspicious that might be linked to a rival gang. Call Candy and give him the info when you're done...yeah, I'm gonna..."

Ida couldn't believe he was standing in her kitchen yakking on the phone as if nothing was wrong. She looked over at poor Izzy. For all she knew, he was dead.

Her eyes narrowed. That son of a bitch. She took her wrapped hands, grabbed the controls of her electric wheelchair, and silently zoomed into the kitchen, plowing smack into the back of the guy's knees.

"Wha...!" He tried to turn around at the last minute but missed his step and fell over and over, crashing all the way to the bottom of the stairs.

He was still.

Ida backed up and headed for the living room. "Izzy! Are you dead?" She took his wrist and felt a pulse. "Thank God. Now wake up, old man! Why should you be sleeping? Do I have to do everything around here?"

She drove over to the phone and with her hands still tied together, took the receiver and put it on the table. Then she pressed the numbers of Bette's cellphone.

It rang and rang. Finally Bette answered. Ida bent over as close as she could get and shouted, "Bette, it's your mother...your mother... can you hear me? Where are you? I can hardly hear you. Well, get off the street and listen to me. There was a man here and he tied your father and me up and he punched...What? Stop laughing. I'm serious. I just killed the guy. Bette, stop laughing. What do you mean I'm trying to make you come home? I'm trying to tell you your father and I had an intruder and...no, I'm serious. Don't go...don't hang up..."

The line went dead.

Ida threw her taped hands in the air and appealed to the ceiling. "Am I such a rotten mother? Do I deserve such disrespect? What is wrong with my children? I'm cursed, I tell you. Cursed!"

She punched 911 into the phone. "I've just killed a man! He attacked me! What? I'm in my living room with a husband who's too busy snoring to help and a daughter who thinks I'm kidding. Does your family treat you like that? What on earth have I done to... What?...I don't know who he was...Isn't that your job? Like I have to do everything for you people?"

The 911 operator finally got Ida to tell her the address and said the police were on their way.

Izzy groaned a little as Ida hung up the phone.

Ida drove over to him. "Izzy? Are you all right? Speak to me."

He groaned again.

"Oy...your nose looks broken. Does it hurt?"

Izzy's groan got worse. He shook his head around.

"Are you convulsing, Izzy? Why is this happening? Why me?"

Izzy finally shook his head so violently, Ida stopped cold. That's when she realized he had duct tape over his mouth. "Oh, I see the problem." She grabbed one end with her tied hands and yanked for all she was worth.

Izzy's scream reverberated all over the neighbourhood. "You stupid woman!"

"Hey, this stupid woman saved your skinny ass. I killed him."

"You killed him? Did you drive him to suicide?"

"You think you're a comedian, don't you?"

"Never mind arguing, old woman. What did he take? Did he rob us?"

Ida grew sombre. "No, he wanted to know where Bette was."

"What? You didn't tell him, did you?"

"I had to. He said he'd kill you. He had a knife."

Izzy rolled his eyes back. "Oh my God. Why didn't you let him kill me? I'm an old man. This is our daughter we're talking about. She comes first."

"Well, this is typical. I get it in the neck for saving your life. Of course I know it's our daughter, but we had to live to warn her, didn't we? To tell her someone is looking for her, even though I can't imagine why."

"Are you sure you killed him? Oh, my nose. I need a cigarette." He tried to stand up but was pretty woozy.

"Yeah, I killed him. I pushed him down the stairs, so let that be a lesson to you. Don't mess with me."

"You're a regular James Bond. I need a smoke. Give me my cigarettes."

Ida drove over to the pack on the coffee table. "How can you smoke? Your hands are behind your back."

"Like that's stopped me before." He reached out his neck and when Ida finally grabbed one out of the package with her linked hands, she put it in his mouth. Then she had to drive over to get a light.

She struggled with the match. "I can't move my hands enough to do this."

"Try."

She did. "Nothing."

"I know, the stove. Help me up." Ida pushed at his back and nearly toppled him over. Then she drove behind him as he wobbled into the kitchen.

"Turn on the gas."

Ida tried to reach the back dial. "I can't do it. It's too far back."

"Get your hiney out of that chair for two seconds and do it. I'm croakin' here."

"What a grouch." She rocked a bit and lunged, turned it on, and poof...set Izzy's eyebrows on fire. His cigarette became a torch. In a flash, Ida reached up and grabbed the back of his head with her bound hands and pushed his face in the sink. Luckily, it was full of hot soapy water. When Izzy finally surfaced with dish-detergent bubbles in his eyes, he sputtered, "Why didn't you let the guy kill me?"

"I should have. You're never grateful for a thing."

Izzy dripped on the floor. "Could you get me a towel?"

She reached for a dishtowel and wiped his face.

"*Ow,* watch my nose."

"You're such a baby. Do it yourself, then." She threw it on the kitchen table and sped towards the top of the stairs. "I called the police. They should be here any minute."

Izzy resorted to bending over to press his face into the towel. "Good, I was about to call them myself, to tell them you're trying to murder me."

"Keep it up. I'll kill you and blame it on the big ape at the bottom of the stairs, and don't think I won't."

"I wish you would. Maybe then I'd get some peace and quiet."

Candy was in a fury. He nearly killed Dumb and Dumber when they came and told him they lost the girl, because now he had to relay that piece of news to his boss, and he didn't like his chances. He couldn't look at their ugly mugs, so he told them to wait outside his office in the warehouse. Candy popped more Life Savers in his mouth. It helped him with his stress levels, but his teeth were starting to rot.

When Freddy the Fish called with the good news, he hollered for his two henchmen. "Get in here."

They opened the door. "Yeah, boss?"

"Fuck this up and you're dead. Go to the Waldorf. That Bette Weinberg is there with a broad named Linda Keaton. I don't care how you do it, but I want those women and that bag brought here by sundown. *Capiche?*"

Dumb and Dumber nodded and left. Maybe Candy could salvage something out of this disaster. But it was only two hours later when the phone rang again.

Candy grabbed it. "Yeah?"

"Freddy bought it."

"Say again?"

"Vince saw the ambulance take his body away. The Weinbergs' neighbours said he broke his neck."

Candy hung up. This was the work of professionals. No doubt about it. Who were these women? He'd never heard of broads doing a job. What was the world coming to?

❋

It was nearly noon when Clive wandered over to Linda's to feed Buster. He put the key in the lock, but when he placed his hand on the knob, it turned and the door opened. He jumped back. That wasn't supposed to happen. What was going on? Then he remembered. It was probably Wes, although he didn't see his car.

He opened the door a little wider. "Wes? Wes?"

There was no answer. Then the hairs on the back of Clive's neck stood at attention. Linda's mail was on the floor, and when he looked down the hallway, he saw a chair on its side. Perhaps Buster had gone on a rampage, but he knew in his heart that wasn't it. When he got to the living room door, he knew for certain. The place had been burgled. But how was that possible? The alarm hadn't gone off.

He ran back to the front door and saw that the wire leading to the contact on the door was cut. Someone knew what they were doing. He ran through the house. All the drawers in Linda's secretary desk were on the floor, papers scattered about. There were open drawers everywhere, but the obvious things weren't touched—televisions, stereos, DVD players. He ran into the bedrooms. Linda's jewellery box looked intact. What were they looking for?

Then he remembered Buster.

"Buster. Buster. Here, pussycat...psst psst psst." He had to find the cat. Linda would be heartbroken if anything happened to him. He searched and searched and had almost given up when he found him crouched behind the washing machine.

"It's okay, Buster. I'm not going to hurt you."

Buster looked like dandelion fluff in his attempt to protect himself. It was quite a battle to get him out. Clive finally resorted to using a mop handle to poke him towards the other side. He grabbed the cat as he tore by. Buster did his best to rip Clive's hands to shreds and Clive, in desperation, dropped Buster into a wicker clothes hamper and shut the lid. He filled a shopping bag with tins of cat food, then took a new bag of kitty litter and ran upstairs with the bags and hamper. Buster growled and hissed the entire time.

Clive hurried over to his house with his cargo. The boys greeted him enthusiastically and then went into a frenzy of sniffing. Buster's howls became more acute. Clive put Buster in the spare room, grabbed a pan and put kitty litter in it, then opened a can of cat food, put it on a plate, and poured some water in a bowl. Finally he tipped the laundry basket on its side, opened the lid, and ran like hell for the door. He shut Buster in. The boys continued their sniffing contest along the crack of the door, but at least Buster was safe.

Clive wasn't sure what to do next. He didn't want to phone Linda and ruin her holiday. He'd have to let Wes know, since he had no idea where Stuart was. So he ran back to the house and grabbed the paper Linda had left on the fridge with all the phone numbers on it. He placed a call to Wes. A voice came on. "The cellular customer you have dialled has their phone turned off. Please try again later."

"Stupid git! Your mother buys you a phone and you never turn it on."

He sat at Linda's kitchen table and stewed. If he couldn't get a hold of Wes within a reasonable amount of time, he'd have to call Linda. He had no other choice.

❋

Stuart had an important seminar on laser techniques for facial reconstruction in a conference room downstairs, but he was missing it thanks to Ryan's stubborn refusal to come out of the bathroom. His pleas fell on deaf ears. When the hotel phone rang he thought it might be one of his colleagues telling him to get his ass downstairs pronto.

He picked it up. "Hello?"

"Dad?"

"Wes?"

"How come you didn't answer your cellphone?"

Stuart took his phone out of his pocket and looked at all the missed call messages. "Sorry, I thought it was on vibrate. I have seminars all day. How the heck did you know where to find me?

"I had to call your office. Is that chick with you?"

"Wes..."

"Forget it, Dad, I'm not interested. I have to tell you something. The house was broken into."

Stuart's hand gripped the phone. "Is your mother all right?"

"She doesn't know, and I don't want her to know."

"What do you mean?"

"She's in New York and I don't want to ruin her good time."

Stuart felt a shiver go up his spine. "Your mother is in New York?"

"Ain't that a kick in the teeth?" Wes said. "She's even staying at the Waldorf. I'm surprised you two haven't met in the elevator."

Stuart's mouth was so dry he had trouble speaking. Linda was here. She was stalking him and terrorizing Ryan. Oh my God. She was having a breakdown and it was all his fault. Who knows what she might be capable of? And her friends were with her. It *was* Bette he'd saw in the doorway, and Augusta and Gemma by the elevator. But how did they know he was going to be in New York? At this hotel? And on this floor? It was probably his office receptionist. She always did have a big mouth.

All this ran through his head in a matter of seconds. Then another thought came to him. "Wes, were you with your mother before she left?"

"No."

"You don't think she's capable of trashing the house, do you?"

"She'd love to slash your suits all to shit and I wouldn't blame her if she did, but Mom would never wreck the house. It was a break-in. Mr. Harris called me. He'd gone over to feed Buster and that's when he saw the mess."

"Was there much damage?"

"Nothing too important, and not much was taken, either. It's like they messed up the place looking for something and then took a few things to make it look like a robbery."

"Wes, I want you to go into my study and look in my filing cabinet. I have a list of our credit cards in there somewhere. I don't have all of them with me. Can you cancel them, just for safety's sake? Don't worry about the American Express. I have that one on me."

"Yeah, all right."

"And then get someone in to change the locks."

"I'll call the security company, too; the wires have been cut."

"Yes. Good idea."

"I've talked to the police. They filed a report but said the chances of finding out who did it are pretty slim. It happens all the time. I'll clean up the house. Chloe and I are staying here for now. I want to be here when Mom gets home, because she won't have a key for the new lock."

"Chloe? Is she your girlfriend?"

"What do you care? You haven't been interested in anything Mom and I do lately. Your attention's been elsewhere."

Stuart flinched. He knew he deserved it, but it still hurt.

"Listen, Dad, I have to go. I just thought you'd want to know. I don't know why, since it doesn't concern you anymore..."

"Wes—"

"Go to another hotel, Dad. Don't parade the chick in front of her. Mom doesn't deserve that."

"Don't hate me, Wes."

There was a long silence. "I don't." He hung up.

❈

They were almost at Saks when Bette took the call from her mother. She stood in the middle of the street with a look of utter amazement. When she hung up and laughingly told her friends the foolish story Ida had come up with to make her feel guilty, they all had a great chuckle, which did a lot to raise their sadly depleted spirits. They gave themselves permission to have a good time in this famous store. They had to, or they'd go nuts.

It was like a dream. The whole first floor was taken up with every cosmetic company known to man. Everywhere they looked, women sat in casting chairs having their makeup done for free by cosmeticians, in the hopes of selling their very pricey wares. Employees also stood at every corner of the aisles handing out coupons or perfume samples. It was easy to get mesmerized, especially when they realized that Gucci, Prada, and other obscenely expensive handbags were on display around the perimeter of the floor.

When Gemma said she wanted to have her makeup done, they all decided to do it. They had a fantastic time being turned into women they didn't recognize. Bette was a real surprise. She only ever used

Chap Stick, and there she was with Sugarplum lips. Linda insisted on taking all kinds of pictures. They even got one of the cosmetic girls to take several pictures of all of them together. It finally felt as if they were on vacation.

Eventually they wandered upstairs to the clothing department. Linda picked out several outfits and four pairs of high heels, which weren't at all practical for traipsing around New York, but she didn't care—she was still in mourning over her favourite Jimmy Choos.

Linda was also unconcerned about the amount on the price tags. The other three were thriftier, even though she insisted they put their purchases on Stuart's card. Gemma picked up a few tops for her kids and Augusta found some pretty jewellery for her girls. Bette grabbed a quilted bed jacket for Ida and a gold-plated lighter for Izzy.

The four of them met back at the cashier.

"As soon as I pay for this," Linda said, "I'm going to run into the dressing room and put on this pantsuit." She held it up for her friends to see. "Isn't it gorgeous? It's DKNY."

"I'm not going to ask how much that is," Augusta said.

"Neither am I," Linda laughed.

The three friends stood aside once they placed their items on the counter. Linda then piled her clothes and chosen shoes on top of them. The clerk ran up the purchases.

"That will be $4,783.26."

Linda passed over the Platinum Visa card and didn't flinch. Her friends' mouths were open. She glanced at them. "What?"

"Almost five thousand dollars," Bette whispered.

Gemma shook her head. "You can't spend that much."

"Why can't I?"

"You better put my gifts back."

Linda dismissed them with her hand. "No indeed. Most of this is mine anyway. We deserve this after the misery we've been through."

The clerk looked up from her register. "I'm sorry, but this card has been declined."

Linda looked at her. "Pardon me?"

The clerk maintained a neutral tone. "It's been declined."

"But that's not possible. Do it again."

The clerk swiped it again with the same result.

Linda's cheeks started to flush. "I don't understand it. This has never happened before."

Bette came forward. "I had that happen once. Sometimes the magnetic strip wears out."

Gemma stepped up too. "That's it, Linda. You've worn it out." She looked at the clerk. "Could you punch the numbers instead?"

The clerk nodded. She punched in the numbers.

Declined.

Linda stamped her foot. "I don't believe it." She rooted through her wallet. "Here. This is my American Express. Put it on that."

The clerk swiped the card and looked up. "I'm very sorry, but this one has been declined as well."

By then there was a lineup of shoppers who were getting impatient or downright nosy about the unfolding drama.

"This can't be happening," Linda said. "I don't understand it. Now you won't get your gifts."

"That doesn't matter," Augusta reassured her.

"Of course not," Gemma said.

Linda's hand suddenly flew to her mouth. "Oh my God, it's Stuart. He's found out about the card somehow. He's doing this to get back at me."

"Is that possible? How would he know about it already?" Augusta asked.

"How does he know anything? He's always one-upping me, the two-timing jerk. I'm almost sure he's behind this."

The clerk looked over Linda's head to the crowd behind. "I'm sorry, but if you're not purchasing these items I'm going to have to ask you to move aside. There are other customers waiting."

Linda stepped away from the counter, pulled out one of the tissues she'd stuffed down her bra that morning, and wiped the corner of her eyes. "What am I going to do? I have no clothes and now I can't buy any."

Her friends gathered up the clothes and shoes she wanted and hustled her off to the side.

"Sure, you can buy some," Augusta patted her hand. "I'll put it on my Visa card."

"I have a little money too," Gemma said.

Bette looked distressed. "I'd give you some if I had any."

"I can't let you do that."

"What are friends for?" Augusta gave her a hug. "Now, what do you really need?"

"A pair of slacks and some high heels. My feet are killing me in these loafers."

"All right, I'll buy your shoes," Augusta said. "How much are they?"

Linda picked up a pair. "Eight hundred dollars."

Augusta cleared her throat. "Perhaps a tad less expensive."

Linda put them back in the tissue-papered box. She held up the least expensive pair. "These aren't costly. They only have a kitten heel."

Augusta grabbed them. "Great. I'll buy these, and I'll get you this nice sweater too." She pulled it out of the pile of clothes. Gemma ended up buying her a pair of jeans, a bra, and some panties with her yogurt money. Linda thanked them profusely. She went into the dressing room and changed into her new duds, stuffing Augusta's jeans and bra and Gemma's shoes in her shopping bag. When she emerged she looked a little more pulled together.

"Let's get out of this store," Linda said. "I have to think about what to do."

They stepped outside and the sun made them squint, so they quickly put on their sunglasses and joined the lunchtime crowd walking briskly down the street. That's when a man in a suit tapped Gemma on the shoulder. She spun around.

"Excuse me, ma'am. Would you mind stepping back into the store?"

"*What?* Why?"

"We'd like to have a word with you."

Bette, Linda, and Augusta talked over each other. "What's the matter? What's wrong? Who are you?"

"Store security."

The blood drained from Gemma's face. "What on earth are you talking about? Are you suggesting I stole something?"

"I'm not suggesting anything ma'am. We'd like to speak to you and would prefer to do it in private, unless you want the whole street to hear me."

"The whole of New York City can hear you for all I care. How dare you accuse me of something so horrible? I've never been so humiliated in my life."

Linda pushed her way between them. "There's been a terrible mistake. We know this woman. She'd never steal anything in a million years."

"If she doesn't come with me right this minute, I'll have no alternative but to call the police."

"That's ridiculous. I've stolen nothing. Get away from me."

The man put his hand on Gemma's arm. Linda took her bag and swung it at him. "Leave her alone."

Suddenly they were all involved as they swarmed around the man demanding an explanation. A whistle got their attention. Two more security guards gestured for their co-worker. "Hurry up...not that fat one, the one running down the street."

"What did he say?" Gemma shouted.

"Sorry, my mistake." The guard ran up the street after his colleagues.

"He called me fat."

Her friends were equally indignant.

"I could sue him for slander. Santa Maria, what is it with me and stores? I never want to go in another one for the rest of my life. People call me gigantic and now I'm fat. Am I?"

They reassured her she wasn't.

"I've had five kids, for pity's sake. I can't help it if I gained a lot of weight with each and every one of them. They were big babies. Like that's my fault?"

Gemma continued her tirade down the street while her friends made sympathetic noises. Then she stopped. "I'm starting to hate this city, and on top of that, I'm getting a migraine."

"Gemma, let's you and I go back to the hotel and you can have a lie down," Augusta said, "and Linda and Bette can go get Bette's passport sorted. We can meet back in the room."

"All right." Linda looked at her watch. "We'll try not to be too long. I've got to figure out what to do about this money situation. Bloody Stuart."

"Here, give me your bag," Augusta said. Linda handed it over and they parted company on the corner of 50th Street and 5th Avenue.

Bette suggested she and Linda grab a coffee and a prune danish before they went to the consulate; Linda looked as if she needed some fortifying. So they sat in a crowded café and took a small table near the window. Linda sat on the chair and Bette scooted around to sit on the padded bench that ran down the length of one wall. She took out her cellphone. "I should call Ma and see if she's in a better state of mind."

Linda dismissed her with her hand. "Don't bother. You'll never make yourself heard in this place."

Bette nodded. "You're right. I'll wait until we get back to the hotel, but can you believe that stunt? Telling me she'd killed an intruder. The woman is insane. When I get that age, do me a favour and shoot me."

"I will."

Bette put the cellphone down beside her on top of her jacket, since she didn't have a purse.

"Bette, what am I going to do about this damn credit card? I was planning on using it all week. I have money in my chequing account but not enough to finance this entire trip the way I wanted to. This was supposed to be a great adventure, an extravagant treat courtesy of my rotten husband but so far it's been nothing but a disaster."

Bette reached over and covered Linda's hand with her own. "Don't worry. So what if we don't spend quite so much on ourselves? You know us; a bottle of wine and some cheese and crackers make us happy. We'll make our own fun. We always have."

Linda smiled. "I don't know what I'd do without you guys."

At that moment, the two ladies sitting beside them left and were very quickly replaced with what looked like three punk rockers, one guy and two girls, all of them sporting numerous tattoos and piercings. Their hair was greasy and the girls wore black lipstick and nail polish. Linda and Bette signalled each other with eyebrow arches and quick nods of the head, code for "get a load of this bunch." It was entertaining to watch them covertly. They spoke frantically into their cellphone, but they kept their hands over their mouths, so Bette and Linda couldn't quite make out what they were saying—which was just as well, since anything these three had to say probably wouldn't be worth listening to.

Bette and Linda quickly finished their coffee and Danish and were about to leave when the guy spilled his drink, not only all over himself, but also the table and Bette's clothes. Everyone jumped, and general chaos reigned for a moment or two.

"Geez, man, watch it," he said to Bette.

"Excuse me? You spilled the drink."

"Oh. Sorry, man."

He grabbed a few napkins and wiped Bette's chest. She slapped his arm away. "I can take care of myself, thank you very much."

"Hey, chill. You got the wrong vibe."

One of the girls spoke up. "Whatcha expect? She's as old as a freakin' goat."

Bette grabbed her coat and her belongings. "Yeah? Well, at least I don't smell like one."

They left in a hurry, and when they got out on the street, the two friends looked at each other.

"Can anything else go wrong?" Linda said.

Bette threw her hands in the air. "I finally get felt up, but it's by a kid who looks like Marilyn Manson."

Linda took Bette by the arm. "You nut. Let's go."

Gemma and Augusta walked back to the hotel at a leisurely pace.

"I don't think I'm a big-city girl." Gemma shifted her purse from one hand to the other.

"We live in Montreal. That's a city."

"Yeah, but New York is New York. I think I'd get swallowed up, like no one would know I was ever here."

Augusta smiled. "I love where I live. Tom bought that house for us."

Gemma glanced at her. "Would you ever consider marrying again?"

"When the girls leave home, maybe."

"Well, well. I never thought you'd say that."

"I get very lonely, Gemma. It's hard. I always felt safest in Tom's arms. I'd like to feel that again. You're lucky to have Angelo, even if he is thoughtless at times. He loves you, and it must be lovely to lie next to that big man every night."

"You know, Gussie, I thought I wanted to come here. I thought I was missing something in my life. But I don't think so. I'd have been just as happy to sit in Linda's family room and drink wine with you guys. I really can't wait to get home."

Augusta laughed. "Me neither, but it'll be our little secret. I don't want Linda to think we don't appreciate everything she's trying to do for us. Of course, maybe we'd think differently about this trip if we were actually having a good time instead of living a never-ending soap opera."

They were in perfect agreement as they walked along, but they stopped dead in their tracks when a young girl suddenly stood in front of them.

"You're Bette Weinberg's friends, aren't you?"

Gemma and Augusta stared at her.

"It's the young girl from the airport," Gemma said. "How wonderful. Do you have Bette's purse? We have your bag with your baby's teddy bear in it. We kept it with us in case you got in touch."

"Is that your little one in your sweater?" Augusta asked. "Where's your stroller, honey? You look exhausted."

The girl put her hands out as if to stop the onslaught of questions. "Please, we don't have much time. You and your friends are in grave danger."

Gemma and Augusta looked at each other and then back at the girl. "Is this a joke?" Gemma asked. "What's your name?"

"It's Gracie. Listen to me. When Bette took my bag by mistake, she took something that I smuggled over the border for...for...some people."

The friends gasped.

"I know it's hard to believe, but it's true. I was desperate and I did it. But now they're going to kill your friend if she doesn't give them the bag. I think they're going to kill all of us. They kept me prisoner, but Keaton and I escaped. I came to warn you."

They looked at the small, slender girl with the pale and frightened face. She was shivering. "There's five million dollars worth of diamonds in that bear."

Gemma's mouth dropped open. "I don't believe it."

"Can you call your friend? I need to warn her."

Augusta reached out and put her arm around Gracie's shoulder. "Of course. Don't worry, sweetheart. We'll keep you and your baby safe. I'll call Bette right now."

Gracie looked like she wanted to cry.

At that moment, a very large and scary-looking man ran up to them as a black car squealed to a stop by the sidewalk. Dumber grabbed Gracie's arm. "Everyone get in the car. Do it now, or the girl gets it." He held a knife against her side.

"Don't hurt her," both women said. They had no choice. They got in the car. Then Dumber pushed Gracie in and jumped in the front seat, as Dumb put his foot to the floor. The car took off like a shot.

CHAPTER EIGHT

After Ida got off the phone with 911, she called her eldest son, Mordecai, who in turn called David, who called Simon, who called Lenny, who called Moshe. Five sons and their families arrived at the scene shortly after the police got there.

There was a stampede up the stairs once the body was removed and the police had finished their interrogation of the Weinbergs. The brothers were in a panic when they saw the state of their parents. Izzy's nose was twice its normal size, and Ida's black eye was turning a lovely shade of mauve.

Mordecai slapped himself on his cheeks. "My God, he tortured Papa. Look at the burns. Did he try and drown you, as well? Oh, this is too much."

Ida and Izzy looked at each other and stayed quiet. They hadn't had this much attention in years. Might as well take advantage of it.

Ida howled. "The pain! The pain I tell you. You have no idea."

Her daughters-in-law rushed about. They made food, swept the kitchen, and one of them even did a wash while another cleaned the bathtub. There were so many people in the house that no one could hear themself think.

Uncle Sid, Izzy's older brother, arrived on his son's arm wailing and gnashing his false teeth. "Oy, thank God Mama and Papa aren't alive to see this terrible day. It would have killed them dead. Dead, I tell you!"

He grabbed Izzy. "Was it awful?"

Ida butted in. "He was comatose for most of it. Ya wanna know what happened, ask me."

Izzy lit a cigarette. "I wasn't comatose when I was trying to get you away from that maniac."

"Well, you were out like a light for the rest of it."

"Not voluntarily."

"Whatever."

"And how did you kill the man?" Uncle Sid asked Ida.

"She browbeat him to death," Izzy answered.

Ida scowled. "Why didn't I leave that damn duct tape on your mouth?"

"You should have. I have no lips now, thanks to you."

Ida looked at her sons. "Did you ever hear anyone complain more than him?"

"So what did the police say?" Uncle Sid asked.

"They asked me why someone would be after Bette, but I told them I had no idea, unless she's up to something in that precious car of hers. You can never get a thing out of her."

"Have you tried to call Bette and warn her about this?" Uncle Sid asked.

Everyone looked at each other.

"Did we?" Izzy yelped. "Did we?"

Ida couldn't tell him that Bette had hung up on her. It was too embarrassing.

"For the love of God, in all this confusion, has no one thought to let Bette know what's going on?"

The family looked at one another.

"Get her on the phone!"

Mordecai reached for the phone and dialled Bette's cellphone. A man answered and said he had the wrong number. Thinking he'd misdialled, Mordecai tried again. The same guy answered.

"I'm looking for Bette Weinberg. Is she there, please?"

"I told you before. I don't know any Bette, so screw off."

"Who is this?"

The line went dead. Mordecai looked at his father.

"What's wrong?"

"A man answered."

"Oh my God, she's eloped," Ida said.

"Eloped?" Izzy said. "Who goes on their honeymoon with three girlfriends?"

Ida drove back and forth over the rug. "How do we know she went with three girlfriends? Maybe this whole thing has been a ruse to cover up her tracks."

Izzy dismissed her. "That slap to the head affected your brain."

"Who's the guy, then?"

"How the hell should I know?"

Mordecai pleaded with his parents. "Enough with the bickering, you two. I know this is difficult, but you need to put everything aside and concentrate on Bette."

Ida drove over to the living room window and looked out. Her shoulders slumped. "Where are you, Bette?"

Bette and Linda were on their way back to the hotel from the Canadian consulate on 6th Avenue. They'd been very helpful and assisted Bette with all the necessary paperwork. It was a relief to have something go smoothly for a change.

And then Bette's phone rang. "I bet this is Ida again. Wonder what she'll make up this time?" She answered it. "Hello?"

"The cock crows at midnight."

"*Hello?*"

"I *said*, the cock crows at midnight."

"Ma? Is this you? Just what the devil do you think you're doing? I've had it up to here with this cloak-and-dagger stuff."

"Who is this?"

"Who's *this?* You called me, remember?"

They hung up.

"Was that your mother?"

"No, some other wing nut."

They continued their journey. "I hope Gemma feels better," Linda said. "Maybe we can actually do something this afternoon."

"Let's hope so."

The phone rang again. "Hello?"

"The cock..."

Bette spoke louder then she intended. "The cock? You again?"

A few people on the street turned their heads and looked at her. "Listen here, you've got the wrong number. I'm not interested in your cock or anyone else's, so give me a break and stop phoning this number." She clicked the phone off and put it in her pocket. She rolled her eyes. "Don't even ask."

✻

Stuart knocked tentatively on the bathroom door. "Ryan. Come out of there, please. I think I know what might have happened."

She yelled from inside. "You think? I *know*. I'm being taken for a mug."

"Stop acting like a child and let's talk."

The door swung open. Ryan stood there in righteous indignation. "Why do you always say that? Believe it or not, I'm allowed to be upset. I do own my own feelings. Age has nothing to do with it."

"Sorry, you're right. Come and sit down."

She flounced by him and threw herself in a chair. "So? What's your explanation? I can't wait to hear it."

"I think Linda's behind it."

"No shit, Sherlock."

"She's here at the hotel."

"*What?*"

"I know. I think she's following me. I think she sent that girl just to upset you." Stuart crossed over to the window and looked out. "I can't believe she'd do something like that, but maybe I drove her to it."

"You didn't drive her anywhere. People are allowed to fall in love."

"Not when they're married."

"Rubbish. No one gets married anymore. It's an ancient ritual that means nothing. The only reason I want to get married is to have a wedding."

Stuart couldn't get his head around that, so he kept his mouth shut.

Ryan crossed her arms. "Who told you she was in the hotel?"

"Wes."

"That's who was on the phone? What did he want?"

"To tell me the house was broken into."

Ryan stood bolt upright. "The house was broken into? Oh God, I hope they didn't take my stereo system."

"Not our house, my old house. Linda's house."

"Oh, that's okay then."

Stuart flinched. "It's not okay."

"You know what I mean."

"Wes doesn't want her to know. He thinks she's here on vacation, but I think she's stalking us."

Ryan ran up to him. "Maybe she wants to kill me. You read it all the time in the *Gazette*."

"I really don't think so."

"Maybe she wants to kill you. That's the more likely scenario."

Stuart shook his head as if to clear it and paced the room. "You're overreacting. But I don't like the thought of her following us. I think it would be best all around if we changed hotels."

"Stupid bitch, screwing everything up like this."

Stuart went over to the closet and took out his suitcase. "Let's go. Then maybe we can have a nice night out. I'll feel better if she doesn't know where we are."

Ryan helped him pack.

❈

Bette and Linda got on the elevator and pushed the button for the seventh floor. The door closed. When it opened again, Stuart and Ryan were standing there waiting to get on. The four of them reeled away from each other in shock.

"Oh, God," Linda cried.

"Don't kill us," Ryan shouted.

Linda stepped out of the elevator, Bette behind her. "Kill you? Are you insane? I wouldn't waste my breath on you, you little homewrecker. What's she talking about, Stuart?"

"Why are you here, Linda? Why are you following us?" Stuart tossed his head towards Bette. "And why did you bring your posse with you?"

Linda put her shoulders back. "Do you honestly think I'm pathetic enough to run around and spy on you two? I can't imagine anything more boring."

Ryan pointed a finger at Linda. "That little trick of yours didn't work, lady."

"What trick?"

"Sending a girl with a baby to my door, asking for Mrs. Keaton. You think I fell for that? What a pathetic bitch you are, pulling a stunt like that. Stuart is well rid of you."

Linda made a face. "I don't know what kind of drugs you're on, missy, but I suggest you take a few more and hopefully overdose on them."

Ryan clutched Stuart's arm. "Did you hear that? She *does* want to kill me."

Stuart stepped closer to Linda. "You don't have to like me anymore, but for pity's sake, look at what you're doing. If you want to keep your dignity, you'll stop with these little charades and go home."

"And when you do go home, I hope you find the robbers stole everything."

"Ryan, don't," Stuart pleaded.

Linda looked at Bette in confusion. "What robbers? Are you telling me my house was robbed?"

"What goes around comes around," Ryan said.

Bette took a step towards Ryan. "Shut up, you little tart."

"My house was robbed?" Linda looked horrified. "Why didn't someone tell me?"

Stuart looked at Ryan. "Go downstairs and wait for me in the lobby."

She started to protest.

"Now."

Ryan stomped into the elevator and stabbed at the button. Mercifully, the doors closed.

"Bette, would you mind leaving Linda and me alone for a moment? I need to clear things up for her."

Bette looked at Linda. "Are you okay with that?"

Linda nodded and Bette walked away. Only when she turned the corner did Linda say, "What happened?"

"Wes called me. Apparently when Clive went over to feed Buster, he found that someone had broken in."

"Is Buster all right?"

"Buster's fine, and strangely enough not much was taken, or even damaged. So Clive called Wes and Wes called the police." Stuart wiped his forehead with the sleeve of his jacket. "Wes didn't want you to know about it. Didn't want it to ruin your so-called holiday."

"It is a holiday. You can think what you like. It makes no difference to me."

"Wes and a girl named Chloe are staying at the house until you get home."

"Chloe? I've met her a few times. I didn't know it was serious."

Stuart shrugged. They avoided each other's eyes; to talk about ordinary things was more painful than anything else.

"I've asked Wes to have the locks changed."

"Good idea."

"And I cancelled all the credit cards, just in case."

Linda's head flew up. "Oh, right."

"Will that be a problem for you?"

"Would you care if it was?"

He closed his eyes. "Don't."

"I didn't, Stuart. You did."

Linda left him standing by the elevator. When she returned to the room Bette was waiting for her. "Are you okay? Did they trash the place?"

Linda shook her head. "Not much was taken. But that's why he cancelled the credit cards. Where are Augusta and Gemma?"

"Maybe they're getting ice or something."

Linda took off her coat and threw it on a bed. "Would they both go?" She looked around. "Our parcels aren't here. Surely they wouldn't get ice holding shopping bags."

Bette looked around too. "They've put them somewhere." She checked the closet and the drawers. Linda looked under the beds and behind the curtains. They both went into the bathroom. They couldn't find a thing.

"They never got back."

Linda bit her lip. "They must have stopped for a drink, or maybe a bite to eat."

"Gemma said she had a headache. I can't imagine them stopping anywhere."

Linda hurried over to her phone. "We'll call them. Augusta has her cell with her." She pressed the numbers and waited. "It's shut off. That's not like her. She always has it on, in case the girls need her."

The two of them sat opposite each other on the beds. "I don't like this, Lin."

Linda shut her eyes. "This is an unmitigated disaster. Why, oh why did we come?"

"Adventure?"

She opened her eyes. "Adventure, yes; punishment, no. Did you see that little madam? Did you see how young she was? She could be Wes's girlfriend."

Bette waved her hand. "Forget her. She's not worth talking about. It's the girls I'm worried about."

Linda folded her arms across her chest and rocked. She did that when she was deep in thought, or very worried. "But what did she mean, a girl with a baby asking for me?"

They had the same thought at the same time.

"The girl at the airport," Bette cried. "She must be looking for us."

"But why me?"

Bette pondered for a moment. "In the ladies' room, I told her we were going to the Waldorf, and I mentioned your last name being the same as her son's name. She must have remembered that and when my name wasn't on the register, she tried yours. She's a clever girl, if nothing else."

"And when she asked for Mrs. Keaton, they told her the wrong one. It makes sense now."

"Well, the poor child, having to deal with Ryan. I'll never get my purse now."

Linda jumped from the bed. "Wait, maybe Gemma and Augusta ran into her. Where's the bag with the bear in it?"

They looked and unfortunately found it right away. "Darn. There goes that theory."

Bette paced back and forth from the window to the bathroom. She looked at her watch. "This is nuts. Where are they? I know darn well they wouldn't have gone anywhere. Gemma was too upset about the store episode. Try Augusta's cell again."

Linda did, and it was still off. "So what do we do now?"

"Wait."

So they waited and waited and waited, and then when they couldn't wait any longer, they still had to wait; there was no word from their friends.

CHAPTER NINE

"Will you shut that kid up?" Dumber yelled at them from the front seat. "He's making me crazy."

"He's scared, that's all." Gracie held Keaton tighter, but he continued to wail.

"He'll be more than scared in a minute."

Gemma leaned forward. "My, that's really brave, threatening a baby like that. Your mother must be so proud."

"Keep your mouth shut, lady."

Augusta leaned closer to Gemma. "Stop pissing them off."

"Sorry. I guess I'm not in a real good mood, what with being taken hostage twice in less than twenty-four hours."

Gracie said, "Twice? What happened yesterday?"

"What *didn't* happen yesterday is a better question."

Gracie's face crumbled. "This is my fault. I got you in trouble and worse, I got my son in trouble too. I'll never forgive myself."

Augusta put her hand on Gracie's arm. "We all make mistakes. Granted, this is a big one. But you'll have your whole life to rectify it."

"Which gives her about twenty minutes, the way this day is going," Gemma said.

"I'm sorry."

Gemma patted Gracie's knee. "Never mind. You're not alone, so that's something to be grateful for."

Keaton continued to let everyone know he was not happy with the situation at all. Gracie rubbed the top of his head and then kissed it. "I don't know what's wrong."

"He knows we're keeping lousy company," Gemma said.

Augusta felt his cheeks. "I think he may be teething. His cheeks are flushed. Do his gums feel hot?"

Gracie rubbed them with the tip of her finger. "I think so."

"Or it could be diaper rash," Gemma suggested. "Is his bum red? Or maybe gas? Or constipation?"

"How are his stools?" Augusta asked.

Dumber turned around with his big moon face. "Shut up. You're making me sick up here."

"Interesting how the big lout has such a delicate stomach," Gemma said. "It must get in the way of all his killing and maiming."

"I'm gonna give you a knuckle sandwich in a minute."

"I like mustard, just so you know."

Augusta hit Gemma on the knee, but it didn't keep her quiet for long. They jolted forward when the car slammed to a stop at a red light. "Don't you know how to drive? My sixteen-year-old drives better than this."

Dumb looked at her in the rear-view mirror. "I got a perfect score on my driving test."

Dumber punched Dumb in the shoulder. "Who gives a shit?"

Gemma looked out the window. "Look at this, Augusta, our own personal tour of the city. Too bad they don't stop at the Statue of Liberty or the Chrysler Building. I always wanted to see them. Instead we get to see the underbelly of life in New York, where the rats play."

Dumber turned around and glared at them. "I'm not warning you again. Zip it."

Gemma mouthed "cellphone" to Augusta, who tried not to make any noise as she rooted through her purse. She gently eased it out and hid it behind her bag, then turned it on and punched in the numbers. With Keaton's screams of outrage covering up her voice, she leaned over and when she thought she heard "Hello," she whispered, "we've been kidnapped. We've been..."

Dumber reached over the front seat, grabbed it out of her hand, and turned it off. "Do that again, and you're dead." He threw the phone in the glove compartment.

The women looked at each other and then straight ahead. There was nothing left to say.

❊

Blue and his girlfriend, Starr, were blasted out of their minds. So when someone phoned and said they had been kidnapped, Blue laughed his head off. But his euphoria didn't last long. There were more pressing issues to deal with, like how to get a stash of drugs to his contact in exchange for...basically nothing. The guy told him if they didn't deliver the goods this time, Blue and Starr would be dead. He didn't offer any other reward for delivery.

They'd screwed up plenty before, and no one was in the mood to take their crap anymore.

Blue had tried to make arrangements over the phone in the coffee shop, but ever since they'd left there, he'd had a series of wrong numbers. Someone looking for Bette. When Blue told Starr, she said, "Wanna bet? Anyone wanna bet?" which she repeated again and again until Blue told her to put a sock in it.

They sat on an old mattress on the floor of a communal apartment. Not so much an apartment as a pigpen. People crashed there day and night and no one did anything to keep it clean. Starr rolled her joint, lit it, and passed it to Blue. He stared at the ceiling. She shoved his arm. "Here."

He reached for it, took a drag, and then knocked back some cheap bourbon. "I think something's wrong. That bastard was supposed to call and tell us when to bring the stuff, and he never did. He's messing with our heads."

Now Starr took the joint. "What's he supposed to say again?"

"The cock crows at midnight." Blue's shoulders shook with laughter. "I thought that up."

"No you didn't. I've heard that before."

"Whatever." He grabbed the joint back and inhaled deeply.

Starr rubbed her nose with the back of her hand. "Where's the stuff, anyway?"

Blue pointed at the ceiling. "It's behind the tiles up there."

"Ahh," she nodded. "Good thinking."

"Why?"

"It's up high...get it...high...you get high...high..."

He grabbed her nose ring and pulled her towards him.

"Ow!"

"Enough with the *high*s."

"Let go or the cock will be crowin' a lot sooner than midnight."

He started to giggle. "Good one."

"Right." Starr got up on her hands and knees and rose to her feet, but she wasn't very steady. "I gotta go to the can." She nearly keeled over when she tripped off the edge of the mattress. "Whoa, we gotta get a new place. The floor is way too crooked in here."

"Gimme a kiss," Blue said.

She blew him one vaguely and then zigzagged to the bathroom, but she forgot what she was there for. She was going back down the hall to ask Blue when some guys passed her going the other way.

"Hey Starr," one of them said. "We got some stuff. Wanna party?"

Starr put her fist in the air. "Rock on, man." She turned around and careened out the door with the rest of them. Blue slid down the wall and fell over on his side. He was out cold and didn't have a clue she'd even left.

❋

The car finally pulled into what looked like a warehouse, one that hadn't been used in a long time. It was dark and dusty and the windows were covered with sheets of plywood. The friends had absolutely no idea where they were, but they kept their eyes open to anything that would stand out later in their memory. It was their only hope.

The two gorillas got out of the car first and then opened the back doors. Gemma slid out one side and Augusta and Gracie went out the other. Gemma carried their bags.

"You won't need those where you're going. Put 'em down," Dumber said.

Gemma did as she was told.

"Get over there with the others."

Gemma walked over to Augusta and put her arm around Gracie. They stood there and waited for something to happen. Soon they heard a door slam in the distance. Footsteps echoed in the vast space as a man with dark greasy hair and a pox-marked face walked towards them.

"He looks like a shark," Gemma whispered. "His eyes are dead."

Candy popped a few more Life Savers in his mouth before he looked at his henchmen. "So? Which one of these two broads is the one I'm looking for?"

Gemma and Augusta glared at him.

"Not sure," Dumber shrugged. "The security guards at the hotel were on our ass. We had to stay in the street."

Dumb jumped in. "Yeah, we saw Gracie run up to talk to them and figured one of them was Bette Weinberg. It was better then nothin'."

Candy gave them a look that suggested Dumb was wrong about that. Then he turned his attention to the ladies. "Who's Bette Weinberg?"

No one spoke.

"I'll say it again. Who's Bette Weinberg?"

"She's not here." Gemma said.

He watched them for a moment. "I don't believe you. You're sweatin' like a pig, which means you're lying."

"I'm having a hot flash. Look at my driver's license if you don't believe me."

The muscle in Candy's jaw worked overtime. "So Bette Weinberg isn't here. Why am I not surprised?"

Dumb became agitated. "Look boss, it was impossible to hang around the hotel lobby. Security was everywhere. It's like that now. Everything's tougher to get into, ya know?"

"Really? I had no idea." Candy reached over and hit the back of Dumb's head. Then he walked over to Gracie and grabbed her out of Gemma's arms. He pulled her back with him, his hand over her throat. "Try anything stupid and I'll kill the kid."

"Which kid?" Gemma said. "The little one or the tiny one, you bastard?"

"Shut up. Now, where do I find this Bette?"

The women looked at him but said nothing. He squeezed Gracie's throat. "Where?"

"You said we couldn't open our mouths, so which is it? You can't have it both ways," Gemma said.

"Dames. What is it with you broads? You twist everything around.

How do I get in touch with this Bette? You should start talkin' before I lose my temper."

"You'll have to call her cellphone," Augusta said.

Candy snapped his fingers and pointed at Dumber. Dumber put his hand in his jacket pocket and produced a phone. He threw it to his boss.

"What's the number?"

They told him. He pressed the numbers and put his ear to the phone. "There's no answer."

Gemma and Augusta looked at each other.

Candy clicked it off. "Looks like we have to wait. Make yourselves comfortable, ladies; you're here for the long haul."

Bette and Linda were scared shitless.

They sat wrapped in the hotel bedspreads because they didn't know what else to do. Finally they couldn't stand it.

"We have to call the police," Linda said. "This is nuts. There's something wrong. They should be back by now."

Bette shivered with fear. "What if something happened to them? They have seven children between them. What will we do, Linda? How are we ever going to live through this?"

"Look, we have to calm down. We're not going to be good to anyone if we get hysterical. We need to think."

Just then the hotel phone rang. They both tripped over each other trying to reach it as they struggled out of their blankets.

Bette got to it first. "Hello?"

"Bette, it's Mordecai. Where the hell have you been? We've been trying to call your cell."

"That's strange. I've had it on all day. Oh, it's so good to hear your voice. Don't tell Ida and Izzy, but it's been a nightmare since we've been here. I lost my purse and Izzy's money and now I don't have a passport. And we can't find our friends—"

Linda wrestled the phone from her and said to Bette, "Don't tell him all that."

"But maybe they can help us."

"From Montreal? We don't want to frighten everyone until we know something for sure."

"Okay, okay." Bette took the phone back. "Mordecai, why are you calling me, anyway? Has something happened?"

"Mama and Papa were attacked."

Bette's mouth dropped open.

Linda poked her. "What's wrong?"

"Ida and Izzy were attacked."

Linda couldn't speak. Bette continued to hold the phone in a vice grip and spoke again to Mordecai. "Are you telling me that Ma's phone call was true?"

"What phone call?"

"She didn't tell you? She called and said she killed a guy and I thought she was kidding, so I hung up on her. You know how she gets."

"She called you?" Bette heard her brother address Ida. "Mama, did you call Bette and tell her you killed a guy?"

Bette heard mumbling in the background and then her brother came back on the line. "She doesn't remember that. She was almost comatose when it happened. She's got two black eyes and they broke Papa's nose. They even tried to burn him."

"Oh my God. That's what I get for going away. The minute I leave them they're brutalized. Why did I go? I feel so guilty."

"Never mind that now."

"Do you want me to come home?"

"Well, you might have to. I've got something to tell you...What? Sorry, Mama wants to tell you. Here she is."

Bette heard the phone being passed over and Ida yelling, "No Izzy, I'll tell her. You were out like a light for most of it. What do you know? HELLO? Bette?"

"Ma, are you okay? I feel awful."

"I told you I'd be dead when you got back, but no one ever listens to me."

"I'm sorry. I shouldn't have gone. Can you forgive me?"

"Well, I'll try. Let that be a lesson to you. Your mother is your mother. You only ever have one, and once I'm gone..."

Her voice disappeared and her father was on the line. "Never mind

that nonsense, Bette. We're trying to tell you that the guy who attacked us was looking for you."

"*What?*" Bette put her hand over the receiver and looked at Linda.
"The guy who attacked them was looking for me."

Linda's eyes bugged out of her head. "Are you joking?"

Bette went back on the phone. "I don't understand. What did he
say?"

"I don't know. Here's your mother."

"Bette? He said, tell me where I can find Bette Weinberg and I said
never and he hit me and then he asked me again and I said never…"

"You did?"

"That's what got me these shiners. So then he pulled a knife on
your father and said he'd kill him if I didn't tell him, so I said you were
at the Waldorf and it was all Linda Keaton's fault."

She looked at Linda. "She told him we were here."

Linda pressed her fingers into her forehead. "Great."

Bette's mother continued. "Yes, I did. I said just because she lives in
Pointe Claire and has a plastic surgeon for a husband she thinks she's
better than anyone else."

"Ma!"

"Well, it's true. So then he looked in our address book and he
ripped out a page."

"Why did he do that?"

"I have no idea. I wasn't about to engage him in small talk, was
I?"

"What page did he rip out?"

Ida yelled for someone. "What page did he rip out of that book?
The *K*'s."

"He must have been looking for Linda's address."

Linda shoved her. "Who? Who was looking for my address?"

"The guy who's dead." She went back on the phone. "How did you
kill the guy, anyway?"

"I pushed him down the stairs."

"You walked?"

"With my chair, you idiot."

"Oh."

"So come home right now. You may be in danger. Did you do something to someone? What sorts of things do you get up to in that precious car of yours? Are you on drugs?"

"Of course not. Look, Ma, I want you to know that I love you and Da, but I have to go now."

"I tell her I'm almost killed and she has to go. What's so pressing?"

"I'll call you again soon. I promise."

"But wait! We need to know..."

Bette hung up and ran to the bathroom, Linda behind her. Linda held her hair as Bette got sick in the toilet. She finally raised her head, threw water on her face, and rinsed out her mouth. Linda passed her a towel.

"Oh my God, something's going on and I can't figure it out."

Linda led her back to the bed. Bette told her what her mother had said. They didn't speak for a few minutes as they tried to process the information.

"Okay," Linda said. "All this can't be coincidence. Ever since we got on that plane, it's been nothing but disaster. There's no way in a million years that all this stuff isn't related. There has to be an explanation."

"What? What could it be? I mean, we didn't do anything. We got in a taxi and left for the city. That's when things started to unravel."

"Who would be looking for you, Bette? No one."

"Thanks."

Linda waved her away. "You know what I mean. You don't have an enemy in the world, and then some guy is looking for you and asks for my address and suddenly my home is broken into. We only got here yesterday, so something had to happen between now and then."

"We had a guy try to kill us. We saw an attempted robbery, you ran into Stuart, we lived through a bomb threat, Gemma was accused of shoplifting, they've disappeared, and I lost my bag. I lost my bag. That's the first thing that happened."

"Everything went downhill from the airport on."

"But it's not like I mixed up my bag up with someone from the mob. It was a young girl and a baby. She had diapers and a teddy bear.

What's so strange about that? And she obviously tried to return it to me today."

"That's true. But you know what still bugs me? How did that driver know our names and where we were going if he didn't work for the cab company?"

Bette's cellphone rang again. She nearly jumped out of her skin. "You get it. I can't take any more bad news."

"Oh, please let this be Augusta," Linda prayed as she raced to the phone on the dresser. "Hello?"

"Where's the stuff?" a voice growled at her.

"Hello? Who is this?"

"Don't mess with me. You know damn well who it is. Now where's Blue?"

"I don't know what you're talking about. What's blue?"

"You better bring the stuff tonight or you're all dead, do you hear me?"

"Yes. Yes, I hear you. Where do you want it dropped off?" Linda looked at Bette and appealed to her silently. Bette hopped up and down and was no help at all.

"Washington Square Park, near the arch."

"Where's that?"

"You're shitting me, right? Be there at midnight. Fuck this up and you and everyone you know are dead meat." The phone slammed down in her ear.

Linda looked at Bette in horror. "He said…"

"…who said?"

"Some horrible man said if we didn't bring him the stuff by midnight, everyone we know will be dead, and then he asked where blue was. What the hell is blue?"

Bette jumped around the room shaking her hands. "Oh my God, oh my God. They must have Augusta and Gemma. That's why they're not here. They've been kidnapped."

"But why? What stuff? We don't have stuff. What do they want?"

"I don't know. What do we do? We have to call the police. We need help, Linda."

"This is a nightmare." Linda paced the floor. "Some guy beats up your parents to find you. Then they go to my house and rob it, but we have no idea why. Your mother tells the guy we're at the Waldorf. They tell someone, and that someone comes and takes Gemma and Augusta away. Then they call and say to give them the stuff or everyone's dead."

Bette nodded.

"So that means only one thing. We must have something they want. We don't know we have it, but we must have it."

"Well, the only thing that's not ours is the baby's bag. But I still don't see how she could be involved."

"Look, does it matter? It sounds like she must have been. There's no other explanation. Where is it?."

Bette ran over and got the bag from the floor beside the closet. She threw it on the bed as if it were on fire. Linda picked it up and turned it upside down. The teddy bear dropped on the bed with a sweater, a few diapers, a soother, a couple of safety pins, some Mentos, a *People* magazine, and a package of baby wipes. Linda looked in there first. She pulled the whole roll out. Nothing.

Then she leafed through the magazine, pushed all the Mentos out of the wrapper, manhandled the soother, flipped the sweater inside out, opened and ripped up the diapers, and even unclasped the safety pins. Then she picked up the bear and shook him. She listened as she did.

"Does this bear seem normal to you?"

"Normal? Yeah."

"It feels a little heavy." Linda examined the seams. "I can't see where they might have opened it up and put something in, but this must be it. There's nothing else."

"Should we open it?"

"God, do you really want to know what's in here? If it's enough to get people killed, I don't want any part of it."

Bette bit her nails. "But what if we're wrong and we get there and this isn't what they want?"

Linda considered it. "I suppose you're right. We can't take any chances."

"But what if they kill us for opening it?"

Linda rolled her eyes. "You just said..."

"I know what I said! I'm not sure, that's all."

They stared at the bear and the bear smiled back at them. Linda turned him over and over. "He's not too squishy, so we can't feel for a lump. His arms and legs move on hinges. Should I try to take a limb off?"

"You might not get it back on."

"Then do you have any nail scissors? I had some in my luggage—but of course my luggage is off in sunny Spain at the moment."

Bette hurried over to her suitcase, lifted the lid, and rummaged through the pockets to produce a nail kit. She unzipped it and sat back down on the bed before handing Linda a pair of cuticle scissors. "But how are we going to sew him back up?"

"Look in the bathroom. They sometimes leave those little sewing kits in there."

Bette rushed to the bathroom and searched through the toiletries. "Eureka, there's one here." She dashed back to the bed.

Linda looked up with the scissors in her hand. "So are we doing the right thing?"

"How the hell should I know? Do we have a choice?"

"Okay." She proceeded to snip one tiny seam thread at a time. When she had an opening about as wide as her finger, she gingerly poked around inside. "I don't feel anything. Oh God, if it's not the bear, then what is it?"

"Cut a little more. You can't get a good feel."

So she did. This time she put two fingers in as deep as she could and suddenly she froze. "I think I feel something."

Bette held her breath.

"I've got something." Linda worked very carefully, not wanting to remove any unnecessary stuffing. Sweat poured down her face as she inched what felt like a plastic bag closer to the hole. "I'm not going to be able to get it out. It's too big."

"Here, then." Bette scampered over to her suitcase and took out a small flashlight.

"Why did you bring that?"

"In case of a hotel fire, but so far that's been the only thing that hasn't happened, knock on wood." She handed it over.

They pulled the bear over to the light and shone the flashlight inside. "It's crystals or something," Bette said.

"Look at that shine. Those are diamonds."

They sat back on the bed in shock.

"This must be Blue. The bear."

"That's it," Bette whispered. "That young girl was carrying diamonds through customs. No wonder she threw her guts up in the bathroom."

"And when you walked out with her bag, she called the driver in a panic and told him my name and where we were going—you told her that in the bathroom. That's why he pulled a gun on us and told us to give him the bags."

Bette jumped up and began to pace. "It's all my fault."

"It's not your fault, Bette. No one in a million years would expect something like this to happen."

"But two of my best friends are in mortal danger, my parents were assaulted, your house was broken into. It's too much."

Linda got up and took Bette by the shoulders. "Snap out of it, Bette. We need to stay focused. The girls' lives are at stake."

Bette reached for a Kleenex in her pocket and blew her nose. "Okay, I'm okay."

Linda reached down and picked up the bear from the bed. "Wait a minute. That young girl came to us today. I wonder if she set a trap or wanted to warn us?"

"She must have set a trap, because obviously Augusta and Gemma walked right into it."

Linda shook her head. "She's only a child herself. How does a young girl's life go so wrong?"

"Who knows?"

"Okay. At least we have some explanation for why all this horrible stuff is happening. Now all we have to do is sew Blue back together, go to this Washington Square Park, give them the diamonds, and get Gemma and Augusta out of there." She put Blue on the bed, went over to her guidebook, and looked up the park. "Oh, fabulous. It's about forty-three blocks from here. I have no idea how long that's going to take."

"I think we should call the police."

"They've been such a big help so far. It'll take ages to explain everything, and by then it may be too late."

"Oh, don't say that."

"Oh shit, how much money do I have?" She raced over to her purse and opened her wallet. "Damn. How are we going to get a taxi?"

"You don't have enough?"

"Oh wait, I know. I'll call Stuart. He's got money."

"Maybe he should come with us. He's a big, strong guy."

"That's all I need. Stuart mouthing off about how I'm always screwing up."

"We don't have a choice, Linda. We need him."

"You're right. We need all the help we can get, even if it is from a two-timing skunk." She ran to her cellphone. "You sew Blue up and I'll call him."

Stuart and Ryan were in the middle of a fancy restaurant. Stuart was doing his best to put the upsetting episode with Linda out of his mind. It was easier as the night went on, now that the first bottle of champagne was turned upside down in the ice bucket.

Ryan looked spectacular in her little black number. When she sashayed to the restroom at one point, he watched other men give her a second and third glance. It made him feel pretty special. He tried to ignore the women who gave *him* the once over, to see who the gorgeous young thing was with. He could tell by the looks on their faces they thought he was old enough to be her father.

Ryan sat across from him and picked up a cherry from her dessert. She licked it with her tongue. "I love cherries, don't you?"

"Stop, you're making me crazy."

Ryan acted surprised. "How?"

"Let's get outta here."

She reached under the table with her foot and put it between his legs. "I don't think you can wait."

His cell went off, which definitely broke the mood. They both sat up straighter in their chairs. Ryan was exasperated. "Don't answer it."

"I have to. There might be a change in tomorrow's venue."

She folded her arms. "Big whoop."

"Stuart Keaton."

"It's me."

Stuart started to rise from the table and then quickly sat down and adjusted his napkin. Ryan looked at him and smirked.

"What's the matter?"

"Everything, and I can't believe I'm going to ask this, but can you help me?"

"Linda, what's going on?"

Ryan made a face. She leaned toward him and waved. "Excuse me, your lady's getting cold."

He held the phone to his lapel. "I'm sorry, I have to take this."

Ryan stood up and grabbed her clutch. "I'll wait by the bar, shall I?" She stormed off.

Stuart couldn't very well run after her. It was unseemly. He put the phone back to his ear and heard, "Stuart? Are you there?"

"Yes. I'm here."

"Where are you, anyway?"

"We're...I'm at the Tavern on the Green."

"Get in a cab and pick me up at the Waldorf and bring lots of money with you."

"What? I'm not going to do anything until you tell me what this is about."

"Augusta and Gemma are missing, and Bette and I have got to go to Washington Square Park and get them back."

"Missing?"

"I'm not playing twenty questions with you! I'll explain it in the taxi. Now are you going to help me or not?"

"Fine, I'll help you. I'll leave now."

"We'll meet you at the front doors of the hotel."

She hung up.

Stuart looked at his cellphone and frowned. What in God's name was going on? And how was he going to explain all this to Ryan?

CHAPTER TEN

While Blue was still out like a light, a girl came in and smoked a joint on one end of the mattress. She kicked him a couple of times to make sure he wasn't dead, but that was as much as she was willing to do. He eventually woke up and could hardly move his neck, what with having been slumped over for a couple of hours. He slowly pushed himself up on his elbow and looked around.

"Hey," he said.

"Hey."

"Where's Starr?"

She shrugged.

He scratched his gelled, spiky hair, yawned, and then took a drink from the bottle of bourbon he still clutched in his hand. "What time is it?"

She looked at her watch. "Almost eleven."

"Morning or night?"

"Geez, how long have you been wasted?"

"Twelve years." He frowned. "I think I'm supposed to be doin' something right about now, but I can't remember what it is." He looked around and then his eyes went to the ceiling.

"Aw, shit." He struggled to get up, but he was so shaky he nearly fell over. He staggered over to a chair and pulled it into the middle of the room.

"Whatcha doin? Gonna hang yourself?"

"Nah, maybe later." He stood up on the chair and had to balance himself for a few moments before he reached up and pushed a tile over slightly. That's when his cellphone rang. He pointed to it on the mattress. "Get that." He meant for her to give it to him. The girl picked it up and answered it instead.

"Hello?"

"We're going to kill your friends unless you bring the bear to

Central Park. Go to 97th and 5th. Walk towards the East Meadow, near the bridge. Have you got that?"

"Yeah, okay."

They hung up. The girl clicked off the phone and tossed it on the bed. Blue waited for her to say something. She went back to smoking her joint.

"Well?"

"Well what?"

"Who was it?"

"How the hell should I know?"

Blue jumped from the chair, nearly breaking his neck in the process. He grabbed the girl by her arm. "What did they say? I've been waiting for a phone call."

"They said they're gonna kill your friends if you don't bring the bear to Central Park."

"*What?*"

"That's what he said, man."

"He said 'the bear'?"

She pulled out of his grasp. "Yeah, the bear. What are you, deaf?"

"Where in Central Park?"

"Um...I forget."

He shook her.

"Chill out, man. I think he said 97th and 5th...walk towards the... um...bridge."

Blue looked around in a daze. "If I want to see my friends alive? Where the hell is Starr? Do I have any other friends?"

"If you do, which I highly doubt, that guy obviously has them."

Blue shook his head. "What the fuck is going on? They've got Starr? How the hell did that happen?" He jumped back up on the chair and threw the tile on the floor, then reached inside and took out the package. He put it under his jean jacket.

"What's that?"

He didn't answer her question. "What the hell is he talking about? What's a bear?"

"It's a brown furry animal with big teeth and claws." The girl cracked her gum. "I'd bring one if I were you. That guy sounds pissed."

"Where am I going to find a bear at this time of night?"

"Use a bear trap."

"Piss off." Blue jumped off the chair, grabbed his phone, and then lurched out the door, panic bubbling up inside his throat.

❖

Gemma, Augusta, Gracie, and Keaton were stuck in a back room that might have served as an office at one point. There were a few filing cabinets around, a table, and a wheeled chair that was crooked and rusty. Some old metal blinds were stacked in one corner and a pile of garbage bags in another. There were windows overlooking the warehouse, but they were frosted. Only shadows were visible through them. That's how they knew that Dumber was standing guard outside the door. Dumb sat on the chair in front of them and looked vacant.

When they were herded into the room, the first thing Gracie did was unwrap poor little Keaton from the sheet around her body. "He needs to get out of this."

"The poor little darling," Gemma said. "He's overheated. Put the sheet on the table, Augusta, and we'll undress him."

"Hey, stop that," Dumb said. "People have to eat off that table."

Augusta pushed past him. "I don't see anyone with a turkey dinner around here, do you? We're not putting this child on the floor."

She spread out the sheet and Gracie laid Keaton down. His head was covered in sweat, but he looked much happier being able to move his limbs about.

"Oh, what a lovely boy," Gemma said. "He's adorable."

"I think so," Gracie smiled.

Gemma turned to Dumb. "We need some water. Go get some."

Dumb pointed at her. "Don't order me around, lady. I don't got to do nothin'."

Gracie quickly took off Keaton's diaper and let the aroma fill the air.

"Aw geez, not the shit again. Is that all that kid does?" Dumb said.

Gracie shrugged. "You'd better get used to the smell if you're not going to give me water to clean him up."

"Why do I get stuck with these broads?" He went to the door and knocked on it.

Dumber opened it a crack. "Wha?"

"Get us some water."

"Water? Where am I gonna find water?"

"A tap," Gemma said.

"Just get it, it reeks in here."

They watched the shadow leave. Dumb stood in front of the door with his gun holster where they could see it, but they didn't pay any attention to him. They were transfixed by the dear little boy who smiled and waved at them, happy to be released from his swaddling sheet.

Dumber came back with a bucket of water. Gracie tore off part of the sheet to clean Keaton off, and she still had a few diapers she'd tucked away inside the sheet. Once he was changed, the friends insisted Gracie sit down on their coats so she could nurse him. They sat on the floor on either side of her and held up the sheet to give her some privacy, since Dumb tried to sneak peeks at her.

Once the baby was fed and growing sleepy, the friends told Gracie to lie down with her baby and try to rest. Augusta used her soft leather purse as a pillow. They put the sheet over the two of them and they were both out like lights in a matter of minutes.

Dumb went back to the chair and sat like a bored gargoyle.

"I feel bad for Linda and Bette," Gemma whispered. "They're going to be frantic when they see we're not back."

"You don't think they'd call home and tell them we're missing, do you? The girls would go out of their minds."

"They're not stupid, and I'm sure they'll think up an excuse if someone calls to speak to us."

Augusta gave her a weak smile. "The girls will wonder why I have the cellphone turned off."

"We'll tell them we went to a movie."

"Gem, what are we going to do?"

Gemma looked fierce. "I won't let these bastards harm one hair on Gracie or Keaton's head. We're the mamas here, Augusta. These children are depending on us. If these were our kids, you know damn well we'd fight these scumbags to our last breath. That's what will keep us strong. I'm not worried for myself. I'm worried about these children. We're going to get out of here because we have to. It's as simple as that."

Augusta sat up a little straighter. "You're right."

They glared at Dumb.

"What did I do?" he yelled when he finally noticed them staring at him. They didn't say a word, just continued to give him the evil eye. He loosened the collar around his neck with his finger. "Stupid women."

There was a family conference at the Weinberg household. Twenty-five people all tried to talk at the same time while the women in the family were busy in the kitchen making meals to feed the troops.

Mordecai repeated Bette's tale of woe.

"She's got no passport and no money?" Ida screeched. "*Oy vey.*"

"She'll have to sell her body in the streets," Izzy shouted.

Ida blew up. "Everything is sex with you, isn't it?"

Just then the phone rang. Ten people lunged for it. Mordecai got there first.

"Hello?"

"Yes, this is Detective Ames with the New York Police Department. I was…"

Mordecai yelled into the phone. "My God, what's wrong?"

Ida tried to grab the phone. "Is that Bette? Gimme the phone."

Mordecai put his hand over the receiver. "It's not Bette. It's the New York Police Department."

Ida beat her chest. "Oh my God, my baby's gone. Why me, Lord? Why me?" She slumped over in her chair.

"Don't be ridiculous, old woman," Izzy barked. "We just talked to her at the Waldorf."

Mordecai put the phone back to his ear. "I'm sorry, officer. Go ahead."

"We had a Miss Bette Weinberg and three of her friends here at the station earlier today and they wanted to report a crime…"

"What kind of a crime?"

Ida sat back up. "A crime?"

Mordecai waved his hand at her to keep quiet.

"They described it as a 'kidnapping, mugging, sudden-death, car-theft, property-damage, gun thing.'"

"Let me get this straight," Mordecai said. "Bette was in the police station today and wanted to report a kidnapping, mugging, sudden-death, car-theft, property-damage, gun thing?"

Twenty-five people in the Weinberg living room became hysterical. Mordecai had to go off in a corner to try and hear the detective.

"That's what they said. I find it a little hard to believe myself."

"So are you going to investigate?"

"Well, the trouble is, we had a bomb threat before I could finish questioning them."

"A bomb threat?"

More hysterics from the clan.

"It was a false alarm, but the ladies fled before they finished filing their report. Miss Weinberg was the only one who was able to give me her address and phone number before we had to evacuate the building. I'd like you to let her know that if they still want to file their report, they can contact me personally. I'll give you my number."

Mordecai snapped his fingers and mouthed, "A pen, a pen."

Ten pens and an old newspaper were produced and Mordecai wrote the detective's phone number down. "I'll tell her. I know she said she lost her money and passport."

"It happens all the time. I don't think there's any cause for alarm. They seemed fine when I was talking to them. Tell her I'll be at my desk in the morning if they'd like to come back in. They can give me a call ahead of time."

"All right then. I'll tell her and thank you for calling."

"Right."

Mordecai clicked the phone off.

"What's going on?" Ida wanted to know. "What sudden death?"

He told them what the detective said.

Uncle Sid shouted above the din. "I think we should go to New York."

"Why do you get to decide everything?" Izzy asked. "I'm the papa."

Uncle Sid pointed to the ceiling. "Because I'm the older brother and Bette is my only niece."

"Shut up, you old windbag," Ida yelled. "Like we need your two cents. I say we go to New York."

Uncle Sid did a double take. "Isn't that what I said?"

"Well, I'm saying it, and I'm the mama."

"What do you mean, we?" Mordecai said. "You're not going."

Ida zipped across the room to sit in front of him. "Like you're gonna stop me?"

Mordecai appealed to his mother. "Ma, be realistic. What help would you be?"

"She's the mama," Izzy said. "If she wants to go, she goes."

Ida crossed her arms and looked triumphant.

"Pop, be reasonable."

"It's decided."

"Are your passports up to date? Are everyone's, for that matter?"

Unfortunately for Mordecai, everyone confirmed that they were.

"I always keep my passport up to date," Ida said. "You never know when you might have to pop over to the Holy Land."

"When was the last time you were in the Holy Land, Ma?"

"Someday I just might go."

Mordecai looked to the heavens. "Fine, but tell me this. What are we going to do when we get to New York? What if we can't get a hold of her? Where do we go?"

"We wait in the lobby of the Waldorf and dare anyone to move us," Izzy vowed. "And then we bring her home."

So that's how one papa, one mama, one uncle, five brothers, and four male cousins all ended up driving to New York City in two vans and a bakery truck.

❀

"Excuse me, Mr. Dumb?" Gemma said.

Dumb ignored her.

Gemma whispered, "I think he's asleep with his eyes open."

"Should we make a run for it?" Augusta whispered back.

Gemma shook her head. "Not yet. I don't know where the other losers are." She cleared her throat. "Hey, Dumb."

Dumb gave a start. "Wha?"

"I need to use the bathroom."

"Too damn bad."

Gemma stared at him. "So what am I supposed to do?"

"I don't give a shit."

"No, apparently not."

Augusta spoke up. "Haven't you heard of the Geneva Convention? Even the enemy is accorded certain privileges, you know."

Dumb got off his stool. "I don't care who this Geneva broad is. I make the rules, not her."

Gemma stood too. "Well, I'm going in the corner, then. Turn around."

Dumb laughed. "Go ahead."

"I'm not joking."

"Right. Do it, lady, I dare ya." Dumb turned his back.

Gemma took the bucket and poured out a stream of water, which meandered across the room and around Dumb's shoes. He looked down and jumped. "Hey!"

"Now, are you going to let me go to the bathroom or not?"

Dumb scowled and went over to the door and opened it. "The fat broad needs to go to the john." He turned back to Gemma. "Go with him, and no funny business."

"I'm not going unless you let the others go too."

Dumb shook his head. "You ain't goin' at the same time. No way."

"I don't mean all together. I mean one at a time."

"Ya got thirty seconds, so move it."

"Be careful, Gemma," Augusta said.

"Don't worry about me." She slipped out the door and Dumber gave her a shove. "Walk in front of me, and don't forget I've got a gun pointed at your back."

Gemma's eyes scanned about as she walked through the abandoned warehouse. She noted two sets of doors, both on the other side of the room. To run for it wouldn't solve anything. There was nowhere to hide.

Dumber poked her shoulder with what she assumed was the gun. "It's straight ahead."

She nodded and walked towards a door with dirty fingerprints all around the light switch. She pushed up the switch with the arm of her sweater, went in, and shut the door in Dumber's stupid, sneery face.

She looked around. "Who leaves a toilet looking like this?" She put her hands together. "Holy Mother of God," she prayed. "Forgive their slovenly ways and may I go home to my family without an infection. Amen." She kissed the gold cross around her neck.

When she got back, Augusta asked her how awful it was.

"Words fail me."

Augusta gave a little shudder. She was the next to follow Dumber into the john. Fortunately, she didn't have to use the horrible light switch; Gemma had left it on for her. She, too, wrinkled her nose at the state of the bathroom. "I'm so glad I never had boys."

Next it was Gracie's turn. But when Dumber escorted her, he spent the whole time commenting on her ass.

"I'd rather have one than be one."

"What was that?"

"Nothin'."

"You got a temper, don't ya? I bet you're one hot chick in bed."

"You'll never know."

Dumber grabbed her shoulder and turned her around. "Don't be so sure about that. The boss ain't here all the time."

Gracie smiled at him. "Well then, be my guest. It'll be my great delight to give you the clap."

He frowned and pushed her towards the bathroom door. "Get in there."

At least walking to and from the bathroom afforded the captives a little exercise. Then they were back to sitting on their coats in a corner of the room. Keaton kept them entertained with happy smiles and giggles, but he stopped the minute Candy stepped into the room.

Candy rubbed his hands. "Well, don't we look all nice and cozy?"

They didn't speak.

"I called your friends."

There was silence.

"I told them where to meet us. They were surprisingly abrupt. Yeah, that's the word I would use—or indifferent. I got that tone, ya know, like maybe I interrupted their meal."

"You're so full of bullshit," Gemma said.

Candy pointed at her. "I can't wait to shut you up."

"And I can't wait to see you try."

Candy laughed. "You remind me of my mother-in-law. Fat and stupid."

"You're married? I feel sorry for your wife."

Candy looked at Augusta. "You better tell your friend to shut her big fat mouth, or you're all done for."

Augusta tossed her head and flipped her hair. "Oh, I don't think I have to do that. You seem like a commanding sort of guy. I'm sure you're not going to let a mere woman get under your skin. Isn't that right?" She brushed her hand over the top button of her blouse. His eyes followed her fingers. He cleared his throat.

"She's not worth my time. Get up. You're coming with me. I can't take the chance of leaving you out of my sight."

As the women struggled to their feet, Gemma muttered, "Good grief, where did *that* come from?"

"I have no idea," Augusta said.

Dumb and Dumber escorted them to the back of a van with no windows. It looked more like a delivery truck. There weren't any seats, so they all crowded in and tried to get comfortable. Candy and Dumber got in the front seats. Dumb looked annoyed that he was in the back, so Gemma rubbed it in.

"They don't like you, do they?"

"Whatcha mean?"

"They always stick you in the back or make you watch us while they go do important stuff. It must bother you. It would bother me."

His frown deepened.

They drove out of the garage and headed up the street.

❊

Blue was frantic. His girl had been kidnapped and it freaked him out. If his brain hadn't been addled by drugs, he might have realized the situation made no sense. Why come and take Starr but not wake him up and demand the stuff?

All he knew was that he had to find a bear in a hurry, and that was no easy task. Not in the middle of the night. He went into some corner stores and ran through their aisles, but no one carried stuffed animals. The closest thing he saw to an animal was a keychain shaped like an American eagle.

Then he had an epiphany. He took off for the street corner where some of his hooker friends plied their trade. He knew Hot Chocolate had a kid; surely the kid had a teddy bear.

She stood under a streetlight, sucking on her cigarette. She looked cold. He ran right up to her and she nodded. "What's up, Red?"

"It's Blue."

"Whatever. Looking for a little action? I'm fuckin' freezing my tits off out here."

"I need something from ya."

Hot Chocolate rolled her eyes. "Amazing, that's what they all say. Get in line."

"Does your kid have a toy? A bear, a teddy bear?"

She immediately looked suspicious. "Say what?"

He grabbed her arms. "I need a bear. It's life or death."

Chocolate yanked herself away. "Get lost, you pervert. You think I'm going to give up my kid's toy? Are you nuts?"

"I'll give you fifty bucks."

She took a drag of her cigarette. "Seventy-five."

"Yeah, okay."

"Follow me."

She marched down the street and around the corner. She told him to stay put and went inside an apartment building that had seen better days. She came out five minutes later holding up a teddy bear dressed in a tutu and ballet slippers.

"Will this do?"

"Yeah." He handed over the money and grabbed the bear. "Thanks."

"Don't you be doin' nothin' weird with that bear, now."

He didn't answer her, just turned around and hightailed it up the street.

❀

Stuart paid the bill and got their coats. He rushed into the bar and took Ryan by the arm. The man who was buying her a drink wasn't impressed.

"Get lost, mister."

"This is my girlfriend."

The man pointed at Ryan. "I thought you said you were alone."

"I *am* alone most of the time. He's being a jerk."

"Ryan, get your coat on and come with me this minute."

She saluted him. "Aye aye, Captain Charisma." She put on her coat and turned to the stranger. "Thanks anyway."

He looked disgusted. "Don't mention it."

Before she could say anything else, Stuart rushed her out of the restaurant and onto the sidewalk. He whistled for a taxi and one instantly pulled over to the curb. He opened the door and steered Ryan toward it.

"What are you doing? Let go of me."

Stuart put his hands up to placate her. "Okay, I'm sorry. Look, something's come up and you have to go back to the hotel. Please, for my sake, I don't want you involved. It's not your worry."

Ryan leaned down into the open cab door. "Thanks anyway. We've changed our minds." She shut the door and the cab squealed away.

"Ryan..."

She stuck a finger in his face. "Listen, mister, why do I get shoved aside as soon as your wife calls? This does concern me, because I'm your girlfriend and you brought me to New York. You can't make me hole up in a hotel room until whatever's going on is over. And by the way, just what the hell *is* going on?"

Stuart took a deep breath and slapped his arms against the sides of his trench coat. "I have no idea. Linda called and said she needed money and I have to go and pick her up. She said she'd tell me then."

Ryan looked incredulous. "And you said yes? Are you a raving lunatic?"

"Stop with the dramatics."

Ryan pointed at herself. "*I* have to stop with the dramatics? You're the one who said she was stalking us, in case you've forgotten. That's why we left the Waldorf."

"Fine. Forget it." He hailed another cab. "Taxi!"

"What are you doing?"

He reached into his wallet and took out some money. He shoved it into her hand. "Here's cab fare. I have to go."

A yellow cab pulled up and Stuart got in.

Ryan stood there with her mouth open. "You're leaving me on the streets of New York in the middle of the night?"

"I have to. I'll see you later." He went to shut the taxi door, but she reached out and grabbed it.

"Don't you dare." She pushed her way into the cab and slammed the door behind her. "Let's get something straight. You're not going anywhere without me."

She plunked herself down beside him and stuck out her bottom lip like a petulant child. Stuart used to think it was cute. Now it irritated the hell out of him.

CHAPTER ELEVEN

Linda and Bette waited with the bear in Linda's carryall bag outside the hotel.

"Hurry up, Stuart. That stupid man is always late."

The words were no sooner out of her mouth when a taxi pulled up. Stuart got out of it and beckoned them over.

"It's about time." Linda and Bette ran towards the cab. "I thought you weren't coming."

"You told me to get money. I stopped at a bank machine."

Linda started to crawl in the back when she spied Ryan. "Dear God." She got out of the taxi and gave Stuart a shove. "Are you kidding me? What did you bring *her* for?"

Stuart grabbed her arm and pulled her to the side. "She wouldn't let me go unless she came too. I tried to get rid of her, believe me."

"You're a complete moron." She yanked her arm out of his grip. "I'm not sitting beside her."

"I'll get in the middle." He turned to Bette. "You get in the front."

Bette looked at Linda. "Don't tell me he brought the bimbo?"

"Can you believe it?"

Stuart crawled in the back and sat beside Ryan. Linda got in after him and gave Ryan a filthy look. "Stay out of my face."

"My pleasure," Ryan said.

The cab driver asked Bette where they were going.

"Washington Square Park. And hurry."

The taxi pulled away from the hotel. No one spoke. The cab driver said, "So, where are you folks from?"

Linda answered. "We're from Montreal, but the one behind you is from Slut City."

Ryan reached across Stuart and tried to hit Linda. Stuart held her arm. "Stop it."

"She has no right speaking to me like that."

"I have every right, since that's what you are."

"Enough," Stuart said. "Now are you going to tell me what this is all about, Linda, or should I get out of this taxi and take my money with me?"

Linda looked past him and stared at Ryan. "I'm not going to tell you a thing. It's none of her business."

"Apparently it is. I'm here, aren't I?"

Stuart elbowed her. "Ryan, be quiet up for a minute."

"Ryan," Linda laughed. "What kind of stupid name is that for a girl?"

"I'm not a girl. I'm a woman. A red hot and sizzling woman, right, Stuart?"

"Will the two of you knock it off?"

The cab driver gave Stuart a pitying look in the rear-view mirror.

Bette turned in her seat and looked over her shoulder. "Linda, do you want to sit up here so you don't have to share a seat with Ronald?"

"Oh, hardy har har," Ryan chimed.

"That's okay, Bette. I'll sit next to my husband."

Bette picked up on it. "How long have you been married, Linda?"

"Twenty-five years this June. Imagine that, Stuart. We were doing it before this slut was even born."

"Stop the car," Stuart yelled at the driver. The driver immediately veered to the right and stopped between two parked cars.

"What are you doing?" Linda shouted.

"I'm getting out of this cab if you two don't shut your mouths. Have you got that?"

"She started it," Ryan said.

"Fine," Linda said. "She's not worth it. We have more important things to worry about. Drive on, please."

The cab driver veered back into traffic.

"So are you going to tell me why I'm driving around in the middle of the night when I should be asleep and getting rested up for my big day tomorrow?"

Linda looked puzzled. "What big day?"

"I'm delivering a seminar on breast implants."

"Well, you *are* an expert on tits. Everyone's but mine."

Stuart's shoulders sagged. He stared straight ahead with a look of resignation on his face. Linda suddenly didn't have the energy to bait him anymore.

"Look, we have to go to Washington Square Park to give something to someone."

"What?"

"Never mind. It's something that belongs to someone. We got our luggage mixed up with theirs and they want it back."

"Why are you meeting in a park in the middle of the night?"

"That's where they told us to go."

"Why are *they* dictating the terms?"

"Because they have Gemma and Augusta."

Stuart sat up. "What on earth are you talking about?"

Bette looked over her shoulder. "You better tell him about the bear, Linda."

So she did. When she finished, Stuart looked at her as if she'd lost her mind.

"Smuggled diamonds? Why haven't you called the police?"

"Because we don't have time. It's a straight exchange. They want the diamonds and we want Gemma and Augusta."

"But..."

"Look, Stuart, we tried five times in the last twenty-four hours to tell the police about the dead guy, and they were no help at all."

"*What dead guy?*"

"She's a killer, let me outta here," cried Ryan.

Everyone, including the taxi driver, told Ryan to shut up.

"I don't have time to tell you about the kidnapping, mugging, sudden-death, car-theft, property-damage, gun thing..."

Stuart grabbed the top of his head. "Okay, now I'm in the twilight zone. How long have you been in New York?"

"We arrived last night."

"And you've had time for all this criminal activity? Even the Mob doesn't work that fast."

Ryan kept trying to open the back door. "I'm being kidnapped, Stuart. Let me outta this car."

"We're nearly there," the cab driver said. "What do you want me to do?"

"Drive to the nearest police station," Stuart said.

"NO!" Linda shouted. "Pull over and let us out. These two can go wherever they like."

"All right, all right," Stuart said. "Pull over, driver."

Ryan yanked Stuart's arm. "Don't you dare get out of this car with them."

"What can I do? I can't let two defenseless women confront diamond thieves."

"But what about me? Don't you care how I feel?"

Stuart shook her hand off. "At this moment, no."

Ryan hit him. "I want to go home. I want my mother."

Stuart gave the driver a handful of money. "Take this pain in the ass back to the Four Seasons."

"Stuart, get back here this minute and apologize."

When Stuart continued to scramble out of the back seat to join Linda and Bette on the sidewalk, Ryan opened her door and jumped out of the car. "You're not leaving me alone. I don't care what you say."

The cab driver shouted after them. "Hey, you want I stick around?"

Stuart stuck his head back in the window. "Would you mind? I'll pay you for your trouble."

"Hey, no problem. I gotta see how this turns out."

"If we come running, get ready to take off."

"You got it."

The four of them gathered on the sidewalk. Ryan punched Stuart in the arm. "Jerk."

He ignored her and turned to Linda. "So what now?"

"Bette and I will go into the park. You and Ronald stay behind in the shadows."

"You're a cow," said Ryan.

Linda pretended she didn't hear her. "If this goes down as planned..."

"'Goes down as planned?' You sound like a mobster. But then, by all accounts you are." Everyone ignored her, so Ryan waved her hand at them. "Hello? I'm right here."

Linda turned to her. "Children should be seen and not heard." Then she addressed Stuart. "Just keep us in sight. If something's wrong we'll give you a signal and you can come running. And call 911 then."

"It will be too late to call then. I think I should call now."

"And what if they come in guns blazing? The bad guys might kill Gemma and Augusta. Let's see if we can't get this over with as fast as possible. It doesn't have to be complicated. They want these diamonds, and the minute they get them they'll disappear into the night."

Stuart didn't look convinced. "What's our signal going to be?"

"Your wife can set herself on fire," Ryan suggested.

"I'll whistle."

"That's original," Ryan said.

"The 'come take me to bed' whistle?" Stuart smirked at Linda.

"How about the 'I belong in a doghouse' whistle?" she shot back. "Now let's go."

The four of them walked towards the park. Linda pointed at some bushes. "You two hide in there."

Stuart went to put his hand on Linda's arm but she turned away from him. "Be careful, Linda."

"Be careful, Linda," Ryan mimicked. "Break a leg, and while you're at it, your neck, Linda."

Stuart took Ryan's arm and pulled her towards the greenery. "Get over here."

Linda and Bette linked arms. "This is it. We've got to do this and be very brave."

Bette shivered. "Do you see anyone who looks like a gangster?"

Linda looked around. "They all look like gangsters."

There were quite a few people around, people Linda and Bette wouldn't ordinarily go near.

"So what do we do now?" Bette asked.

"Walk forward slowly and keep your eyes peeled for lowlifes."

They took tiny steps, as if they were eighty. Linda looked to the left and Bette looked to the right. They shuffled closer to the arch itself and got some pretty weird looks from the young people who were about, but no one approached them.

"Well, where are they?"

"How should I know?" Linda said. "Let's stand right in front of this arch. Someone will come up to us eventually."

"I hope Augusta and Gemma are here. Please, please."

They stood like statues and peered into the night. All around them people went about their business, some of which looked pretty unsavoury.

"I feel like a fish out of water," Bette said. "Any minute now, we're going to be robbed or raped or both."

"Stop it. That doesn't help."

Bette glanced at her watch. "It's almost midnight. Are you sure he said this was where we were supposed to go?"

"Yes."

Two drunks stumbled up to them. "How much?"

Bette and Linda held each other closer. "Go away, we're not prostitutes," Linda said.

"Are ya sure?" one of them laughed as he hung on to his friend.

"Quite."

One drunk looked at the other and made a face. "Oh, she's *quite* sure."

"Well, as long as she's *quite* sure."

The two men nearly fell down, they laughed so hard, but fortunately they had to stagger away to keep themselves upright. They soon disappeared.

"This is nuts," Bette said. "Let's call the police. We're going to be dead meat in a minute."

Linda let go of her arm. "I know." She unzipped the bag and pulled the teddy bear out. She held it in front of her. "This should bring them out of hiding."

They waited for another few minutes. People came and people went, still giving them odd looks. One man even threw them a quarter.

Linda shoved Bette's arm. "Look. Over there."

Bette squinted. "Where? I can't see a thing."

"There are two guys directly in front of you by that tree. They've been there for a while now. They're smoking, but they haven't moved. It must be them."

"Are you sure?"

Linda got cross. "Of course I'm not sure. It's an educated guess."

"Well, wave the bear around and see if they respond."

Linda held up the teddy bear and made it dance in the air. The two guys looked at her, all right. They looked at her like she was nuts.

"Oh, come on, you idiots." Linda continued to prance the bear in the air.

"Maybe they're waiting for other people to leave."

"If that's the case, we'll be here all night. We have to go over to them. Maybe they're as blind as you are."

So they linked arms once more and took baby steps towards the two horrible-looking characters. One man was shaved almost bald and the other had long, stringy hair down to his shoulders. They both wore clothes that looked like they hadn't been washed in weeks.

"I always thought Mafia types wore nice suits. Just goes to show you can't believe everything you see in the movies."

Linda squeezed Bette's arm. "Will you shut up? I'm trying to concentrate."

"Concentrate on what? The fact that we're going to be killed any minute now?"

"I'm trying to stay sharp."

"And I'm dull?"

Linda stopped.

Bette stopped too. "I'm sorry, Lin. I'm nervous. You know me. I run off at the mouth when I'm nervous."

"You run off at the mouth like your mother. Being nervous has nothing to do with it."

"Are we going to have an argument? You're picking on me *now*?"

"Okay, I'm sorry. Can we keep moving?"

They picked up a little speed and crossed over nearer to the men in question, who sort of backed up as the women continued to advance.

"Excuse me. Excuse me. I have something for you." Linda lifted the bear higher in the air and jiggled him up and down. "Is this what you're looking for?"

The two men glanced at each other. One threw his cigarette on the ground and was about to say something when Linda interrupted him. "Aren't you the ones who called us? Are you waiting for Blue?"

The two men were instantly alert and took a step closer. "Where is he?" one of them said.

Linda and Bette snuck a peek at each other. "Well, he's here." Linda offered him the bear.

The guy ripped the bear out of her hand. "Stop with the bullshit. Who are you? How do you know Blue?"

Linda and Bette recoiled before Linda spoke. "We're the ones who got our bag mixed up with yours. You want Blue, so we're bringing him to you. You called us a few hours ago and told us to come here. Don't you remember? Where are our friends? Please, take the bear and let our friends go. We don't want any trouble. We'll just walk away."

The guy looked at the teddy bear. "Are you telling me the haul is in this bear? That's it? That's all there is?"

"Yes. It's all there. I made sure." Linda clapped her hand over her mouth. She forgot she wasn't supposed to say that. She looked at Bette and Bette tried to give her a reassuring smile, but it turned into a grimace.

The two men looked at each other and cursed. "That dumb asshole screwed it up again."

The man with the long hair grabbed Linda by the arm and the other one grabbed Bette. "I suppose you're his mommy?"

Bette struggled. "Whose mommy? Let go of me."

"Not until we clear this up. You're going to get on the phone and tell him to meet us or you're dead meat."

"More killing? Is that absolutely necessary?"

"We're trying to cooperate. We've done everything you've asked," Linda said. "Please, let us go."

The creeps ignored their pleas. Linda tried to whistle, but her mouth was so dry she couldn't do it. Their only hope was for Stuart to run after them.

Unfortunately, just as Linda and Bette were being grabbed, Ryan got her heel stuck in some mud and took a header, twisting her ankle in the process. *"Ow...*oh, my God, my ankle. It's broken. And it's all your fault."

Stuart reached down to pick her up while Linda and Bette were being frog-marched over to a beat-up car that was parked along a side street. He didn't see them being pushed into the back seat, but when a car horn start to honk incessantly he dropped Ryan in the mud and ran towards the taxi. The driver yelled out his window and pointed. "They've got your wife."

Stuart turned around, just in time to see the car take off with a piercing squeal that left a smell of burnt rubber in the air.

"LINDA!"

He ran back to a crying Ryan, picked her up, and ran towards the taxi, yelling, "Follow that car!"

Stuart threw Ryan in the back seat of the taxi.

"Ow. I hate you, you stupid man."

Stuart jumped in the front and the taxi driver took off. "I still see him," the taxi driver yelled. "He turned left at the lights."

They gave chase for about fifteen blocks before they lost them.

❁

Blue scurried along 5th Avenue until he got to 97th Street, where he turned right into Central Park. He had to go to the first walkway. He carried the coke and the bear inside his jacket, which made him look pregnant. He ran up to where Flea and Tony were supposed to meet him. He looked around, but there was no one there except a guy who looked like a shark and another guy who looked like a sneering bouncer.

They glanced at him and then looked away. Blue hopped up and down to stay warm. Where was everyone? That stupid broad better not have told him the wrong address.

He waited for five more minutes. The other two waited as well. Finally the shark guy gave him a dirty look. "You waitin' for someone? If not, scram."

Blue's head was pounding. There was no one around, no one but these guys. It suddenly occurred to him that maybe Flea and Tony had stayed behind to watch Starr. Maybe they sent these guys instead. He decided to risk it.

"Hey."

The shark and bouncer turned at the sound of his voice.

"I am waitin' for someone."

The shark said, "Like I care?"

"Someone who wants some stuff."

"Stuff?"

"Yeah...stuff...and a bear."

The shark and bouncer rushed over and grabbed him by both arms. "Did you say *bear*?"

Blue struggled, but he was no match for these two. "Yeah."

The bouncer squeezed his arm.

"Hey, man, be careful. I've got the stuff. There's no need to get nasty."

"Where it is?"

"In my jacket. Listen, where's Starr? What have you done with her?"

They ignored him. They ripped off the first two buttons of his jean jacket and grabbed the bear and the package of coke.

"What's this?" the shark said.

"It's a bear."

The shark smacked him across the face. "What's in the package?"

Blue ears were ringing. "Your stuff, man. I'm delivering your coke. This is where we were supposed to meet, isn't it? I've done my bit. Now let Starr go. She's done nothing to you."

The shark was still for a minute. "Where did you get this?"

"The usual courier."

"Who told you to come here?"

"You did."

Shark grabbed his shirt collar. "I talked to a woman on the phone. Who the fuck are you?"

"I couldn't reach the phone so a friend answered it, that's all. Don't hurt me."

The shark let go and turned his back on them. He took a knife out of his boot and slashed the bear open. The stuffing fell around his feet as he ripped it to shreds. He turned around with a crazed look. Even the bouncer seemed afraid of him.

"Where's my bear?"

"I got you that one. You told me to do it, so I did. Please, you've got to believe me. You have your coke. Just let me go."

The shark held his knife at the tip of Blue's nose. "There's no way in hell I'm letting you go. There's something going on here and I won't be made a fool of. Do you hear me?"

"I hear ya, I hear ya."

Before he knew what was happening, Blue was being pulled along with the two men on either side of him. They walked at a fast clip, so fast that Blue stumbled a couple of times, but they kept right on dragging him down the street. They soon reached a van. The bouncer knocked on the back door three times. The door opened and they shoved Blue inside. He couldn't believe his eyes. Another bouncer, two old broads, a cute chick, and a baby all looked at him in surprise.

"Well, well," said the fat broad. "Let's have a party, shall we? Did you bring dessert?"

Blue stared at her. That dope he had earlier must have been bad. There's no way this wasn't a complete and utter hallucination. It was almost enough to make him consider giving up weed altogether.

❀

Linda and Bette held on to each other and trembled the entire time they were in the filthy car. The smell of tobacco and piss was enough to make them sick.

"Try and remember which way we're going," Linda whispered in Bette's ear. "I have my guidebook in my purse. It's thanks to stupid Stuart that we're in this predicament. Why didn't he come after us?"

"To be fair, he did try to get you to call the police."

"It's his fault anyway. Keep your eyes peeled."

Bette nodded. There was nothing they could do but keep track of their surroundings, but they were soon hopelessly lost.

"Why are you doing this?" Linda ventured at one point. "We can't hurt you. We just want to go home to our families."

"Shut up back there."

Now Bette whispered in Linda's ear. "We still have the cellphone. We'll call for help when we get a chance."

Linda nodded.

The car finally pulled up behind a rundown house. The men dragged the women out of the car and hustled them into the building as quickly as possible, then made them sit on kitchen chairs around a table that was littered with ashtrays, empty beer cans, and old pizza boxes. The stench of sour milk was overpowering, and the musty, filthy mop by the door didn't help matters.

"Tony, you stay here with the broads. I gotta call somebody."

"Who?"

"You're too nosy for your own good." The man with the buzz cut seemed to be the one in charge. He left the room with the bear in his hand.

Bette looked at their babysitter. "So you're Tony? What's the other guy's name?"

"Flea."

"His name is Flea? Gee, I can't understand why."

"Tony, you should let us go. We can't possibly help you," Linda said.

Tony lit a cigarette and shook out his match. "Sure ya can. You can do the dishes."

"Are you serious?"

Tony laughed. "You should see how serious I can get." He walked over to Linda and grabbed her chin in his hand. "And I'm getting pretty serious about you."

Linda tried to turn her face away, but he held on.

"You're hot. I think I could dig you. Would you like that?" He lowered his head and tried to kiss her.

Lucky for her, Flea walked back in. "Leave her alone. We've got trouble."

Tony backed off, and Linda wiped her chin with the back of her sleeve and glared at him. Flea put the bear in the middle of the table and turned to Tony. "If we don't deliver by morning, they're coming after us."

"Who?" Bette asked.

Flea gave her a look. "What's it to you? Shut your yap."

Tony took another drag of his cigarette and then threw it in the sink. "Well, we don't got it all, that's for sure. It wouldn't fit in that." He pointed to the bear.

Flea went to a drawer, opened it, and took out a knife. He reached for the bear and made a small incision in the seam. Then he pulled and ripped it up the side. A package dropped on the table. Everyone looked at it.

"What's this?" Flea grabbed the bag and peered at it. He paled. "Is this what I think it is?"

"What is it?" Tony said.

"Diamonds."

"Holy shit."

"You see," Linda said. "They're all there. The bag was never opened. We never took any of them. They're all yours. All you have to do is let us and our friends go and you can take them. You'll never see us again."

Bette joined in. "We'll never tell the police. We don't even belong here. We live in Canada. Once we cross the border, we disappear forever. You have our word."

Now it was Tony's turn to grab the bag. Both he and Flea were speechless. They ignored the ladies and kept their eyes glued on the sparkling gems. Then they started to giggle like schoolgirls.

Flea wiped his eyes. "I must be seein' things." He took the knife, cut a hole in the bag, and poured the diamonds into the top of an empty pizza box. He pointed at them. "These are real?"

Linda looked puzzled. "Don't you know they're real?"

Flea put his hands on his head. "Wait a minute." He sat down on a chair and Tony stood behind him. "Who are you people?"

"We keep telling you," Bette said, "we have nothing to do with this. Our bags got mixed up at the airport, that's all."

"This is what you wanted," Linda insisted. "This is Blue."

Tony and Flea looked stunned.

"What's wrong? I don't understand. Isn't this Blue?"

"Of course it's not Blue."

"But you told us to bring the stuff to the park or you'd kill our friends. Was there something else in the bag we missed?"

Flea slammed his hand on the table and jumped up. "What the

fuck are you talking about? You're driving me crazy. This is not Blue. We didn't take anyone…"

"You kidnapped us," Bette said.

"Besides you," Flea yelled. "Blue is a guy. He's supposed to deliver a bag of coke. A bag I'm still going to need if I want to stay alive in the morning."

Now the four of them looked confused. Everyone tried to digest the new information. No one said a word for a good minute. Then Linda pointed at Flea. "Hold on a minute. You're not the Mafia?"

Flea's eyes widened. "The Mafia? This shit belongs to the Mob?"

Bette nodded. "And they're pretty anxious to get this back, so if I were you, I'd let us go, so we can take it to them. They have our friends, who are worth a lot more than that little pile of rocks."

Tony raked his fingers through his long hair. "Christ. We're dead. I don't like this; I don't like this at all."

Flea shoved Tony's shoulder. "Shut up and stop panicking. There's got to be a good explanation. I have to think."

"Difficult for a drug addict, I imagine," Bette said.

Flea and Tony were so preoccupied with their own thoughts that they didn't notice the insult. Flea sat on the chair again and rubbed his shaved head. Tony paced back and forth, smoking.

Linda folded her arms. "Well, it's obvious."

Flea looked up at her. "What's obvious?"

"There's been a mixup."

"Ya don't say! What do you think I am, stupid?" Flea drummed his fingers on the table. "I called you. You answered. How's that possible?"

"Who did you think you were calling?" Bette asked.

Tony stabbed the air with his index finger. "Blue."

Flea tapped his own forehead. "Right, right. We called Blue, but you answered the phone. The lines must have crossed."

"The lines crossed?" Linda frowned. "I doubt that. What's his phone number?"

Tony took a piece of paper out of his pocket and put it on the table. "Here."

"Well, maybe the lines *did* cross, then. I don't recognize this number at all."

Flea looked at her. "What phone did you get our call on?"

"My cell." As soon as Bette said it, her shoulders slumped. She could have cried. "I'm sorry, Lin."

Linda patted her hand.

"So where is it?" Tony wanted to know.

Bette pulled it out of her coat pocket. Their one shot at escape, and she blew it. Flea grabbed it.

"So this is your phone?"

"You saw me take it out of my pocket, didn't you?"

Flea jumped up from the table and turned the phone on. "So if I call Blue on his cellphone, this shouldn't ring, should it?"

"That's right."

Flea went over to the kitchen phone and called Blue's number. They all jumped when Bette's phone rang.

"This is Blue's phone. How the hell did you pick up his cellphone?"

Linda and Bette sat with their mouths open. "I don't believe it," Bette said. "Let me see that."

Flea handed her the phone and she pressed a couple of buttons to check her menu. She looked at Linda. "This isn't my cell. Why do I have someone else's cellphone?"

Linda shook her head. "I don't know."

Tony still paced. "So does that mean Blue has her phone, or did she just pick up Blue's?"

"You're making me crazy with the blues," Flea shouted. "Shut up for a sec."

Linda snapped her fingers. "I know. Does Blue have piercings and tattoos, spiked hair, and a really bad sense of style?"

"I don't know about the last thing, but yeah, he's covered with tats."

Bette caught on. "Those weirdos in the coffee shop. When he spilled coffee all over me, he was talking on the cellphone. We must have switched them by mistake."

Linda covered her face with her hands. "This goes from bad to worse."

"Tell me about it," Flea said.

"Did you phone about a cock crowing at midnight?" Bette asked him. "Was that a signal or something?"

Tony pointed to himself. "I thought that up."

"No you didn't, you lamebrain," Flea said. "That was Blue's dumb idea."

"Oh."

Flea pointed at Bette. "So if you call your cellphone now, Blue will answer?"

"I guess so."

"Oh my God, Bette," Linda said. "If the Mob phoned us about the bear and this Blue character answered and didn't know what they were talking about...they might have hurt Gemma and Augusta." She turned to Flea. "You have to give these diamonds back. We have to save our friends."

"And what do I get out of it?"

"Well, you're no worse off. If Blue was supposed to deliver a bag of coke to you, he's probably still waiting for your instructions. You'll get your bag of coke." Linda bit her lip as she tried to keep her story straight. "Then you can take a few of these diamonds as a reward. When Blue shows up with the drugs, we'll exchange cellphones and the Mob will get in touch with us and we'll give the diamonds back and save our friends. Everyone can go on their merry way."

Flea smiled at her. "Well, I have a better idea. I'll get the drugs, keep the diamonds, get rid of you two, and *then* go my merry way. I like that plan a whole lot better."

Tony couldn't keep still as he cracked his knuckles. "I don't know Flea. I don't wanna mess around with the Mob. Once those wise guys are on your ass, you're dead. And that pile of ice there must be worth a fortune. They're not going to give up until they get it back."

"Don't be such a chickenshit," Flea growled.

"He's right," Bette said. "They'll track you down, so you'd better not make any hasty decisions. They might have Blue right now, *and* your drugs. Didn't you say someone was going to kill you if you didn't deliver those drugs by morning?"

Flea didn't say anything; Bette must have touched a nerve. Linda kept it up. "If they do have Blue and the drugs, you guys could swap—diamonds for coke, and vice versa."

"You make it sound like we're swapping school lunches," Flea shouted. "It's a little more complicated than that."

Bette shrugged. "Not really. You have what they want and they have what you want. Once you're all straightened away, we can go home and forget this ever happened."

"She might be right," Tony said.

Flea looked at his watch. "It's gettin' real late. Call your cellphone and see who answers."

Linda and Bette weren't sure they'd heard correctly, but Bette wasn't about to make a second mistake. Before Flea could change his mind, Bette pressed the buttons on the cellphone. Only she didn't call her own phone. She called home.

Stuart couldn't believe it when they lost the car. He slammed his hand on the dash. "I told her. I told her to call the police, but she's always so goddamn stubborn."

"Will you be quiet about your stupid wife?" Ryan shouted. "What about me? I'm in agony back here. Take me to a hospital."

"I'll take you to a hospital after I go to the police."

"You're going to make me wait?"

Stuart twisted around in his seat and gave Ryan a look of incredulity. "My wife has been kidnapped from under my nose, and I let it happen. I think her situation is a little more urgent than your sprained ankle."

"I hate you. You are never coming near me again when we get back home. I'm going to another plastic surgeon when I want bigger breasts. I don't care if you are the best boob man in the city."

The taxi let them off at the police station. "Good luck, man. I hope you find your wife."

Stuart shook his hand and pressed several bills in it. "Thanks for all your help."

The taxi driver looked at the money. "Hey, this is more than I need."

"You chased that car. I owe you."

"Thanks."

He helped Ryan out of the taxi; she couldn't walk without hanging on to him. She made him stop while she brushed the dried mud off her coat. "You're going to pay for my dry cleaning, too."

"Ryan, please stop. I've got a colossal headache and you're not making this any easier."

"Is it my job to make it easier? You've dragged me around New York all night and broken my ankle in the process. What do you want me to say?"

"Nothing. I want you to say nothing."

"Nothing, nothing, nothing."

He resisted the urge to yell at her. He managed to get her up the stairs and into the precinct with much moaning and groaning on her part. He sat her on the bench that was along one wall and walked up to the large man at the front desk.

"Excuse me, officer."

The man held up his finger and barked into the phone. Then he wrote something down and finally looked at Stuart. "May I help you?"

"My wife has been kidnapped."

"Excuse me?"

"My wife. Two men grabbed her and her friend and took off with them. We chased them for a while, but we lost them."

"Did you get their license plate number?"

Stuart rubbed his forehead. "We tried, but they were too far away."

"And why would someone want to kidnap your wife?"

That's when Stuart's professional veneer began to unravel. "I have no idea what's going on. She said she was meeting diamond smugglers so she could exchange the diamonds for her friends, who have apparently been kidnapped as well. And then she started to talk about a kidnapping, mugging, sudden-death...."

"...property-damage, gun thing?"

Stuart blinked. "Yes, how did you know?"

"Four women were here today to report just that. Let me get Detective Ames on the phone. He's still here. We're pulling a double shift since the bomb threat."

"Bomb threat?"

"Have a seat. He'll be down in a minute."

But Stuart didn't sit down; he paced. He didn't need another earful from Ryan. Detective Ames came down the stairs and walked over to him. "I'm Detective Ames. I spoke to your wife earlier today. We can go upstairs and you can fill me in."

The two of them started for the stairs.

"Excuse me. Did you forget about me?"

Stuart turned around. "Ryan, you stay here. I'll be down in a minute."

"I don't think so. I've been traumatized too, in case you've forgotten."

Stuart looked at Detective Ames. "Would you mind helping me? She's turned her ankle."

They went back and Ryan put her arms around their shoulders. They hopped her over to the stairs and started up. Detective Ames told her not to worry, that they'd find her mother.

"She's not my mother. She's the loony wife of my boyfriend here."

Stuart turned a lovely shade of red.

Detective Ames looked at the floor. "Sorry, my mistake."

They finally dumped Ryan in one of the chairs in front of the detective's desk. He went around it and sat down, pulling a sheet out of his pile. He took a pen from the inside pocket of his suit.

"What's your wife's name?"

"Linda. Linda Keaton."

"And she has a friend named Bette Weinberg, I believe."

"Yes, that's correct. Bette was with her when they were taken."

"Do you have a picture of your wife?"

Stuart extracted his wallet from his back pocket and took out a picture. "Here's Linda." He passed it over and began to babble. "We were on vacation in Florida. That's Wes, our son. He was only fourteen at the time. He's twenty-five now. Nice boy, never any trouble. Does his mother proud."

"Thanks. I'll need this to send out a bulletin." The detective examined the picture. "She hardly looks a day older."

Stuart nodded. "Linda's a striking woman. Always has been."

"'A striking woman?' Well, isn't that nice. Start complimenting your wife right in front of my face, why don't you? You really are a piece of work, Stuart, did you know that? Here I sit with my ankle swollen, and has anyone offered me so much as an ice pack? You men are all the same. I really want nothing more to do with either of you."

She crossed her arms and looked away.

Detective Ames glanced at Stuart's downcast face before he looked at Linda's picture again. What a shame. Who would cheat on such a lovely woman?

❁

Ida and Izzy's daughters-in-law, Miriam and Esther, stayed at the apartment in case Bette called. They curled up on either end of the living room couch and tried to stay awake and alert, but it had been an exhausting day and they soon nodded off. When the phone rang, the two of them popped up and looked about like gophers out of a hole. Miriam got to the phone first. She never even had a chance to open her mouth.

"We've been kidnapped, we're a half an hour north of Washington Square Park…" There was a scuffle and the line went dead.

Miriam's face registered shock.

"Was that Bette? Is something wrong?" Esther asked.

Miriam's hands started to shake. "Oh my God, it was Bette. She said they've been kidnapped and they're a half an hour north of Washington Square Park. And then the phone went dead like someone ripped it out of her hand."

Esther's knees buckled. "Call the police."

"Call the police here?"

Esther picked up the newspaper Mordecai had written on. "No, call that detective. His number is right here."

"And then we have to call Mordecai."

❁

Mordecai was driving one of the vans through the night. His father was sitting in the front seat, while his brother David was stuck in the back with their mother. Mordecai couldn't decide if his father's smoking or his mother's voice was the most irritating part of the trip. He finally concluded that it was a tie.

He led the convoy, while his uncle, brothers, and cousins were behind him. Someone had had the good sense to take along three walkie-talkies, so they could communicate with each other without tying up their cellphones.

They made good time; traffic was light in the middle of the night. Large transport trucks zoomed along, but cars were few and far between.

Izzy lit another cigarette.

"Geez, Pop, give it a rest. The ashtray's overflowing as it is."

"Leave your father alone," his mother said. "If he wants to smoke, let him smoke."

Mordecai caught his brother's eyes in the rear-view mirror and they shook their heads ever so slightly. Ida noticed.

"What? You want I should I tell your father to quit smoking? I'd be dead in two seconds. He'd kill me for sure."

"He should cut down," David said. "I can't bring the kids over to visit because of their asthma."

"Why can't they stay on the balcony?" Izzy said. "They'd get plenty of fresh air out there. Kids need fresh air."

"I'm going to send my kids out to play on a balcony thirty feet off the ground? You're crazy."

"Don't call your father crazy."

"Why? You do."

"I'm allowed."

"But I'm not?"

"No, you're not."

"That's right. Listen to your mother," Izzy coughed.

Mordecai reached for the radio and turned it up full blast, so he didn't hear the phone ring, but he felt it vibrate in his pocket.

"You call that music?" Ida said. "Where's Perry Como when you need him?"

"Mama, hush. The phone." He turned down the radio and reached into his pocket. There was instant silence. "Hello?"

"Oh, baby, it's me," Miriam cried into the phone.

"What's wrong?"

Ida shouted behind him, "Something's wrong?"

"Ma, be quiet for a sec." Mordecai put the phone back up to his ear. "What is it? Tell me."

"Bette called—"

"Oh, thank God."

"No, you don't understand. She called to say she'd been kidnapped and they were being held thirty minutes away from a place called Washington Square Park. Then the phone went dead. I called that detective, so the police are looking for her right now."

"I can't believe this."

"*What?*" Ida and Izzy shouted.

Mordecai put the phone against his chest. "I'll tell you in a minute. Let me talk." He returned to his phone. "Did you tell the detectives we're on our way?"

There was an intake of breath. "No, I didn't. I forgot all about it. Should I call them back?"

"Not yet. I'll call you when we're closer to the city. There may be more news by then. In the meantime, stay calm. Everything's going to be all right."

"You didn't hear her voice. She sounded frightened."

Mordecai had a hard time seeing the road with the tears that welled up in his eyes. "It's okay; we're going to get her."

"Please be safe. Don't let anything happen to you."

"We'll be fine. There's safety in numbers. I better go. Love you."

"Love you too. Call me as soon as you hear something."

"Will do." Mordecai turned off his phone and held his hand in the air to ward off any questions. "That was Miriam. Bette called—"

Shouts of joy rang out. Then he told them what Miriam said. The shrieks were deafening.

Izzy grabbed the walkie-talkie. "Car one calling car two, over."

Uncle Sid's voice crackled, "Go ahead, car one, over."

"Bette's been kidnapped! Over."

The crackling came on with only uproar in the background. Mordecai looked out his side-view mirror and saw the van behind them almost go off the road.

"Papa, they're panicking. Don't say anything else. We'll pull over at the next gas station."

"My brother needs to know. He's the head of the family."

Mordecai glanced at him. He suddenly saw his father as a younger brother who needed his big brother right away. "Sorry, Pop."

Ida's sobs in the back were heartbreaking. David did his best to console her.

Car two must have called car three, because suddenly the bakery truck careened from behind car two and roared up beside Mordecai. His crazy cousins shouted at him through the glass, as if he was going to hear them as they sped down the road.

"Tell them to stop at the next gas station," Mordecai yelled at his father. "They're going to cause an accident."

Izzy relayed the message and one of his cousins gave him the thumbs up, but they still beat it down the highway, so Mordecai sped up. Car two stuck to his bumper like glue.

CHAPTER TWELVE

When Candy and Dumber threw Blue into the back of the van and drove off, Gemma and Augusta couldn't figure out what on earth was going on.

"Are you involved with all this, or are you just a hitchhiker?" Gemma asked.

"I don't know these people. Who the heck are you?"

"We're the welcome wagon. So what's your name?"

"Blue."

"As in the colour blue or the wind blew?"

"As in suede shoes." Blue turned to Dumb. "Where's Starr?"

Dumb looked dumbfounded. "Who?"

"My girlfriend. They said they'd kill her."

"Who said?"

"You."

"Me?"

"Yeah."

"Not me."

"Then who?"

"Give it a rest, you sound like a couple of kids," Gemma grumped.

"Shut up," Dumb said. "Don't talk."

"Shut up and don't talk mean the same thing."

"Can it."

"Good one. Can you make it four?"

"Shut your face."

"Thank you."

Dumb rubbed his head. "You're givin' me a headache."

Gemma started to open her mouth, but Augusta reached over and grabbed her arm. "Stop antagonizing him," she said under her breath.

"I know what I'm doing. Trust me." Gemma cleared her throat. "Dumb, I think you're getting the raw end of the stick."

He furrowed his brow. "Huh?"

"You've got a headache because you're carsick. You're stuck back here on the floor with the rest of us prisoners, while those two up front ride in comfort. I think you should demand your fair share. When we get to wherever we're going, Dumber should be the one who has to watch us. I think it's only right."

Blue spoke up. "Did you say Dumb and Dumber?"

Gemma nodded.

"Now I know that dope was bad."

Dumb didn't say anything, so Augusta started in. "She's right, you know. I think they take advantage of you. I didn't want to say anything before, but...".

"Ya think?" Dumb frowned.

"Oh yeah," Gracie added. "I heard them laughing about you when we got in the truck. I thought it was mean."

Dumb gave his neck a little twirl to get the kinks out. "Ya don't say."

Blue didn't know he was being helpful when he said, "That sucks. I hate people who do that."

They fell quiet, to let the conversation sink in. Poor old Dumb's face was a sea of emotion. They could practically see the wood burning.

Gemma wiggled herself a little closer to Gracie, who held her sleepy baby. She hardly moved her lips. "If we go back to where we were, I'm going to cause a ruckus. The car we first got into was parked by this van. I'll keep people busy on one side of the van and I want you to sneak around and get Augusta's cellphone out of the car's glove compartment. Then come back to us."

Gracie nodded. Gemma sidled up to Augusta. She nodded too.

It took awhile before the van stopped. Gracie handed the baby over to Augusta. He snuggled in her arms. They waited for the doors to be opened.

Dumb banged on them from the inside. "Hurry up."

Dumber finally got the back door opened. "What's your problem?"

They spilled out as Dumb, who jumped down first, jabbed his finger into Dumber's shoulder. "I ain't got a problem. *You're* gonna have the problem."

"What are you yammerin' about?"

Candy looked perplexed. "What's goin' on?"

"I'll tell ya what's goin' on." Dumb kept pushing Dumber. "He's an asshole."

Candy went over to break them up. "What is this?"

"He's right," Gemma said. "You have no business…

"…I can attest to the fact that…" Augusta chimed in.

Blue jumped about. "This is freaky, man."

Tiny Gracie slipped undetected around the back of the van and opened the car door as quietly as she could. She quickly opened the glove compartment and grabbed the phone, sticking it down inside her bra before she leaned on the door to close it and slipped back into view, immediately adding her two cents to the discussion.

It was over as soon as it started. Candy fired a gun into the air. They jumped out of their skins. Poor little Keaton let out one almighty scream and his mommy was there to comfort him.

"Move it. *Now.*"

Everyone was herded into the old room at the back of the warehouse. Dumb and Dumber glared at each other. Candy looked furious as he crunched on his Life Savers. He pointed at Gemma and Augusta. "I have a sneaking suspicion you two have been stirring the pot."

Blue held his hands up. "Hey man, I gave you coke, not pot."

"Shut up, you dough head."

"Who is this kid?" Gemma asked. "Are you collecting innocent people just for the hell of it?"

Candy pointed to Blue. "This idiot tried to give me a bear with nothing in it."

The ladies looked at each other.

"What do you mean?" Gemma asked. "I thought you said you talked to our friends. What's he got to do with it?"

"That's what I'd like to know." Candy stepped closer to him. "Tell us again, genius. What happened tonight?"

Blue rolled his eyes. "I told you guys already. I waited for a phone call to tell me where to take that." He gestured to the package Candy still had in his hand. "The phone rang and I couldn't reach it. A girl I know picked it up and said some guy told her he'd kill my friends if I didn't take a bear to Central Park. And since Starr is missing, I figured I better do what he said, even if it didn't make no sense."

Candy looked at Gemma. "Did you give me the wrong number? Because so help me…"

Gemma got annoyed. "As if. I want you to have your dumb bear more than you do, so I can get the hell home to my family. Why would I give you the wrong number?"

Augusta said, "Maybe it's your fault. Maybe you dialled incorrectly."

Candy opened his mouth as if to speak and then shut it again.

Dumb rubbed salt in the wound. "Yeah."

Candy spun around to face him. "Did I tell you to open your trap? Did I?"

Dumb looked at the floor.

"Or maybe our friends got their cellphone mixed up with Blue's somehow," Gemma suggested.

Candy took his cellphone out of his breast pocket and pointed at Blue. "So if they got their cells mixed up and I call your friend's number again, this idiot's phone is going to ring, right?"

Gemma nodded.

A hush fell as Candy punched in the numbers. Blue's phone rang. His eyes lit up. "Maybe it's Starr." He reached into his pocket. "Hey babe, is that you?"

"Yeah, it's me," Candy answered.

"You sound weird. Are you okay?"

Candy shut his phone. "Someone kill this moron."

Blue put his hand up to cover his ear. "Hey Starr, are you there? I can't hear you." He looked up. "I lost her."

They had to pull Candy off him.

Once the dust settled, everyone went back to their corners. Blue was very indignant and Candy's face was the color of a mottled plum. He took a few deep breaths, threw more Life Savers in his mouth, and tossed his head from side to side, as if to chase out the cobwebs. "Okay, so that means…"

"…the cellphones got mixed up. It's as simple as that," Gemma said.

"So where's my phone?" Blue wondered.

"I don't care about your phone," Candy exploded.

Augusta put her hand up.

"What?"

"Maybe you should call his number. Bette may answer."

Blue groaned. "Oh boy, I'm in trouble. If Flea and Tony called an old lady, my ass is cooked."

Gemma stamped her foot. "Bette is not an old lady. She's my age."

"Yeah, that's what I said. Old."

"Smartass." Gemma turned to Candy. "Call the number and see if Bette answers. Do you want me to talk to her? I'll tell you if it's Bette or not."

"I ain't givin' you a phone."

Gemma shrugged her shoulders. "Whatever. The last time a woman answered, you thought it was Bette, and look what happened. We have Blue here instead."

Candy hesitated. "All right, but no smart moves." He adjusted the gun that was shoved down the front of his pants.

Gemma and Augusta exchanged glances. Just to hear Bette's voice would be enough. Candy passed Gemma the phone. Her hand trembled as she pressed the numbers and the phone started to ring.

Bette and Linda's situation was now desperate. They couldn't move.

When Bette screamed into the phone to Miriam, Flea jumped across the kitchen and batted the cell out of her hand. It landed on the pizza box filled with diamonds, and the gems were scattered across the room.

Greed overrode anger as a distracted Flea and Tony scurried around and made sure they had all of the precious stones. Once they were gathered inside an empty jam jar, Flea turned his attention on his prisoners.

"That was a dumb move, lady."

He tied Bette and Linda to their chairs and turned them back-to-back before he roped the chairs together. It made things worse, not to be able to see each other, but they entwined their hands together to keep their spirits up.

Once the women were taken care of, the men weren't sure what to do. They stared at the diamonds in silence.

Bette got impatient. "Do we have to sit in this kitchen for the rest of our lives? You have to give those back. Haven't you ever seen *The Sopranos*? Believe me, you don't want to mess with these people." Flea sat there biting his thumbnail. Tony smoked one cigarette after the other.

Linda spoke up. "You know, you should play it this way. You stumbled on these through no fault of your own and expect a reward for their return. Tell them you didn't have to give them back, but you are. Would that help?"

Tony gave Flea's shoulder a quick flick with the back of his hand. "That makes sense."

Flea slammed his fist on the table. "What makes sense is to take these diamonds, leave the country, and never be heard from again."

Tony looked fed up. "We've got enough trouble. We have to get that coke to you-know-who; they'll hunt us down if we don't deliver. We don't got a lot of time."

That's when the cellphone rang.

The four of them froze for a few seconds, then Flea said, "No one touch it."

"It's probably Blue. They've no doubt figured it out by now." Linda said. "Answer it. It's not like they know where you live, if that's what's bothering you."

Flea hesitated at first, and then grabbed it. "Hello?"

"Is Bette there?"

Flea put the phone to his chest. "Someone wants to know if Bette's here."

"So tell them I am."

Flea spoke into the phone. "First tell me if Blue's there?"

"Not until you tell me if Bette's there."

"No."

"Yes."

Flea cursed. "Yeah, she's here."

"Let me talk to her. I can't know for sure until I hear her voice."

He held the phone to Bette's ear. "Hello?" she said.

"Oh Bette, it's Gemma. Are you okay? Don't worry, Augusta and I are together..."

"Yes, Linda's with me..."

Flea took away the phone. "Where's Blue?"

A man answered him. "He's here."

"Let me speak to him, to make sure."

A voice came on, "Hello, Flea?"

"Blue, you stupid bastard..."

The other male voice came on the line. "Who's this?"

"Who's this?"

"Cut the crap," Candy said. "Who am I dealing with?"

"Well, who am *I* dealing with?"

"Look, I think we both know what's happened. I believe you have something of mine and I have something of yours. Am I correct?"

"Maybe."

"Stop with the fucking games."

"Hey, I didn't ask for this," Flea yelled. "It fell in my lap, and you need my cooperation."

"And you need mine."

"I think you need mine more than I need yours. Your something is a whole lot more than my something. I think a reward is coming to me, don't you?"

Silence. Flea waited him out.

"What kind of reward?"

"The memorable kind."

"Don't push your luck."

"*Sayonara.*" Flea clicked the phone off.

"Whatcha do that for?" Tony yelled.

"I'm the brains of the operation. Wait for it."

Two whole long minutes went by before the phone rang again.

"Yeah?"

"Let's talk."

❈

Stuart painstakingly told Detective Ames everything he knew about what his wife had been up to. Ryan yawned and moaned a lot.

"Can we get out of here? My ankle is throbbing."

He whipped his head around. "Just five more minutes, please. Please."

"You said that ten minutes ago."

The detective's phone rang. Ames picked it up. "Detective Ames."

"Yes, hello, Detective. My name is Miriam Weinberg. You were talking to my husband, Mordecai, earlier this evening about my sister-in-law Bette."

"Oh yes, Mrs. Weinberg. Did you get a hold of her?"

"Well, she got a hold of me, in a matter of speaking."

Miriam told him about Bette's call, and how Bette's family was driving to New York and would get in touch with him when they arrived.

He thanked her for calling.

"Please find her. You don't know my in-laws. This will kill them."

"I'll do my best, Mrs. Weinberg."

He hung up the phone and looked at Stuart. "Bette called home. She's been kidnapped. She's a thirty-minute drive from Washington Square Park."

Stuart rose from his chair. "I told you where we last saw the car. We chased them for probably five minutes anyway. Did she say anything about Linda?"

"No. It was only a moment's conversation and then the line was severed."

"What can we do now?"

"'We'? What do you mean, 'we'?" Ryan complained.

"I have to do something, Ryan. How am I going to explain to my son that his mother is missing and I let it happen?"

"You tell him his mother is completely stupid and wouldn't listen to a thing you said. It's not like you didn't warn her."

Stuart dropped back into his chair and sighed.

Detective Ames said, "You can't do anything at the moment, Mr. Keaton. Just keep your cellphone on in case she calls you, and let me know right away. I have your number. If I find out anything, you'll be the first to know."

"All right." Stuart stood again and held out his hand. "Thank you for all your help, Detective."

"Sure."

Detective Ames hurried away after signalling to another detective to come with him. They both went out the door.

Stuart and Ryan looked at each other.

"So *now* do I get some attention?"

He frowned. "Let's go."

"Are you taking me to the hospital?"

"Of course I'm taking you to the hospital. That's where you want to go, isn't it?"

"I guess so, but what I'd really like to do is to go to Tiffany's. Maybe a nice ankle bracelet will make me forget the throbbing pain." She reached down and rubbed her ankle ever so lightly.

"Ryan, it's the middle of the night. Be sensible."

Ryan folded her arms across her chest. "You just care about your *striking* wife. Well, I can go on strike too, ya know."

This was definitely the longest night of Stuart's life.

❋

Flea finally finished his negotiations with Candy. It was a long, drawn-out process, and Linda and Bette became increasingly tired as the nonsense went on. Flea finally got off the phone, jumped up, and hit Tony in the shoulder.

"Right, we've got to go. We're meeting them at the Bronx Zoo."

Tony pointed at the women. "What about them?"

"Leave them here. They'll be more trouble than they're worth in the car. We'll take care of them when we get back."

"What do you mean, take care of us?" Bette asked.

"Mind your own business."

"I believe it *is* our business if you plan on killing us."

Flea put his face next to hers. His bad breath almost made Bette retch. "You've got such a big mouth, lady. I can't wait to shut it forever." He straightened up. "Let's go."

The men hurried out the door.

Linda squeezed Bette's hand. "Don't worry, Bette. We're going to get out of here."

"How? We're tied up like hogs."

"Hogs don't know how to use a knife. Let's jump over to the cutlery drawer."

"Which one is the cutlery drawer?"

"One of them has to be. Jump in the air when I say three and lean to the left."

"Whose left? Mine or yours?"

"Mine."

"Okay."

"One, two, three." They pushed off with their strapped feet and managed to move a whole half an inch.

"This is going to take forever," Bette wailed.

"Don't give up. Do it again and don't stop. One, two, three..."

They hopped and hopped but didn't get very far.

"I don't think this is working."

Linda pinched her arm.

"Hey, stop that. How would you like it?" Bette pinched her back.

"Bette, focus. I think the problem is that we're headed in two different directions. Let's follow this row of tiles over to the counter, the third row from the wall." She jerked her head to indicate the row she meant.

"Okay."

"One, two, three." They leapfrogged over to the sink. By the time they got there, they were covered with sweat.

"Great," Bette said. "What now?"

"Look for a knife, of course."

"How do we do that?"

"Grab the drawer knob with your teeth."

"Are you kidding me? Do you know how many germs live on those handles?"

Linda knocked the back of her head into Bette's. "Would you rather be shot or have a cold sore?"

"Oh God." Bette grabbed the handle of one drawer in her teeth and slowly drew it open. Then she let go and spit on the floor. "Gross."

"What's in it?"

"Damn. Looks like a junk drawer."

"No doubt they're all junk drawers. Is there anything in it we can use?"

"A nail, a clothespin, a candle…"

"Maybe we can burn the rope."

"I don't have a match, do you?"

"Okay, I'll try this one." Linda pulled at the drawer nearest to her. She peered inside. "There are clean tea towels in here. One of these jerks must have a girlfriend. Jump backwards and I'll check the next one."

They hopped over to another drawer and finally found a small knife.

"How will you reach it?"

"Any way I can." Linda tried to stick her head inside the drawer, but she couldn't extend her neck far enough, what with the rope around her arms and legs.

"Damn."

"I know," Bette said. "Pull it right out and let it fall on the floor."

"Good idea." Linda grabbed the knob in her teeth and pulled for all she was worth. The drawer slid out slowly, but not all the way. "Oh perfect. Close, but no cigar."

"Grab the last bit with your chin."

So Linda strained her neck once more and tried to grab the end of the drawer with her bottom jaw. She managed to pull it out completely and the drawer fell to the floor with a clatter. They peered at the dirty tiles and looked for the knife.

"There it is." Bette shook her head to the right. "Over there by the table leg."

"Okay," Linda said. "Be brave. Any way we do this, it'll hurt. We have to tip over and land on the floor. Are you ready?"

"Wait. Are there any sharp objects about?"

"They're all sharp objects."

"I mean, are there any sticking up? We don't want to impale our-selves on a vegetable peeler."

"Not that I can see. So, are we ready?"

Bette nodded.

At the count of three, they leaned over to one side and fell to the floor with a resounding thud.

"Oh God, my shoulder," Bette moaned. "I think I dislocated it. Are you okay?"

"My elbow's broken, but other than that, I'm fine."

Bette gave a little yelp.

"What's wrong?"

"Lin, don't look up under the table. You wouldn't believe it."

Of course, Linda looked under the table. "Oh, good lord, are those wads of gum or old wasp colonies?"

"I don't want to know."

"Okay, let's shimmy over to the knife."

They tried to crawl on their sides using a modified breaststroke without their arms and legs. It was rough going, but Linda finally managed to get the knife in her hand.

"Okay. Pull as tight as you can on the rope and I'll try and saw this back and forth."

"Don't slit my wrists, Lin. I don't want to die on a dirty floor."

"Stop talking about dying. We're not going to die. I refuse to, do you hear me? Absolutely refuse."

"Okay."

"We have to get out of here and save Gemma and Augusta. They have seven children. Seven babies who need their mothers!"

"It's okay, Lin."

Linda's voice trembled. "You guys are my family. I can't lose any of you. I can't."

"It's okay, honey. Don't worry. We'll make it."

Linda started to cut the rope.

❀

Candy, Dumber, and Blue went to the Bronx Zoo to make the exchange with Flea and Tony. They had to leave immediately, as it was almost dawn.

Dumb was left behind to watch the prisoners, and he was like a bear with a sore paw.

"What happened?" Gemma asked him.

"Whaddaya mean?" Dumb paced up and down.

"I thought you were going to stand up for yourself. You're in the right, not them."

Dumb's eye started to twitch. "I got my orders, that's all."

Gemma shook her head. "As far as I can see, you're better than Dumber."

Dumb looked at her. "Yeah?"

"Yeah. You're Dumb, but he's Dumber."

"You're right."

"So tell Candy you're not going to put up with it anymore."

Dumb paced and hit his fist in his open hand. "Yeah."

"And by the way, aren't you a tad upset that your boss calls you Dumb? I'm sure that's not your real name."

"My name's Jethro."

"I should've guessed."

Keaton was starting to get a little fussy. The women tried to keep him entertained, but he was having none of it. He began to cry, and he kept it up. Dumb held his hands up to his ears as he walked around the tiny room.

"Jeez Louise. Enough already."

Gracie did her best to quiet Keaton, but he only wailed louder. She began to fret. "I think he's been in this diaper too long. I think his bum is sore."

Gemma and Augusta concurred. "Let's get it off him."

Dumb rolled his eyes. "Not the shit stuff again. Is that all he does?"

"He's a male," Gemma shrugged. "All he does is eat, burp, fart, and shit."

"And grab boobs," Gracie added.

Dumb grinned. "Hey, that was good."

"Thanks."

They lay Keaton down, and sure enough, his little bottom was raw. The women gathered round and made sympathetic noises, or at least that's what Dumb thought. Actually, they made plans. Gracie pulled the cellphone out of her top and passed it to Augusta, who quickly dropped it down her cleavage.

Gemma whispered, "This is the best chance we have to get you out of here, Gracie. We'll distract Dumb. I want you to grab this child and run. Keep running until you can flag a cab or get to a phone." She slipped her a roll of money. "Use this, and when you're safe, call the police and tell them where we are, as best you can."

Gracie's eyes filled with tears. "But I can't leave you."

Augusta said under her breath, "You have to. We'll keep the cellphone in case we can use it, but you're the best chance we have."

Gemma nodded. "The only thing that matters right now is getting this darling baby out of danger. You're a brave girl, Gracie. We know you can do it."

Gracie wiped the tear that trickled down her face. The ladies tidied Keaton as well as they could, and his mother wrapped the sheet around him. She jiggled him up and down as she walked closer to the door.

Gemma suddenly gasped and grabbed the front of her dress. "Ahh..."

"Gemma, are you okay?" Augusta cried.

Gemma lurched forward and hit the table, then rolled over and fell to the floor. "My heart..."

Augusta screamed at Dumb. "Do something, she's having a heart attack. Please, help her."

Dumb hurried over and knelt beside Gemma, who writhed on the floor. Augusta kept up her barrage of desperate pleas and Gemma joined her with gasps and groans.

Gracie opened the door and did what they told her. She ran like hell.

Dumb didn't see or hear a thing, what with both women making such a racket.

Augusta grabbed Gemma's hand and patted it. "She's going to be all right, isn't she?"

"How the hell should I know?" Dumb said. "Where does it hurt?"

"Right here." Gemma pointed to her heart. "I can't take the stress. I can't. You have to let us go. I should see a doctor."

"You need to exercise, that's all."

Augusta grabbed Dumb's hand. "Feel her pulse."

"What?"

"I bet you're an athlete. You know these things."

Dumb preened a bit. "I know a little."

Gemma grabbed his other hand and put it on her neck. "Feel it. Am I dying?"

Dumb pressed his enormous fingers against her skin. "I can feel a pulse."

"Oh, you're so smart," Augusta said. "What would we ever do without you?"

Gemma covered her forehead with her arm. "It's true. I feel safe around you. I bet you're a good son. Do you love your mother?"

"That ain't none of your business."

Augusta patted his knee. "I'm sure she's very proud. Does she know what you do for a living?"

"A mother always knows," Gemma said. "You don't have to tell us anything. I bet she's worried about your profession. Don't break your mother's heart. Become an accountant."

Dumb felt a draft of air and looked around. The door was open, and Gracie and the baby were gone. He jumped up. "You guys tricked me! Get up off the floor." He reached down, grabbed Gemma by the arm, and dragged her to her feet.

"Hey, don't be so rough with a sick woman."

"You're not sick, you old bat." He shook her. "Do you want to get us killed?"

"Exactly the opposite.."

He pushed her away and rubbed his head. "I can't go after her. You guys will leave."

Augusta nodded. "What did we tell you? You're very smart."

He paced the floor. "What do I do?"

"Let us go."

"No."

"Please."

"Shut up."

Gemma put her hands on her hips. "Listen here, I'm old enough to be your mother. Would you like some big goon pushing your mother around? Wouldn't that make you mad? Candy's a bully, but you're not. You're a good boy at heart, isn't he, Augusta?"

"Oh yes. A good boy who takes too much crap from that horrible man."

"Both of you shut up and let me think."

"There's a first time for everything," Gemma muttered.

CHAPTER THIRTEEN

The Weinbergs drove until they found a gas station. The clan piled out of their vans and truck, all of them talking over each other. Uncle Sid rushed over to embrace Izzy. He tried to do the same to Ida, but she hit him with her handbag.

"Get away from me. You're acting like she's dead." Ida's sons put her in her wheelchair so she could use the bathroom. She rolled away from them in a hurry.

Mordecai looked at his uncle. "Forgive her. She's very upset."

Uncle Sid looked to the heavens. "Your mother's been upset for as long as I've known her."

David frowned. "Why *is* that?"

"She never got over the incident."

Izzy pointed his cigarette at his brother. "Don't talk about the incident."

The brothers and cousins looked at each other.

"We don't have time for this," Izzy insisted. "We have to find Bette. What do we do when we get to New York?"

"We call the detective and ask him where they want us to go," Mordecai said. "We want to help, not be in the way."

Uncle Sid pointed at him. "We should be in the way. We're family."

Mordecai shook his head. "I don't think they've ever run into a family like this one. And they've certainly never run into a mother like Ma."

They filled up their gas tanks, and by then Ida had returned from the washroom. She emerged from the door at top speed and was nearly run over by a car pulling into the station.

"Get outta my way," she yelled at the driver as she careened into the gas platform. She almost toppled over but righted herself at the last minute and charged ahead over to her sons. "Get in the car. What's wrong with you? Move it, move it, move it!"

They scrambled to put her back in the van and fold away her wheelchair. Sid decided he wanted to be in Mordecai's van in case his brother needed him. They were about to pull away when Izzy remembered he needed more cigarettes. He ran into the station.

"Where is that man going? I'm going to kill him."

"He's doing a good job of killing himself with those cancer sticks," David said.

"Well, he's not doing it fast enough. If something happens to my Bette, it'll be his fault."

"Don't say that, Ida," Sid pleaded. "It doesn't help the situation."

"I can say whatever I like. I don't need a lecture from you."

Everyone kept their mouths shut. Izzy rushed back to the van and was so out of breath that he coughed for the next half hour, and by then everyone in the van wanted to kill him.

As the Weinbergs drove into the city, Ida couldn't stand it anymore. She demanded Mordecai give her his cellphone.

"I don't think that's a good idea."

"Why not?"

"Someone might be trying to get through."

"I'm the mama."

Mordecai knew better than to argue with that logic. He handed it over. Ida called Bette's cellphone over and over again. Her heart sank every time the operator said the customer had the phone turned off.

"You're going to wear the numbers off those buttons if you're not careful," Izzy said between puffs.

"Never mind," Uncle Sid said. "It keeps her quiet."

Ida turned to look at her brother-in-law, who, if it was possible, was even thinner than Izzy. "Who asked you?"

She tried once more and lo and behold, the line was busy.

"It's busy!"

Izzy turned in his seat. "Bette's phone?"

"No, Frank Sinatra's. Who else do you think I'd be calling?"

"Well, that's a good sign," Izzy grinned.

"Try again, Ma," David said.

She did. "Still busy. At least that means she's alive, doesn't it?"

Mordecai said over his shoulder, "Of course she's alive, Ma."

The phone remained busy for quite a while. Ida tried once more and it rang.

"It's ringing! It's ringing! Oh my God. Please answer, Bette. Please."

They held their breath.

A man answered. "Candy? Is there a problem?"

"Candy? Who's this?"

"Who's this?"

"What have you done with my Bette? Please. We have ransom money. We'll give you money. As much as you want."

The voice hesitated. "Ya don't say. How much?"

"Fifty thousand dollars."

Izzy almost fainted. "What? We can't get out hands on…"

Ida brushed him away with her hand. "Shut up, I'm negotiating." She spoke into the phone. "Tell us where Bette is and I'll give it to you."

"No, no, no. You give it to me and then I'll tell you where she is."

"Okay, okay. Where can we drop it off?"

"Give me a number I can call and I'll get back to you about where and when."

Ida gave him Mordecai's cell number and the guy hung up. She closed the phone. "I can't believe it. I talked to a kidnapper."

"I can't believe it either. Where are we gonna come up with that kind of money?" Izzy said.

Ida glared at him. "Do you have a better idea? Why do I have to do all this crime stuff myself? I kill men for you, I talk to kidnappers…"

Mordecai said, "Did he say he had Bette?"

"Yeah, sort of. He said he'd tell us where she is once he has the money."

"Of course he did. He'll say anything to get money. But who is he?"

"Well, he has Bette's phone. He must have had some contact with her."

"Even if we do meet this guy, we don't have the money," Izzy insisted.

"We'll gather up as much as we can and make it look like more," Ida said. "They do that all the time in the movies."

"But how much money have we got?"

Everyone started to look in their wallets.

"We go to a bank machine," Ida insisted. "We each take out our limit and pool the money together. Why am I the only one thinking? You're all useless. Now hurry up, Mordecai. My daughter's been kidnapped."

❖

Flea and Tony couldn't believe their luck when Flea answered the phone and some woman offered them fifty grand.

"This has got to be the weirdest day of my life," Flea said. "After we deliver the diamonds to these people and get our coke, we'll arrange to meet this dame. Where do you think?"

"Washington Square Park gave us a lot of luck. Why not go back there?"

"Yeah, I suppose so."

"Are you gonna tell them where the women are?"

Flea made a face. "What do you think? We gotta get rid of those dames."

Tony took a drag and looked out the window at the traffic going by. "I don't think we should. I mean, we're not murderers."

Flea yelled at him. "Well, I'm gonna be one if you don't stop with the soft routine. These women have seen our faces. If we don't play our cards right, we'll go down not only for the coke but smuggled diamonds as well."

Tony didn't say anything.

They drove from Astoria to the Bronx and soon found themselves in the parking lot of the Bronx Zoo. It was too early for the zoo to be open, so they easily spotted the car with three men in it. They pulled up about a hundred feet away and waited for someone to do something.

The three men got out of the car.

Flea shook his head. "Look at that asshole, Blue. If I never see him again, it won't be too soon."

They got out of their beat-up car and stood beside it. A guy who looked like a shark held out a package. Flea took the bag of diamonds out of his inside jacket pocket and held them out as well. Minus his cut, of course. Candy had offered him three diamonds for his inconvenience. He crammed them in his sock. And then he took three more. One was in his jeans pocket and the other two were in a film canister in the car. By spreading them out, he thought he was covering his tracks.

The two groups walked forward. They looked around to see if they were being watched, a reflex developed by their criminal lifestyles. When they got to within ten feet of each other, they stopped.

Candy shoved Blue towards them. "I believe this idiot belongs to you."

Blue tripped and nearly fell at Flea's feet.

"You can kill him, for all I care," Flea said. "He's too stupid to live."

"Where's Starr?" Blue asked. "Did you take her?"

"I wouldn't take that loser anywhere," Flea laughed.

"Hey, that's my girlfriend you're talking about."

"Shut up." Candy held out the package of coke. "Give me my diamonds."

Flea held out the bag. Candy grabbed it and tossed Flea the coke. Candy looked in the bag and then up at Flea. "I think you've made a mistake."

Sweat appeared on Flea's upper lip. "How's that?"

"There's a few missing."

"How the hell do you know that? Ya didn't even count them."

Candy grinned and poked Dumber in the ribs. "How do I know? Because that's what I'd do."

He and Dumber whipped out their guns. Flea, Tony, and Blue jumped back and put their hands in the air.

"Hey, man..."

"Give me the coke," Candy demanded. "*Now.*"

Flea passed it over.

"Search him." Dumber went over and patted them down. He found the four diamonds and gave it to Candy. Candy looked at it. "Well, well. You're stupid, too. There's only four here."

"We're not stupid. We have two more in the car," Tony said. Then he looked at Flea. "Aw, jeez."

Candy gestured with his gun to Dumber, who went over and searched Flea's car. He came out with the film canister and passed it to his boss. Candy shook his head. "Boys, you've got a lot to learn about wheeling and dealing. Never, and I mean never, try to pull a fast one. It's the quickest way to get killed."

He pointed his gun and shot Flea in the leg. Flea grabbed his calf and fell to the ground. "Oh shit, oh shit, oh shit."

Candy and Dumber sauntered back to their car with both the diamonds and the coke, and then they revved their engine and with tires squealing, left the parking lot.

Tony and Blue were shocked. They didn't move, not until Flea started to rant: "Get in the car, get in the car."

The two of them hurried to the car.

"Get me first, for Christ's sake." They turned around and picked Flea off the pavement, then wobbled back over to the car. They struggled to get Flea in the back. He screamed in agony. "Follow those bastards."

Tony got in the driver's seat and barely gave Blue a chance to jump in the front seat before he tore out of the parking lot after Candy's car. "I think you should go to the hospital."

"With a bullet wound? Don't be so fucking stupid."

Blue looked over the front seat at Flea. "You should put a bandage on that."

"No shit. Give me that thing around your neck."

Blue untied his filthy bandana and passed it over. Flea tied it around his calf as tightly as he could. He couldn't contain his anger. "I shoulda known better. This pisses me off."

"I say you're lucky. They're wise guys and the Mob usually shoots to kill."

"Maybe he was in a good mood," Blue said.

Flea hit him on the head from behind. "I'd be in a good mood too, if I took off with a package of cocaine I didn't pay for."

"Whadda we do?" Tony shouted. "Keep following? They could shoot us."

"They already did, you genius. Of course keep following. We're dead if we don't deliver that coke."

"But how are we gonna get it from them?"

Flea pulled at the back door panel until it came off. He reached inside and pulled out a gun. "I'm not gonna be so stupid next time."

Gracie ran out of the warehouse as fast as she could. She panicked at the sight of more low, rundown, and abandoned warehouses with broad parking lots between—she was so exposed. What if Candy and Dumber came back? She needed to get to a street, preferably a residential one.

Poor little Keaton cried at being jostled. "Some day, little guy, I'm going to tell you how sorry I am." She kissed his head and kept moving, even though she stuck out like a sore thumb. A few trucks went by, but Gracie stayed in the shadows. She wanted nothing to do with big, burly men.

It was daybreak. People would be about soon. She'd have to keep moving until she found someone who could help her; there were hardly any cabs on the street at this hour. She turned a corner, and at the other end of the block on the opposite side she saw a diner.

"Please be open," she whispered against Keaton's hat. She hurried closer and saw two people inside, but when she went to open the door, it was locked. She knocked and the man turned around and yelled, "Come back in twenty minutes."

She knocked louder. "Please, help me."

A large woman, obviously the waitress, pushed past the man and came to open the door.

"Thank you."

"Girl, whatcha doin' at this time of day with that poor baby in your arms? Ya wanna give that child pneumonia?"

Gracie stood and shivered and suddenly couldn't talk.

"Lord, child. It's all right. Don't mind me and my big mouth. You come on over here."

The waitress led Gracie over to a booth and made her sit down. She turned to look at the cook. "Get me some hot coffee."

"I'm goin' broke feeding all your strays," the cook muttered, but he did as he was told and delivered the coffee with a piece of pie. "You look like you're starvin'."

Gracie could only nod.

"Give me that baby," the waitress demanded, "and you eat up."

Gracie passed Keaton over and that's when she realized how heavy he was. She took a sip of coffee and it warmed her. She was back in the real world. Gracie cleared her throat. "I'm sorry, I need to call the police. Can I use your phone?"

"The police?" the cook said. "Didn't I tell you? These waifs are always trouble. You mark my words."

"Shut your mouth. Don't mind him. He's always saying dumb stuff. Of course you can use the phone. There's a payphone right over there." The waitress nodded her head to the left.

"Thanks." Gracie ran over, picked up the receiver, and called 911. "Hello? My name is Gracie Martell and I need to talk to the police. I've escaped a kidnapping and my friends are still being held. Please hurry."

The cook and the waitress stared at her with big eyes, their mouths agape. It even sounded unbelievable to Gracie when she said it out loud, but she knew it was all too real, and it was all because of her. The guilt bubbled up from somewhere deep inside and Gracie was overcome with tears.

❀

Candy shot out of the parking lot, turned right on Bronx Park South, left on Crotona Parkway, and right again onto East Tremont Avenue. He headed for his warehouse in the Bronx. He thought they'd lost the bozos in the parking lot but soon saw the junky car trailing them a few blocks away, exhaust pouring from its tailpipe.

Candy drove as fast as he dared and tried to lose them. Then his cellphone went off. He reached for it in his inside pocket. "Yeah?"

"It's me."

Candy drew a sharp breath. "Dumb, you better not tell me you've lost someone, or so help me…"

There was a pregnant pause. "Uh…"

"What?"

"I've lost someone."

Candy slammed his fist into the steering wheel. Dumber wrinkled his brow. "What?"

"He lost someone."

Dumber hit his own forehead.

"Who'd ya lose?" Candy shouted.

"Gracie and the brat."

"*Again?*"

"Sorry, boss."

"You fucking idiot. Take the two broads to the safe house. If you lose them, I'm gonna cut your nuts off and shove them down your throat, have you got that?"

❇

Dumb closed the cellphone. "I have to take you somewhere right now."

"That's the extent of your thinking? You call Candy and he tells you what to do? I'm not impressed, Jethro," Gemma said. "Not impressed at all."

"Stop yappin' and get movin'."

"Where are we going?" Augusta asked.

"You think I'm gonna tell you?"

The women sighed and grabbed their purses. "Can we take our parcels?"

"No."

"If they're here when the police come, they'll know you kidnapped us," Gemma said.

He rolled his eyes and picked up the parcels. Then he pulled out his gun and pointed it at them. "Let's go."

They walked ahead of him into the empty warehouse, their footsteps echoing in the vast space. As they crossed over to the van, Gemma whispered to Augusta. "Remember the license plate."

Dumb herded them into the front of the van. "I can't risk leaving you two alone in the back."

They looked at each other. Drat. No chance to use the phone yet.

Dumb got behind the wheel and started the engine. "Get down, the both of you."

"But I have arthritis," Gemma said.

"That's not my problem. Hurry up."

So Gemma and Augusta scooted down in the seat as far as they could, with groans of protest from Gemma. Dumb revved the engine and off they went. They drove past the diner and headed for parts unknown.

❋

Linda sawed at the rope for what seemed like forever. Her wrist was numb and so were her fingers. Bette took over for a while but didn't get very far. The angle of the blade was on a slant, and without being able to see where they'd cut, they only succeeded in whittling down some of the outer strands.

Finally, in utter frustration, Linda dropped the knife. "This is hopeless. They'll be back before long and we'll still be here. We have to think of something else."

"Why don't we try yelling?"

So they did that for awhile, but got no response. Bette couldn't stand it any more and thrashed about. "IhatethisIhatethisIhatethis!"

She bumped the table leg and a half-empty glass of coke with two butts floating in it fell off the table and crashed to the floor.

Shards of glass scattered around them. They didn't dare move.

"Oh great, now we're going to bleed to death," Bette said.

"No, this is perfect." Linda jerked her head. "Do you see that big piece of glass? Come slowly my way and you might be able to grab it."

"But we'll cut ourselves on this stuff."

"Bette, honest to God, do you ever think positively?"

"Oh, shut up. You can afford meditation classes and yoga retreats. I live in the real world, where people yell at you all day. It makes a difference, you know."

"Just be quiet and grab that glass."

Bette inched her hand forward and picked it up. "Now what?"

"Hold it firmly. I'm going to rub this rope back and forth. You can't move now, or you'll slit my wrists."

"Now there's an idea."

"I'm not going to dignify that with an answer." Linda set to work and this time things sped up considerably. Before they knew it, they felt the rope start to give. With a final almighty yank, the rope broke.

"Oh, thank you, God," Bette yelled.

"Quick, cut the rope around your ankles and then give it to me."

It wasn't long before they were free, but because they'd been tied up for so long in one position, they could hardly move. And of course there was the dilemma of broken glass everywhere. Inch by inch they gingerly rose to their feet, and once they were up they gave each other a big hug.

"I'm sorry I yelled at you," Bette said. "I didn't mean it."

"I didn't mean it either. Now let's get out of here."

"There's a phone. Why don't we call the police first?"

"We can't tell them where we are. Let's go before they come back."

"Okay."

They started for the back door and to their horror saw a car pull up into the back driveway.

"Oh my God, they're back."

"No, that's not them. It must be the dealers, come for the coke. Quick, Bette, we have to hide."

Linda grabbed Bette by the hand and pulled her out of the kitchen. They raced up the stairs just as two thugs threw open the back door. They yelled as soon as they entered.

"Give it up, Flea, I'm warnin' ya."

Linda and Bette ran into the bathroom and hid behind the shower curtain. There was an almighty crash from downstairs, as if one of the thugs had turned the kitchen table on its end. Suddenly the shower curtain seemed too flimsy.

"Come on." Linda grabbed Bette's arm again; Bette seemed incapable of making a move on her own. The yelling continued and Linda heard the dealers climb the stairs just as she and Bette made it into a bedroom. She yanked open the closet door, but there was not enough in it to hide behind.

"Shit."

"They're coming, Lin. They're going to kill us. Oh God, I don't want to die."

Linda yanked her arm. "Will you stop with the dying thing?" She looked around frantically. "The window." She pulled Bette over to the windowsill and tried to open it. It wouldn't move. "Open, damn you."

"It's locked." Bette reached over and undid the lock at the top. Linda shoved at it again and pushed it up. The men were almost at the door.

"Get out, quick." Bette went first and Linda was right after her. They had to hop down a few feet to a slanted roof, and then they slipped and slid towards the gutters. They made it to the edge and saw a six-foot drop into a bush. They looked at each other.

A roar of indignation came through the window. "They're getting away!"

"Okay, go." Linda pushed Bette ahead of her and then jumped herself. They landed in a heap of vegetation. Bette moaned. Linda had the wind knocked out of her, but she got to her feet quickly. She rushed over to Bette.

"Get up, get up."

"I'm trying. It's my ankle."

Linda grabbed Bette by the arms and pulled her up. "Lean on me. Hurry."

They limped out of the bush and started up the back driveway. There was the car the dealers drove up in. Linda glanced through the window. "There are keys in there. Get in, quick."

Linda shoved Bette into the front seat and ran around to the driver's side. She started the car just as two furious men crashed out the back door of the house. Throwing the gear shift in reverse, Linda stepped on the gas and the car fishtailed down the driveway. Linda had to turn around, so she yanked the steering wheel as far as it would go and shoved the car into drive.

The men caught up to the car and were clawing at the back bumper.

"Quick!"

Linda floored it. The car hurtled out of sight and left the men in a shower of gravel.

CHAPTER FOURTEEN

Detective Ames got a call from his precinct that a Gracie Martell and her baby had escaped a kidnapping attempt and Bette Weinberg's name had come up. They thought Ames might be interested.

He was.

"Where's Gracie now?"

"They took her and the baby to St. Barnabas Hospital to check them over. She was pretty upset when we got there."

"So she turned up in the Bronx? I think I better have a talk with her."

Detective Ames left his partner to continue looking for Linda and headed straight for the hospital. He identified himself and was taken into a room where a girl of about eighteen was lying on a bed, a baby in a crib beside her. She turned her big eyes to him as he came in.

"Hello, Gracie. I'm Detective Ames from the NYPD. I'd like you to tell me what happened to you."

Gracie told him everything she knew, everything she could remember, and anything that might help him at all. "It's my fault they're in trouble. I hope Candy didn't get Bette and Linda Keaton."

"I'm afraid they've been taken as well."

Gracie covered her face with her hands. "Oh my God. What am I going to do? How will they ever forgive me? They were so nice to me. They were on vacation, just minding their own business."

She cried so hard that Detective Ames had to get a nurse.

❀

Candy finally shook the drugged-out idiots in the other car by racing down back alleys and through stop signs. He knew this neighbourhood like the back of his hand, and when he was sure he'd lost them for good, he sped towards the safe house, where he'd told Dumb to take the women. He wanted to get there in a hurry; he didn't trust Dumb not to screw up again. He had to get rid of those women and find Gracie or his goose was cooked. The only thing that gave him a little satisfaction was the fact that he had a hefty package of coke he could sell for a little pin money. He didn't plan on sharing it with anyone. It was payment for the aggravation he'd been through in the last two days.

But his nightmare continued. When he and Dumber arrived at the safe house, the van was nowhere to be seen. They rushed into the apartment. Empty. They tried to call Dumb's cellphone. It wasn't on. Candy picked up an empty beer bottle on an end table and smashed it against the wall. "Where is that fucking idiot? I'll kill him."

Said idiot was about to be tied up in the back of the van.

It was a delicate operation, but Gemma and Augusta's maternal abilities to instill guilt paid off. They hounded poor Dumb about everything under the sun as they crouched down in the front seat.

"Do you love your mother?" Gemma asked him again.

"What's it to you?"

"I think he loves his mother, don't you, Augusta?"

"I bet she made good things to eat. Did she bake cookies?"

Dumb stared straight ahead.

"Did she come and kiss you goodnight?" Gemma asked. "Did she make homemade soup when you were sick?"

He drove on.

"My kids love it when I make them cookies," Augusta sighed. "Especially chocolate chip."

"My babies hug me every night. They must be so worried that I haven't called. They're probably crying right now. They don't know where I am."

"My girls, too. They lost their father, you know. He died in front of them. They've never gotten over it. Neither have I."

Dumb looked down at them. "My father died in front of me too."

They tsked and shook their heads. "Isn't that awful, Augusta?"

"That's awful. What happened? But don't feel you have to talk about it if it's too painful."

Dumb hesitated. "No, that's okay. He…he…"

"Yes?"

"He tried to kill this guy, but the gun jammed. He shot himself in the face when he looked down the barrel to see what was wrong."

Augusta and Gemma looked at him in horror. "And you were there? He dragged you along to an assassination attempt?"

"It was Take Your Kids to Work Day."

Dumb unexpectedly pulled over to the side of the road and covered his face. He cried his heart out. Gemma and Augusta crawled up on the seat and Gemma put her arms around him. "There, there, sweetheart. It's all right. It was a long time ago and your father's in"—she rolled her eyes—"heaven."

"The last thing he said was, 'What's wrong with this fuckin' thing?' He never told me he loved me."

Gemma patted his back. "I'm sure he did, dear. I'm sure of it." She grabbed his gun. "Don't move."

He looked up in confusion. "What?"

Augusta opened her door and the two of them scrambled out, Gemma keeping the gun pointed at his head. "Don't move or I'll kill you."

Dumb wiped his eyes. "I thought you guys liked me."

Augusta rushed to say, "We do. It's got nothing to do with you personally, but we need to get home. Being kidnapped is very inconvenient."

"Toss me your cellphone," Gemma said.

He threw it at her. She passed it to Augusta, who turned it off.

Gemma went around the front of the van to the driver's side. She noticed a man walking his dog out of the corner of her eye. Then she noticed the man scoop up his dog and run down the street.

"Gussie, open the back of the van. Dumb, do as I say and you won't get hurt. We're going to put you in the back. I'm afraid we'll have to tie you up."

"This is just great."

"*Move it.*"

He jumped out of the van and walked around to the back, Gemma's gun on him the entire time. Augusta opened the door and he crawled in. She picked up a roll of duct tape. "We can use this."

Gemma gestured with the gun. "Dumb, use the tape to tie your legs together."

"Aren't *you* supposed to do that?"

"Don't argue with me, unless you want a swat."

Once he did it, they made him turn around so Augusta could tie up his hands. She also put a strip across his mouth. "That's not too tight, is it?"

"Get out of there. He's fine. See you later, Jethro."

They slammed the door shut and hopped back in the van. Augusta looked at her friend. "You are without a doubt the smartest woman I know."

"Tell that to my mother-in-law. Right, get on the phone and call the police."

A car roared up the street, and they recognized it right away.

"Oh damn, it's Candy. Hurry, Gemma!"

Gemma threw the gear shift into drive and gunned it. Their heads flew back and then jolted forward as they careened towards Candy. Poor Dumb was crashing around in the back making a hell of a racket as he smashed into the sides of the van. They clipped Candy's car as they roared by.

"Call the police, Augusta." Gemma glanced in the rear-view mirror and saw Candy turn on a dime and chase after her. "Oh no you don't, you bastard. I'm going home to my family."

Augusta called 911. "Hello? You've got to help us. We're being chased by mobsters. What? I don't know." She turned to Gemma. "Where are we?"

"How the hell should I know? Tell them we passed a sign for Yankee Stadium."

"We passed a sign for Yankee Stadium...what?" Augusta turned to Gemma. "Which direction are we headed?"

"We're headed *away* from the gangsters trying to kill us. For God's sake, tell them we're being chased. We don't have time to consult a map."

Augusta screamed into the phone. "We're in a white van and we're driving much too fast. There's a black car on our tail...what kind?... Uh...it's big and sort of creepy looking. Well, I'm sorry if I can't be more specific. Do you want me to poke my head out the window and get it shot off?"

"Tell them I just saw a sign for a museum."

Augusta repeated Gemma's observation and turned to look at her. "They say that means we're headed north."

"Good. If we keep going we can make the Canadian border." She glanced at the dashboard. "Damn, we're almost out of gas. Candy's a cheapskate as well as a dick. Tell them to hurry up."

"Hurry up! You have to help us. These horrible men are after us. They want us dead. What? I'm Augusta Ramsey and I'm with my friend Gemma Rossi. We don't know where our other friends are—"

Gemma turned the wheel to go up a one-way street and caught the edge of the sidewalk. They bounced in the air and the cellphone flew out of Augusta's hand just as Candy's car drew up beside them.

"Duck!" Gemma grabbed Augusta's head and pushed her down. A shot rang out and the driver-side mirror disappeared. Gemma saw the gun on the floor and reached for it.

"Gemma, don't! You might kill someone."

"That's the idea."

Gemma fired it but in her panic forgot the side window was up. The noise of shattered glass made both women cry out. "Get out of the van, Gussie. I'll cover you."

"I'm not going anywhere without you."

Candy yanked open the passenger-side door, reached in, and grabbed Augusta by the hair. "Put that fucking gun down or I'll blow your friend's head off."

❁

Flea was furious with Tony for losing sight of Candy's car. He leaned over the front seat and gave the back of his head a whack. "Now what are we supposed to do? We've lost everything."

"It's not my fault," Tony said. "This piece of junk belongs to you. I told you to get a tune-up."

Blue raised his hand. "Since we're not chasing anyone anymore, can I leave?"

Now it was Blue's turn to get a smack on the head.

"This is all your doing, you moron. Do you think I'm going to let you get away with it? The minute I can stand up, you're dead."

"So what do we do now?" Tony asked.

"The only thing we can do. Get the money from that crazy woman on the phone and get the hell outta town."

"But what about the broads at the house?"

"When you-know-who comes lookin' for us and we're not around, they're done for. That's one job I don't have to worry about."

"I don't like this," Tony admitted. "I don't like this at all."

"Who cares what you like?" Flea grabbed his leg. "Oh, this is killin' me."

"Want somethin' for the pain?" Blue asked.

Flea hit him again. "You've got somethin' and you never gave it to me before? Hurry up, jackass. Hand it over."

Blue rummaged through his pockets and came up with some powerful painkillers. "These are good." He handed them over his shoulder to Flea.

Flea swallowed three pills without the benefit of water and nearly choked. "This better work…"

"…or I'm dead meat. I know. Ya said that before."

Another smack on the head for Blue.

The Weinberg gang were in the city and they were lost. Not one of them had ever been to New York. Added to that was their general anxiety about when the kidnapper would call again.

"We should call the detective and tell him we're here," Mordecai said. "Maybe there's been some progress on the case, and he can tell us where the heck we are."

That's when the phone rang and everyone shouted. Mordecai had a hard time keeping the van on the road. "Stop panicking, you're going to get us all killed."

Ida answered the cell. "Hello?"

"Ya got the moolah?"

"Yeah, I've got the money. Where's my daughter?"

"Furs things furs."

"What? What are you saying? I can't understand you. Hello?"

There was nothing but giggling.

"There's nothing funny about this. My daughter is missing and I want you to tell me where she is." Ida put her hand over the phone.

"This guy's laughing."

Izzy grabbed the phone and started to say something, but his cough kicked in and he couldn't get the words out. Mordecai yanked it from his old man and put it to his ear.

"Where do we meet you?"

"Wha?"

"Where do we meet you? Where do we drop off the money?"

"Money? What money?"

"Are you trying to be a wise guy? This is a serious situation."

"Whoa. Whoa there cowboy. Hold your horseseseses. I'm gettin' to that."

"Your voice keeps fading away," Mordecai shouted. "Talk to me." He heard a struggle and arguing. "Hello? Hello?"

Another voice came on the phone. "Meet us at Washington Square Park, under the arch. Come alone. If you call the police, she's dead."

"But where is she? Will she be there?"

"Who are you? Where's the woman?"

"She's here." Mordecai passed the phone to his mother. "He wants you."

"Yes? What is it?" Ida said into the phone.

"I only want you there."

"Fine. No problem."

"Meet us in half an hour."

"Will Bette be there?"

"Yeah."

"Okay. Okay. Don't hurt her." The phone went dead. "How far away is Washington Square Park?" Ida asked.

They consulted their maps. Everyone but Izzy agreed that Ida was the go-between and that the rest of the family would stay in the shadows and pounce if something went wrong.

"I don't think your mother should be out in the open like that. What if they kill her?"

"Then they'll finally accomplish what you've been trying to do for years."

Mordecai protested. "Ma, don't say such horrible things. You know you don't mean it. He's worried about you."

"So he says."

"I am. I am worried," Izzy yelled at her. "First my daughter goes missing and then they kill my wife?"

Ida thawed a little. "Gee, I didn't think you cared."

"Of course I care, you stupid woman. Who'll feed me and clean the house?"

Ida threw the cellphone at him. It smashed against the windshield and broke into pieces.

❁

Linda and Bette drove like maniacs but had no idea where they were going. Linda tried to break every traffic rule in the book, but it went unnoticed.

"How come there's never a policeman around when you need one? If I did this on any other day, I'd have a SWAT team after me."

Bette kept her eyes peeled. As peeled as eyes can be without their glasses. "I don't see a phone booth or anything. We have to get to a phone."

They rushed down several more streets. Bette squinted as best she could. "Wait, I think there's a phone booth up ahead."

"That's a bus stand."

"Oh."

"Wait. What's that?" Linda pointed straight ahead.

Bette leaned into the windshield and peered intently through the glass. "I don't see anything."

"There. There. At the stop sign. There's a guy on a bike using a cellphone. Roll down the window and grab it from him."

"Are you serious? Can't we ask him to use it?"

Linda shouted at her. "We don't have time. Lean out the window and grab it from him. Hurry up, Bette. It's our only chance."

So Bette rolled down the window and hung out over the side. Linda slowed down and steered as close to the man as she dared. He never looked at them, just continued to natter away. Bette reached out and tore the phone from his hand.

The guy was momentarily stunned. "Hey...hey...gimme that."

"Go!"

Linda stepped on the gas, which caused Bette to lose her balance and drop the phone. "Bloody hell."

The man chased them on his bike, cursing. He picked the phone off the pavement and waved his fist at them until they disappeared.

Bette sank back in her seat. "Sorry."

"Never mind." Linda pulled over to the side of the road and shut off the car. "We must be far enough away from those maniacs. Let's ask someone in those houses over there if we can use their phone to call the police."

"I don't think people open their doors to strangers anymore."

"Well, we have to try. Gemma and Augusta are counting on us."

They got out of the car and walked up to the first duplex that had a car in front of it. They rang the doorbell. A bevy of barking began, along with a man's voice. "Shut up, the lot of ya."

Linda and Bette looked at each other.

"Maybe we should go somewhere else?" Bette said.

They didn't have time. The door opened and a slovenly looking man with the world's biggest beer belly stood there, his undershirt barely concealing his body. They stepped back.

"What do ya want?"

Only they weren't sure what he said, because there were five rabid-looking miniature dachshunds slipping and sliding up the hallway towards them.

"Never mind." Linda grabbed Bette by the sleeve and pulled her away from the door. The two of them ran from the porch to the sidewalk as the wiener dogs poured over and down the steps, yapping and snarling.

The women sprinted down the street, but the dogs gained on them until their owner let out a sharp whistle—then they stopped on a dime and strutted back to the front door, their mission accomplished.

When Linda could breathe again, she hollered, "Keep your dogs on a leash."

"That'll teach ya to stay away from my property." The man slammed the door shut as soon as his canine terrorists were back inside.

Bette stood there panting, and when she looked at Linda her shoulders started to shake.

"Don't cry, Bette."

Bette wasn't crying. She was laughing. She was laughing so hard she wasn't making a sound. Linda hit her arm. "Stop that. You're hysterical."

"Oh my God, I wonder what normal people do on their vacations."

Linda didn't answer her. She was running after a police car that had appeared, waving her arms, yelling, "STOP! STOP!"

❧

The Weinbergs scrambled out of the van, and not very gracefully. Ida insisted on being taken out immediately, and as luck would have it her wheelchair had a wonky tire, no doubt thanks to her mishap at the gas station. "Hurry up, you numbskulls."

"Ma, do you want to scare the kidnappers away?" Mordecai said. "Lower your voice."

"Stop ordering me around. Where's the money? Someone give me the money."

"We're trying to. Hold your horses."

Izzy passed Mordecai the knapsack filled with twenty-dollar bills. They hid a sweater at the bottom of the bag to bulk it up a bit and covered everything up with the cash. It looked like a lot more than seven thousand dollars, and hopefully the ruse would work long enough to grab Bette and run. Mordecai put it in Ida's lap.

They stood as a group to listen to last-minute instructions. They were oblivious to the curious looks being thrown their way.

"Remember, I'm going in alone," Ida said. "They only want me."

"Maybe we're wrong," Uncle Sid said. "They might grab the money and run away from you."

"I know that, you birdbrain. I wasn't born yesterday. If that happens, everyone tackle them. We have enough for a football team."

"Look at us." Uncle Sid pointed to his sons and nephews. "We're skinny Jews from the city. We have an accountant, a mortician, a dentist, a doctor, a banker, a baker…"

"…a candlestick maker…shut up already. Even wimps like your boys can trip someone if they have to."

"*My* boys?"

"Never mind." The ashes from Izzy's cigarette fell on Ida's head. "Sid, you and yours go into the park. Pretend like you're walking."

Ida swivelled around to look at her husband. "Pretend like they're walking? How do they do that? If they're walking, they're walking."

Mordecai wrung his hands. "Will you two knock it off? This is serious. Everyone disperse. I'll be closest to Ma. Pop, you stay back. If you start to cough you might spook them."

"Wait a minute…"

Ida started to roll away. "Do as you're told, Izzy."

Twelve members of Bette's family went every which way. Ida led the charge and Mordecai and his brother David had a hard time keeping up with her. She whizzed past the arched gate and made several loops around the entrance, peering at anyone who came near her. Izzy and Sid found themselves behind a bush, as Bette's cousins and other brothers paraded around trying to look inconspicuous.

They were a disaster waiting to happen, and it didn't take long.

Not far away, Tony pulled into a parking spot. Flea was having a hard time keeping his eyes open, thanks to the painkillers, and Blue was just plain bored.

"Can I leave once we have the money?" Blue asked. "I don't want a share."

Flea went to hit him on the back of the head but missed. "You wasn't getting any, no how."

"I better go get the money," Tony said. "You can't limp into a park with a bloody leg. Wait here and I'll come back."

Flea put his gun to the back of Tony's head. "I don't think so, partner. You might take off, and then where would I be?"

"Put that away. Do you want the cops crawling all over us before we get the dough?"

Flea grinned. "You worry too much." He shoved the gun down the back of his pants. "Let's go."

Tony turned around in his seat and glared at Flea. "You honestly wanna walk down the street with a dripping kerchief around your leg?"

Flea kept grinning. "This is New York, my friend. No one will notice, especially since freak boy is coming with us."

Blue folded his arms. "I resent that."

"Do I care?" Flea opened the back door. "Come and help me, freak boy."

Blue got out of the front seat and stood there with a mutinous look on his face. Flea grabbed his jacket and hopped a few steps before he attempted to put weight on his foot.

"*Ow*. Jesus Christ, come here, Tony."

Tony went over and Flea grabbed his arm too. Between the two of them they sort of dragged him down the street. They looked almost normal, if you didn't count the fact that they were walking unnaturally close to each other and leaving a trail of blood behind them.

"How do we know who they are?" Tony asked.

"We look for a woman with lots of money. Maybe she's wearing a mink coat. Whatcha think?"

"I think I shoulda given you only one of those pills." Blue flinched in case Flea hit him, but he didn't. He looked at his feet instead, as if to make sure they were still there.

They hauled Flea into the park and then stood there and looked around. There were quite a few people about for so early in the morning, but they weren't going anywhere, just aimlessly wandering.

"I don't like this," Tony said under his breath.

Blue pointed. "I think I see someone behind that bush."

"They're havin' a piss," Flea assured him. "Don't get paranoid."

"I don't see no woman, unless you count that maniac in the chair." Tony tossed his head to the right and they all saw an old crone barrelling down on them at about twenty miles an hour. They stared at her with incredulity as she headed straight for them.

Stuart paced in a cubicle in the outpatient department of Mount Sinai Medical Centre while Ryan had her ankle wrapped by a young intern. She oohhed and ahhed just enough to keep him wrapping longer than necessary.

"You have such strong hands."

"Give it a rest," Stuart said.

Ryan threw him a look. "Mind your own business. At least this nice gentleman is being kind to me, unlike some I could mention."

Stuart stuck his hands in his pockets. "I'll be in the hall."

He went out the door and walked to the end of the corridor. When his cellphone rang, he quickly went to an out-of-the-way corner to answer it.

"Hello?"

"Mr. Keaton, it's Detective Ames here."

Stuart resisted shouting at him. "Did you find Linda?"

"Yes."

His hand went to his heart. "Oh, thank God. Where is she?"

"I believe they're on route back to the station house. I'm in the Bronx interviewing the young girl who was held hostage with your wife's other two friends. They're still missing, unfortunately. The information was passed to me about your wife. I haven't seen her yet."

"May I see her?"

"I imagine she'll be tied up with our unit for a while answering questions, but if you come to the station house, I'm sure they'll let you see her for a few minutes."

"I can't thank you enough for all your help."

"I wasn't much help. Your wife and her friend managed to escape on their own. Very resourceful ladies, I must say."

"That's Linda. She's quite a gal."

"I must go. I'm still in the middle of this. I'll be in touch if I have any news about the others."

"Thank you. Thank you so much."

Stuart turned off his phone and sagged into a corner. He was glad he'd resisted the temptation to give Wes a call. Hopefully his son would never have to know about this horrible episode.

Tears welled up. He quickly wiped them with the back of his hand, put his cellphone in his pocket, and hurried down the hallway. He burst into the cubicle. Ryan had her hands on the intern's arm. They jumped apart at the sight of him.

"Linda's been found."

"Oh, goody, there is a God."

"You could at least be relieved."

"I am relieved. Relieved this nightmare is over. I have to go back to the hotel and put my foot up, don't I, doctor?"

The intern backed away from her. "It would be wise. Ice it every so often and take some painkillers. You'll be fine."

"Thank you so much."

The intern nodded and quickly fled.

"Okay, let's go. We have to get to the police station."

Ryan glared at him. "You heard him. I need to be off my feet."

"You can be off your feet after I talk to Linda."

"You have got to be the most selfish man I know. I can't believe the way you treat me. Absolutely no regard for my feelings or my welfare whatsoever."

"I do worry about you, Ryan, and we'll definitely go back to the hotel after I take a minute to reassure myself that Linda's all right." He hurried over and put his arm around her waist. "Let me help you."

"Let me go, you big jerk." She pummelled his shoulder with her fists.

"Fine. I'll see you later." He let her go and marched out the door.

"Get back here!"

He poked his head back in. "Are you coming with me or going back to the hotel on your own?"

"Looks like I don't have a choice."

"That's right."

"Fine, I'll come with you. But I'm not happy, Stuart. I'm not happy at all."

He pushed her in a wheelchair until they got outside, and then he handed her a cane he'd bought from the hospital. He hailed a cab and she hobbled over to it.

On their way to the police station, Stuart suddenly looked at his watch. "My speech is in two hours."

"I'm exhausted. I need my beauty sleep."

He didn't bother talking after that.

Bette and Linda sat at a table in a small room drinking coffee. A box of doughnuts was open between them, but they were too worn out to eat more than one.

Bette sighed. "I'm so tired, I'm not tired."

"I know what you mean." Linda looked around. "How long do you think they'll leave us here?"

Bette shrugged. "It doesn't matter. I'm not leaving this station until I know Gemma and Augusta are safe."

"They have to be. They just have to be."

There was a knock at the door and Stuart poked his head in. Linda jumped up from the table and flew into his arms. She didn't notice Ryan limping behind him with a scowl on her face.

"I'm sorry, you were right," she snivelled into his shirt. "I should've called the police."

"It doesn't matter now. You're safe."

They held each other for a few moments and then Linda suddenly realized what she was doing. She practically pushed him away. "Sorry. I'm not thinking." She went and sat down again. "I see you brought your lapdog with you."

"You're so clever," Ryan smiled at her. "So clever that someone kidnapped you in a matter of minutes. I believe your friends are missing as well. They must be as clever as you are."

"You and your big mouth can leave," Linda said.

Bette slapped her cheeks. "Speaking of big mouths, I haven't called home yet. Ida must be frantic. Stuart, do you have your cellphone?" Stuart passed it to her and she placed the call.

Miriam and Esther were still on the couch, fighting to keep their eyes open, but as soon as the phone rang, they sprang to attention.

Miriam reached for the phone. "Hello? Hello?"

"Who's this? Miriam?"

"Bette?"

"Yes, it's me."

"Oh, praise God!" Miriam smiled at Esther. "It's Bette."

Esther shook her hands in prayer.

"Are you all right?" Miriam shouted in her excitement.

"Yes, I'm at the police station."

"Oh, that's wonderful. Is everyone with you?"

"No, only Linda. We're still waiting to hear about Gemma and Augusta."

"Oh dear, that's terrible. But I meant the family."

"What family?"

"Your family."

"*My* family?"

"Yes. Obviously you haven't hooked up, then."

Bette rubbed her forehead. "I must be overtired. I don't understand you."

"When we heard you were in trouble, the family went to rescue you."

"*Rescue* me?"

"Of course. Did you think we'd just leave you there?"

"Who's we?"

"Everyone. Ida, Izzy…"

"*What?*"

"All your brothers, Uncle Sid, and your cousins."

"How did they get here?"

"They drove all night."

Bette held her hand over the phone. "My entire family is here in New York."

"I don't understand," Linda frowned.

"You don't understand? Me neither." She took her hand away. "Miriam, why in the name of God did you let Ida and Izzy loose on the streets of New York?"

"Sorry, Bette, there was no stopping them. They love you. We all do."

Bette fell into the nearest chair. "I don't believe this."

"I'm going to call Mordecai and tell them where you are," Miriam said. "Give me the address."

Bette found out what it was and gave it to her, along with the phone number where she could be reached. Miriam then called Mordecai, but the operator kept saying there was no service. "That doesn't make sense. I know he has that phone on."

"Maybe they're not in range," Esther said.

"Why don't you see if David's cellphone works?"

Esther took the phone from Miriam and phoned her husband. He answered.

CHAPTER FIFTEEN

Whenever the Weinbergs remembered the events of that day, it seemed to all of them as if everything had taken place in slow motion. Only Ida's wheelchair remained speedy—in fact, she seemed to be everywhere at once. It was as if she had lost control of her powered wheelchair, but it could have been the wonky wheel.

Whatever it was, she covered a lot of ground and was on top of the three Stooges in no time, while everyone else circled around the perimeter.

She whizzed up to them and asked them flat out: "Are you the kidnappers?"

Flea laughed. "Got it in one, lady."

"You don't look like kidnappers. You look like losers."

"I'm starting to get a complex," Blue shouted. "I've never been insulted by so many people in one day."

"Get used to it. Where's my daughter?"

"Where's the money?" Tony asked.

Ida picked up the backpack from her lap. "It's here, but I'm not handing it over until I see my daughter."

Flea started to giggle. "You're a bossy old nag, ain't ya?"

She glared at him. "Got it in one, loser."

Flea frowned. "I'm getting tired of you. Hand over the cash and make it snappy."

"No, not until I see Bette."

Tony got nervous. "Listen, lady, don't make this difficult. We've got your daughter in the car. Give us the dough and we'll take you to her."

"I don't believe you. Where's the car?"

"I've had enough of this old bitch. Gimme that." Flea lunged at Ida, obviously forgetting about his bum leg. He went down like a ton of bricks and hit the pavement with a sickening thud. Tony and

Blue couldn't believe it, so they stood frozen to the spot—along with a small crowd of spectators, a.k.a. Weinbergs. Everyone waited for someone to do something, and they all jumped when Flea reached out and grabbed Ida's chair.

"Let go of me." She hit him on the head with the backpack.

He held on with one hand and attempted to wrestle the bag from her with the other. "Gimme that dough, lady."

"In your dreams."

Just then David yelled from thirty feet away. "*Ma,* Bette's at the police station. Bette's safe at the police station. Get outta there."

"Why, you little bastard, trying to steal my money." Ida put her chair in gear and zoomed away, dragging Flea with her.

Everyone started to run in twenty different directions. There was mass confusion as the Weinbergs shouted and coughed and pursued the speeding wheelchair. But when the gun went off, everyone stopped dead.

"Unless you want me to kill this old bitch right now, everyone back off," Flea screamed. He trained his gun on Ida's face from the ground. "No one come near us, do you hear me?"

Everyone stayed put.

He gradually managed to get into a sitting position. "Throw me that bag, lady."

"You want I give you the money? Fine. Here's your money." She threw it in his face.

He grabbed the bag and then hobbled to his feet. "Tony, Blue, get over here and help me."

They hesitated.

"Get over here now, or I swear to God I'll kill you too."

They hurried over.

"Anyone ever tell you you're a schmuck?" Ida yelled at Flea.

He sneered at her. "If I'm such a schmuck, how come I got your money, eh? Answer me that."

"Here's your answer."

She kicked him right in the nuts. Flea went down with a crash, his gun flying. The bag of money fell and Tony took off. Blue put his hands up. "I was kidnapped too. Don't hurt me."

The Weinberg boys ran from every direction and pounced on all three of them, not that Flea put up much of a fight. He writhed on the ground, moaning in pain.

Izzy and Sid rushed over to Ida.

Izzy patted her head. "Are you all right?"

"Of course I'm all right. You didn't think I'd let a little wiener like him bother me, did you?" She waved him away. "Stop that. I'm not a dog."

Sid was incredulous. "How did you do that, Ida? I couldn't believe my eyes."

She dismissed him with her hand. "Every so often, God give me strength."

❊

Ames was summoned from his interrogation of Gracie by an important phone call from his partner, telling him that a 911 operator spoke to a woman named Augusta Ramsey, who said she and her friend Gemma Rossi were in a white van and they were being chased through the Bronx by someone they described as a mobster, a mobster with a gun.

His partner picked him up at the hospital and they hit the streets—they didn't have a moment to lose. They headed for the last known location.

"I hope this has a happy ending," Ames said.

"Odds don't look good. Two naive housewives trying to outwit and outrun the Mob? I don't like it."

"Well, the other two seemed to keep their wits about them."

Ames's partner frowned. "Not really. They never called the police, did they?"

"True."

A voice crackled over the radio telling them the white van had been located. They looked at each other and stepped on the gas.

When they approached the scene, police cars were everywhere and traffic was being held up. The front of the van was up on the sidewalk, resting against a mailbox, and the passenger door gaped open. There was a shot-out window and the driver-side mirror was in pieces on the ground.

They ducked under the police tape and approached an officer.

"Are they here?" Ames asked.

"No sign of them."

"Damn."

"Witnesses say they saw two women being pushed into a black car."

Ames sighed. "They could be anywhere."

They were interrupted by a shout. "Detective Ames, over here."

He hurried over to the van. "Find something?"

"Yeah." The policeman held the back door open and pointed inside. He peered into the van. There was a huge, dumb-looking guy, tied up, gagged, and looking madder than a wet hen.

Candy and Dumber took the women back to the safe house, nearly yanking their arms off as they escorted them from the car into the apartment. They threw them onto the living room floor. Candy paced around them, crunching on his mouthful of Life Savers.

"Where's Dumb?"

"I told you," Gemma said. "He took off."

"He wouldn't do that."

"Well, he did."

Candy wiped at the sweat on his face.

"Are you feeling okay?" Gemma asked. "You're sweating like a pig."

He pointed a finger in her face. "Shut your mouth."

"Did you know that's sometimes the first sign of a heart attack?" Augusta said. "You should get out of this stressful business, or you'll be dead before you know it."

"No, *you'll* be dead if you don't shut up."

"My mother had a heart attack," Dumber said.

"That's terrible," Augusta said. "Did you have a chance to say goodbye?"

"No. One minute she was beating us with a belt and a shoe, the next minute she was on the floor."

"Well, that explains your personality. You never had a chance."

Dumber looked at her. "Whaddaya mean?"

"Well, they say that…"

Candy picked up a lamp and smashed it against the wall. "This ain't Dr. Phil,"

"You know Dr. Phil?" Augusta asked. "How odd."

"What's so odd about it?"

"You're a criminal, for heaven's sake. Have you considered reading his book *Relationship Rescue?*"

"Forget that," Gemma said. "Tell him to read *The Ultimate Weight Solution.*"

"Like you should talk," Candy fired back.

"Hey, my husband happens to like my love handles. All the more to grab."

"Well, he's a fuckin' idiot, then."

Gemma stood up. "What did you say?"

Augusta looked at Candy. "I think you'd better run."

Candy shook his head in disbelief. "Are you serious?"

"You don't want to see Gemma in a rage."

"No, you don't want to see me in a rage." She tapped her fingers on her forehead. "And I've had it up to here with you two."

Candy and Dumber looked at each other and burst out laughing. That's when Gemma took a flying leap at Candy and knocked him off his feet. Dumber tried to grab Gemma, but as soon as he turned away from Augusta, she picked up a heavy ashtray and threw it at the back of his head. He crumpled to the floor.

"Grab his gun," Gemma screamed as she tried to keep Candy under her.

Augusta made several attempts, but Candy squirmed his right arm out and held her off.

"You're dead," he growled, still fighting to get Gemma off him.

"Remember what Oprah said, go for the eyes!"

Gemma gave him a jab and he howled. "I'm going to kill you, you bitch."

She put her hands around his neck. "I'm going to kill you first, for talking about my husband like that." She banged his head on the floor as she choked him. "You good-for-nothin' piece of…"

Police officers kicked in the front door and swarmed into the room,

Ames leading the charge. They couldn't believe what they saw. A Mob boss on the floor having the life throttled out of him by an Italian housewife, and a bodyguard knocked out cold beside him, an art teacher sitting on his back.

Despite the police presence, Gemma kept it up. She banged Candy's head against the hardwood floor. "Don't you ever say that again about my Angelo! Do you hear me?"

Ames rushed over and grabbed her. "It's all right. Let go."

Gemma ignored him and kept it up. "I'm tired." Bang went his head. "I'm hungry." Bang. "And if you ever come near any of us again, I'll cut your balls off." She threw his head back on the floor and got off him. "He's all yours."

Augusta got up too. "Oh, thank you...how did you find us?"

"Your man in the van gave them up." Ames grabbed Candy's gun, turned him over, and cuffed him.

"He did?"

"He said it was last time he'd ever sit in the back of that van. He was pretty banged up."

Gemma and Augusta stepped over Dumber and gave each other a big hug.

"We did it, kiddo," Gemma said.

"We sure did. I'd never have made it without you, Gem."

"The feeling is mutual."

Augusta quickly turned to the detectives. "Please tell us our friends are okay, and Gracie and the baby."

"They're all safe. Linda and Bette are at the police station, and Gracie and the baby are in the hospital. She's a tough little cookie, but she was pretty distraught about you two."

"That poor child," Gemma said. "She's only a baby herself. Can you take us to her?"

"Later," Ames said. "We have to get you two back to the station. We'll need your statements."

"Anything. As long as it locks up these two bastards for the rest of their lives."

❁

Linda and Bette, Stuart, and the reluctant Ryan sat around the table in the lunchroom not knowing what to do. Linda told Stuart he should go.

"I'd like to see this through. You did ask me for help, if you recall."

"A fat lot of good you were, letting those freaks carry us off."

He leaned across the table. "You were the one who insisted on meeting those freaks, if you remember."

"He came to my rescue," Ryan gloated. "He rushed back for me, not you."

"And he's very welcome to you. But don't forget. Any man who'll cheat on his wife will sure as hell cheat on his girlfriend."

"Will you both stop talking about me as if I wasn't here?"

Linda couldn't sit still any longer. She got up to look out the window. "Where the hell are they? Why hasn't anyone come back to tell us anything?"

"My stomach's in knots," Bette said. "How long do we have to sit here?"

There was a quick knock on the door and Detective Ames came in.

Bette stood up. "Is there any news? We've been worried sick."

"I have something for you." He stepped aside and revealed Gemma and Augusta. The four friends ran to each other. There were lots of hugs and kisses and tears.

Ryan rolled her eyes and filed her nails. "You'd think they just came back from darkest Africa."

At that point another officer came in and addressed Detective Ames. "We've got a situation downstairs. Something to do with your case. It's the mob from Washington Square Park, demanding to speak to Bette Weinberg."

Bette turned at her name. "It must be Ida and Izzy."

Gemma did a double take. "Ida and Izzy?"

"They're here?" Augusta said. "I can't believe it."

"You know those two. They never leave me alone."

The commotion downstairs rose in volume, so everyone hurried out of the lunchroom and rushed down the staircase. There were the Weinbergs, milling around the lobby, talking and gesturing while Ida shouted at the desk sergeant that she'd lodge an official complaint if her daughter wasn't produced forthwith.

"Ma."

Ida turned at the sound of her voice.

"Bette!" Ida pushed herself out of her chair and wobbled across the lobby toward her. "You scared me half to death! What kind of a daughter scares her mother half to death?"

She grabbed Bette by the shoulders and shook her. "What did I tell you about getting lost? Didn't I tell you you'd get lost? Why don't you ever listen to me?" She hugged Bette for dear life and kissed her several times on both cheeks.

"Ma, stop it, I can't breath."

Ida slapped her hands together and appealed to the ceiling. "What did I do so wrong that my daughter runs away from home and gets lost? Why do I put up with such disrespectful behaviour?"

Bette shook her. "Ma, you walked! You walked!"

Ida's eyes widened. She looked around and saw everyone with their mouths open, staring at her in disbelief. She shrugged. "What? You've never seen a miracle before?"

The Weinbergs rushed towards Ida, but she held them off. "Wait a minute, I want a word with Linda Keaton. Where is she?"

Linda raised her hand cautiously. "I'm here, Mrs. Weinberg."

Ida came after her in slow motion, teetering on her clunky black shoes. "You're going to pay for this, you terrible woman. Who do you think you are, dragging my daughter to sin city only to have her kidnapped?" She advanced on Linda with her arms in the air.

"Stop it, you crazy woman," Bette shouted.

Linda kept backing up the stairs. "I'm sorry, Mrs. Weinberg. I had no idea any of this was going to happen."

Everyone tried to intervene, but it was the sergeant at the desk who finally got their attention.

"*Enough.* If you do not cease and desist this instant, you will all be carted off to jail. Is that understood?"

Everyone but Ida nodded. She appealed to the ceiling. "Why oh why does this always happen to me? That God should hate me so much I have to come to New York and get yelled at by a bigmouth."

The sergeant pointed at Detective Ames. "Put that woman in a holding cell."

The family all started shouting at once. It wasn't until Mordecai gave a sharp whistle that things quieted down. He appealed to the sergeant. "My mother has suffered great emotional trauma and she's not quite herself. If we promise to remove her quickly, and never darken your door again, can you see your way to letting her go?"

The sergeant gave Ida a look. "Get her out of here now. You've got thirty seconds."

Ida's sons grabbed their protesting mother and put her in her wheelchair. As they wheeled her out the door she shouted, "What have I ever done to deserve such disrespect?"

CHAPTER SIXTEEN

Gemma knocked on the hospital room door. "Hello? Is there a really great kid named Gracie in here?"

"Come in!"

Gemma, Augusta, Linda, and Bette rushed into the room bearing gifts.

Gracie held out her arms. "I'm so glad you're all safe."

They hugged her and made a big fuss over Keaton, who was asleep in the crib beside his mother's bed.

"I thought I'd never see you again." Gracie wiped her eyes with tissues.

Gemma and Augusta sat on either side of her bed, while Linda and Betty gathered two chairs and pulled them up close.

Augusta patted Gracie's leg. "Did you really think we wouldn't come to see you? If it wasn't for you, no one would've been looking for us."

"If it wasn't for me, none of this would've happened. I can't tell you how sorry I am."

Gemma grabbed her hand. "We know you are."

"You learned a hard lesson," Augusta said. "And a lesson learned is never in vain."

Gracie nodded.

"No more tears," Linda smiled. "Open your gifts."

Gracie reached for the first brightly coloured package. She opened it up and took out a soft squishy teddy bear.

"We thought maybe Keaton was missing his old one," Betty said.

"Thank you. I've never in my whole life had anyone be so nice to me."

"Nonsense." Gemma passed her another present. "Open this one."

Gracie opened a Baby Gap box. It was filled with gorgeous little outfits for Keaton. "They're beautiful."

"You can thank Linda for her taste in clothes," Augusta laughed.

Linda reached out and gave her another box. "And we didn't forget you."

They bought her a soft cashmere sweater, a pair of jeans, and a warm jacket.

"It's all too much. Thank you."

"You're very welcome," Gemma said. "Now tell me, dear, have the police said anything to you yet?"

"Not much, but social services will be paying me a few visits to assess my ability to parent."

"Augusta and I can tell the caseworkers that you're a wonderful little mother, so I don't think you have anything to worry about. It's nothing we can't handle."

Augusta spoke up. "In the meantime, we've been given permission to tell you that your charges have been dropped."

"What? How?"

"Dumb came to our rescue in the end. He's turned informant on all of Candy's activities and he told the authorities how Candy coerced you into being their mule, as it were."

"That's the reason we're cleared to go home, too," Gemma said. "In light of the circumstances, they know that we accidently killed that man in self-defence."

Gracie's eyes got big. "You killed a man?"

"I sprayed that horrible airport driver with mace. The foolish man had an allergic reaction and died."

Gracie looked down at her hands. "I'm such a loser."

"Don't be silly," said Augusta. "Where's your family, honey?"

"I was raised by my grandmother, but she died two years ago." Her eyes filled with tears. "The only reason I got into this mess in the first place is because I had no money. Keaton's father left me with nothing. He said we were going to start a new life in Montreal, but he got mixed up with drugs and he disappeared. Someone told me he left the country. I'll never see him again. Not that I ever *want* to see him again. He doesn't deserve to see Keaton anyway."

The friends exchanged glances. Gemma said, "Shall we tell her?"

They nodded.

Gracie looked up. "Tell me what?"

Gemma held her hand. "How would you like to live with one of us?"

"What do you mean?"

Linda jumped in. "I think you should live with me. I have a huge house with no one in it. But I know I'm going to have to wrestle Gemma and Augusta for you."

"I'd love to have you too," Bette said, "but I wouldn't wish my parents on anyone."

Gracie's eyes sparkled. "Do you mean it?"

Gemma patted her knee. "Of course we mean it, *bambino*. But don't be so quick to be happy. You'll have four mothers breathing down your neck."

"I can't wait." Gracie looked over at Keaton, who stirred in his sleep. He lifted his head and blinked with sleepy eyes, looking for his mother. When he saw the ladies, his lip went down and he started to cry.

All the friends tried to hush him, but it was his mother he wanted. Gracie lifted him out of his crib. "There, there, baby boy. Everything's going to be all right now. Everything's going to be just fine."

Keaton stopped crying once he was in his mother's arms. He hid his face in her neck and peeked out from time to time. The friends made funny faces and played peekaboo, and finally he turned towards them. He stuck his thumb in his mouth and gave them a big grin.

❋

Uncle Sid and his sons left for home after their visit to the police station. Everyone else wanted to go home as soon as possible too. The police still needed more information from Gracie, so they made arrangements for her to follow her new mothers to Montreal later that week. Linda said she'd use that time to get a nursery set up. Gracie was so excited she clapped her hands like a little kid.

The Weinbergs insisted Bette drive back to Montreal with them, and since Gemma said she'd never fly again in a million years, they offered to take her back too. The police returned Bette's passport. They'd found it in Candy's warehouse, which was a bonus. There wasn't enough room for Augusta and Linda to accompany them, but they said they'd be fine flying back together, as soon as they could get a flight. Fortunately, Linda's suitcase arrived at the hotel in time for their departure.

They were about to get in their taxi for the airport when Linda spotted Stuart on the sidewalk in front of the hotel. Linda told Augusta she'd be right with her, then walked over to Stuart.

"You're all alone?"

"Ryan left for the airport as soon as we got back to the hotel."

"I see."

"She's not too happy with me at the moment, but I still have two days of meetings to go to."

"Were you able to reschedule your speech?"

"Fortunately, yes. I told them I had a family emergency."

They glanced away from each other for a moment and then Stuart cleared his throat. "I'm glad you're okay. Whatever you might think, I'd never want any harm to come to you."

"I know that."

"I'm sorry, Linda."

She didn't say anything at first. "Whatever happens between us, I don't want your relationship with Wes to disintegrate. I expect you to be there for him as always. Can you promise me that?"

"Of course."

Linda took a deep breath. "And since this is the first civilized conversation we've had in a while, I want to tell you that I paid for this trip for all of us with your Visa; the one you left in your sock drawer."

Stuart's eyes popped for a moment and he almost said something, but he obviously thought the better of it.

"Doesn't matter."

"Goodbye, Stuart. I hope she makes you happy." She turned around, walked over to the cab, and got in. He watched the taxi until it was out of sight.

❊

They got into Montreal late that night. Everyone was exhausted but supremely happy to be home. Someone must have been on watch in the front window at Gemma's house, because as soon as the

Weinbergs pulled up and Gemma got out, the entire family poured down the porch stairs. Anna jumped in her arms and wouldn't let go, so Gemma had to kiss and hug everyone with Anna on her hip.

Angelo smiled and gave her a big hug. "Hey, beautiful."

She was speechless for about five seconds. "Who's been plying your father with wine?"

He put his arm around her shoulder and escorted her to the house. "I missed you and we have a surprise for you."

"Goodness, what is it?"

"It's in the kitchen," Anna told her.

They trooped in as a unit. The only thing Gemma saw was her dratted mother-in-law.

"Hello, Nonna."

Nonna stood stiffly at attention. She looked at Angelo for encouragement. He nodded at her. She came forward, leaned in, and kissed an astonished Gemma on the cheek.

"*Benvenuta*, Gemma."

"Th-thank you."

"We buy you a present to make you happy," Nonna said.

Anna ran to where her grandmother had been standing. "Look, Mama. Instead of you buying a gift for us, we bought one for you."

Anna moved aside and there was a brand-spanking-new, top-of-the-line dishwasher.

Gemma's hands flew to her face. "Are you serious? A dishwasher?"

Angelo nodded proudly. "Yeah, isn't that great? Why did we buy it for her, Mama?"

He waited for her to say her rehearsed line. Nonna struggled before she opened her mouth. "You work hard."

"And..." Angelo prompted her.

"You a good mama."

Tears sprang to Gemma's eyes. "Why, thank you, Nonna. I appreciate that."

Anna hopped around the machine. "Quick, let's cook something so we can dirty the dishes."

Nonna, relieved to have that ordeal over with, immediately ran to the fridge. "I get some dinner."

The kids rushed around to set the table. Gemma hugged Angelo. "Thank you."

"Hey, I gotta keep my woman happy so she doesn't leave me again."

"If this is what's going to happen every time I go away, I'll be gone every weekend. I need a new dryer, too."

They laughed together.

❀

When Bette and entourage arrived home, all the Weinbergs were there with a handmade sign drawn by her nieces and nephews: "Welcome Home Aunt Bette." Every relative she had in the world came out of the woodwork to be there. There was food and wine, a family reunion.

Naturally everyone had heard of Ida's miraculous achievement and clamoured for all the details. She held forth in the middle of the room and then demonstrated her new-found ability. She got out of the chair and hobbled around the room for a few minutes. Everyone clapped and cheered.

Bette and her sisters-in-law found themselves in the kitchen replenishing trays of food.

"I can't believe how happy and grateful I am to be back in this dingy apartment," she smiled.

Miriam laughed. "It's life-altering, I'm sure."

Bette took a drink of wine. "I'll never take my life for granted again, that I can tell you."

"It's like having a new start," Esther agreed.

Bette nodded happily.

Miriam looked around the room to make sure no one was listening, and then she took Bette by the arm and pulled her into the corner, Esther right behind her.

"Listen, Bette, I think now is the time to break away from your parents. Your mother can get around now."

"But who knows how long that will last?"

Esther pointed at her. "You don't demand enough for yourself. You should have your own place."

"But…"

"Bette, dear, stop putting up roadblocks," Miriam interrupted. "You know perfectly well the boys can help with expenses and what-not, if we have to hire someone to come in from time to time. I know Mordecai has suggested that before, but you always have an excuse. Don't waste the second half of your life, Bette. You've been given a second chance. Take it."

Bette looked worried. "You're right. Ma will never want me to go out again."

"Exactly," Esther said. "Think of the hell your life will be."

"I'd strike while the iron's hot," Miriam said. "She's so grateful you're alive, she'd say yes to anything."

Bette gulped the last of her wine. "Do you think?"

They both nodded their heads.

Bette looked off in the distance. "My own place." Then she shook her head. "She'd never let me."

"*Let* you?"

"You don't know what she's like. She'll make me feel guilty."

Miriam squared her shoulders. "Right, I don't care if you think I'm an interfering busybody. This stops today. Come with me." She grabbed Bette by the hand and pulled her into the living room. Bette looked beseechingly at Esther, who said, "Go, go."

"I need more wine."

Esther ran to get a bottle and poured Bette a large glass.

Miriam clapped her hands. "Excuse me, excuse me, everyone."

The room went quiet.

Miriam smiled. "I just wanted to say, on behalf of all of us, how happy we are to have our Bette back safe and sound."

Everyone clapped and cheered. Bette raised her glass to them and then downed it.

"And I'd like to make an announcement."

Bette looked green.

"Ida, we're thrilled that you've been given the chance to be up and running again."

Everyone clapped and cheered again. Ida soaked it all up.

"Now that you're a little more independent, Ida, I'm sure you'll agree that this would be the best time for Bette to move out on her own. I think its God's way of letting you know that Bette can fly away now. He's given her wings and you feet!"

Everyone clapped and cheered once more. Everyone but Ida. Her face went as dark as a thundercloud. She stood still for only two seconds before she appealed to her favorite altar, the ceiling.

"What have I done to deserve this? My daughter goes missing, so I have to kill a man, and then I nearly get shot so she can come home and what does she do but go missing again? I can't take it. Oy, the pain, the pain."

She staggered a little before collapsing back in her chair. "My legs… my legs. I can't feel my legs."

There was silence. Ida looked around. Everyone was stony-faced.

"What? You've never heard of a relapse?"

David, the doctor, spoke up. "I find it awfully convenient, Ma, that the minute Bette tries to exert her own will, you get a relapse. Odd, don't you think?"

"What's so odd about it? It happens."

No one answered her. Bette held out her glass. Esther poured the wine to the brim.

Izzy came forward. "Ida, give it up."

She threw daggers at him. "Give what up?"

"This charade. You know you can walk."

There was a gasp from everyone and they all started to talk at once. Bette handed her wine glass to Esther. She put her two fingers in her mouth and whistled. Silence descended once more and she walked over to her mother.

"Is it true?"

"Is what true?" Ida clasped her hands and twirled her thumbs and looked everywhere but at Bette.

"So, it's true then," Bette said sadly.

Ida shrugged.

"Why? Just tell me why."

Ida looked at Izzy. He nodded at her to go on, but Ida shouted instead. "You tell her, then, since you're so smart."

Bette turned her head to look at her father. "Tell me what?"

Izzy lit a smoke before he spoke. "Your mother had a baby girl when she was fifteen."

No one said a word. Ida looked at the floor.

"In those days, that sort of thing was frowned upon, as you can imagine. Her parents made her give the child away. Your mother never got over it. We had five sons and loved them all, but the one thing she wanted was a girl. Then you came along, Bette, with your big brown eyes and your red hair, and your mother knelt by her bed every night asking God not to send away another daughter."

Bette looked at her mother, but her father continued. "I'm afraid I am as much to blame. I've loved having you here too. It made your mother happy. It wasn't so much of a lie. She does have trouble walking, but we never should've let this go on for as long as it has. It wasn't fair, and I can see that now. I'm sorry, Bette. I hope you can forgive us. You should have your own home. You're not a little girl anymore, and I think you proved that in the last couple of days." His eyes filled up. "We were so afraid of losing you…" He couldn't continue.

Bette went over and hugged him as her mother hid her face in her hands. Then she knelt by her mother's chair. "Ma, even if I get a place of my own, you're never going to lose me. I'd be over here a lot. You know that, don't you?"

Ida sniffed and nodded. "I guess."

Mordecai walked over and put his hand on his mother's shoulder. "We love you, Ma. We're all here for you and no one is judging you. Let Bette go. You have five other children that would love to help, if you'd let us."

Ida nodded. She wiped her eyes and looked at them. "What do you want me to say? I'm sorry?"

There was quiet.

"I'm sorry, okay."

Izzy rolled his eyes. "That's as much as you're going to get, folks."

"Hey! Enough with the sarcastic comments. You're no saint. Did you know he has *Playboy* magazines under his bed?"

Everyone burst out laughing.

"What's so funny? I don't think that's funny."

"It's funny, Ma," Bette smiled.

Her mother winked at her. "It's hysterical, but he doesn't need to know that." Then she shouted, "Does everyone have enough food? I have a cheese ball in the fridge. I'll go get it."

She drove away.

❋

When the taxi dropped Augusta off, she stood outside on the sidewalk with her suitcase and gazed at the wonderful house she and Tom bought together. The red maple Tom planted was going to be glorious someday. It was comforting to have a permanent reminder of the future they had planned together—a future that was altered by a twist of fate, but a future nonetheless.

"I'm home, Tom." The leaves on the tree rustled in the evening breeze. "I felt your presence with me the entire time I was away. You're always with me. Thank you."

She walked up the stairs, opened the front door, and couldn't help but smile. The messy pile of shoes was still messy, thank heavens. The smell of chocolate cake wafted through the air. Her mother had no doubt let the girls bake her a surprise. The stereo blared out the *Moulin Rouge* soundtrack over the hair dryer in the girls' bathroom. She heard Summer's off-key voice singing, "Hey sister, soul sister."

Augusta shouted, "I'm home."

Shrieks of joy came from everywhere. Her mother ran from the kitchen, Raine hightailed it in from the family room, and Summer jumped down the stairs two at a time. It was all a wonderful blur. She wrapped her arms around her girls and her mom and it was the happiest she'd been since Tom's death.

Later, after nearly half the cake had been consumed and two pots of tea and hot chocolate drained, they sat together around the kitchen table and talked of everyday things—not earth-shattering to anyone else, but to Augusta, it had the feel of a painting; colourful, dazzling, and creative. Her girls' voices were splashes of light across the canvas of her life. She'd always thought of Tom as the easel, the one who held them up, kept them from falling. She realized then that an easel has more than one leg, and she and her mother were as important to her girls as their father had been.

They were complete.

"Why did you come home so early, Mom?" Raine asked. "I thought you wanted a holiday."

"I got homesick."

"Weird."

Augusta clasped her hands and put her elbows on the table. "Girls, I have a big, fat, juicy idea."

Raine laughed and rubbed her hands together. "I love your big, fat, juicy ideas."

They looked at her expectantly.

"How about all four of us go somewhere special?

"Where?" said Summer and Raine together.

"Disney World."

The girls jumped up and started cheering. Augusta laughed. "I think they like the idea, Mom."

"You can say that again," Dorothy grinned. "What made you change your mind?"

"Daddy always wanted us to go, right girls? So I think it's high time we did, don't you?"

They nodded happily.

"Life is short and for the living. So let's live."

❀

Linda got out of the taxi and saw Wes's car in the driveway. She was relieved, not wanting to come home to an empty house, knowing that her friends were enjoying a great reunion with their extended families. The door was unlocked so she let herself in. She dropped her well-travelled suitcase on the floor and grinned when Buster came from nowhere at a great clip and jumped up in her arms, his motor already going a mile a minute.

"Hello, little friend. Mommy's sure glad to see you." Then she hollered, "I'm home."

"Mom!" she heard from upstairs.

She waited for it. The sound she loved; the sound of Wes's big feet stomping down the stairs. He came at a run and gave her a big hug and kiss. "Hey, Mom, it's good to see you. Did you have a nice time?"

"Very nice. You sure look happy. Is it my homecoming that's put such a sparkle in your eye?"

"Chloe's here."

Linda took off her coat. Chloe walked down the stairs and Linda watched Wes watch her. Aha. Something was up.

"Chloe, it's lovely to see you again, dear."

Chloe gave her a hug, which surprised Linda. It felt nice. "Hi, Mrs. Keaton. Did you have a good time?"

"It was short but eventful."

Wes pulled Chloe to him. "You'll have to tell us all about it, Mom, but we have something to tell you first."

Linda felt her head spin. "Okay, honey, but can I sit down for a second?"

They both looked appalled at their thoughtlessness. "Of course."

They hustled her off into the kitchen and Chloe made tea while Wes took out a box of crackers and cut up some cheese for a snack. "You must be hungry."

Linda nodded as she sat at the kitchen table. Buster immediately planted himself on her lap and rubbed the top of his head against her chin. At that moment, Linda was so happy; happy to be doing nothing and going nowhere in her beautiful kitchen with her cat and her son and his girl.

Life was good.

And then it got great.

As she sipped her tea, she got the feeling that Wes and Chloe were dying for her to finish, so she put down her mug and sat back. "So, tell me what's been happening with you two—"

"We're getting married—"

"—and we're pregnant!" Chloe said.

It was the final straw in what had been a very long day. Linda immediately covered her face and burst into tears. She couldn't have stopped if her life depended on it.

So of course, then Chloe started to cry. "She's upset...oh God, we shouldn't have told her."

Wes was flustered. "Mom, for God's sake, I thought you'd be happy. Don't you want us to be happy? I love her, Mom. I love her and I'm marrying her and I don't care what anyone says."

Linda waved her hands around, trying to signal for someone to get her a Kleenex, but they couldn't figure out what she wanted.

"Mom, what is it? Are you having a panic attack?"

"I'm sorry, Mrs. Keaton," Chloe bawled.

Wes dithered between the two of them. "This sucks. Will one of you stop crying?"

"I'm sorry." Linda got up and rushed to the kitchen sink, where she splashed some water on her face in an attempt to stop the tears. She grabbed a tea towel and buried her head in it. The kids stood in front of her and were at a loss. Finally she lifted her head, mascara running down her cheeks. "You don't understand—"

"No, you don't understand, Mom. I'm a grown man and I have to make my own decisions. I love Chloe—"

"*Stop.*"

He stopped.

Between her jagged breaths and runny nose, Linda said, "I'm so happy. I'm so very, very happy. A daughter-in-law and a grandchild. I can't believe it. Thank you. Thank you. Thank you."

She reached out and they both ran to her.

As if by a fairy godmother's wand, Linda's life turned completely upside down and inside out. She was so full of joy, she couldn't sleep. Even after she said goodnight to them and went to her room, she looked out her window at the moon and marvelled how, with just a few words, her life was changed forever.

"A little girl...or boy...that would be nice too...but a little girl to dress up. I could brush her hair and buy her shoes." Linda pinched herself and then remembered that Gracie and Keaton were soon going to be part of her family as well. As she gazed outside she realized she'd never known such utter and complete contentment. How lucky she was.

She ran herself a hot bath, desperate to wipe away the horror she'd been through. As she stripped off, she heard a tiny ping against the floor tiles. She thought she'd caught her earring, so she looked at the floor. A diamond sparkled at her feet.

Linda picked it up and held it in the palm of her hand. "How did you get here?" She wrestled with her conscience for a moment. Should she give it back? Nah. It had travelled home with her against all odds. She and her friends had earned it. Then a perfect solution came to mind—of course, not without the Book Bags' approval. They all owned a piece of this particular rock, so they would all have a say. But she had no doubt they'd agree to have Chloe's engagement ring made with it.

After a wonderful night's sleep in her own glorious bed, she came downstairs to find Wes and Chloe busy in the kitchen making her breakfast, though Chloe soon had to excuse herself.

"I suddenly hate the smell of bacon. Oh, I'm going to be sick." She took off.

Wes started to go after her, but Linda waved him down. "Never mind, leave her be. It's morning sickness, that's all. A rite of passage."

Wes nodded and went back to his bacon. "I have a lot to learn, I guess."

Linda took a sip of coffee. "Understatement of the year."

Buster hissed at the patio doors, and the sound of Winnie and Churchill barking alerted Linda to the fact that Clive was out puttering around in his garden already.

"Excuse me for a sec, I'll be back in a minute."

Linda got up, shooed Buster away from the door, and carried her coffee outside to the deck. She watched Clive for a while before he spotted her. He raised his hand in greeting.

"Good morning, Linda. You're back early."

"Yes." She went down the steps and walked over through the hedge to his backyard. "Thank you, Clive. You were a brick with all this robbery business. I'm sorry you had to worry about all that."

"It wasn't a problem. As soon as I got in touch with Wes, he handled everything. He's a very capable young man once he turns on his cellphone."

They laughed together.

"I'm so excited this morning, Clive. I'm bursting to tell someone. Wes and Chloe are getting married and they're having a baby."

"Well, that's exciting news! Congratulations. You'll make a wonderful grandmother, won't she, boys?" The boys concurred by wiggling their back ends.

She beamed. "Yes, I will."

"Young people are so clever these days. They have weddings and babies all at the same time. Saves a lot of bother, I should imagine."

"You're right."

"I suppose I'd better get back to my digging. I have great plans for the southern end of the garden. There's never a dull moment around here."

"Yes, Wes is making my breakfast. Anyway, thanks again."

"My pleasure."

Linda walked away and was on the porch when she turned around and shouted, "Would you like to come to dinner tonight? The kids are going out for the evening and the only thing I have on my agenda is a game of Solitaire."

He gave her a big smile. "I'd like that very, very much. Thank you."

"Until tonight, then." She waved and disappeared through her patio doors.

Clive adjusted his tie and cleared his throat before looking down at Winnie and Churchill.

"Don't wait up tonight, boys. Your father may be late."

❁

Lesley Crewe is the author of *Ava Comes Home* (2008), *Shoot Me* (2006), and *Relative Happiness* (2005), which was shortlisted for the Margaret and John Savage First Book Award. Previously a freelance writer and columnist for *Cape Bretoner Magazine*, she currently writes a column for *Cahoots* online magazine. Born in Montreal, Lesley lives in Homeville, Nova Scotia.

www.lesleycrewe.com